THE GIFT
OF ROME

THE GIFT
OF ROME

A NOVEL BY JOHN
AND ESTHER WAGNER

An Atlantic Monthly Press Book

LITTLE, BROWN AND COMPANY
BOSTON • TORONTO

ATLANTIC—LITTLE, BROWN BOOKS
ARE PUBLISHED BY
LITTLE, BROWN AND COMPANY
IN ASSOCIATION WITH
THE ATLANTIC MONTHLY PRESS

Published simultaneously in Canada
by Little, Brown & Company (Canada) Limited

PRINTED IN THE UNITED STATES OF AMERICA

For those we can never repay: parents, teachers.

MARGARET *and* WALTHER BUCHEN
ELLEN *and* ANTON WAGNER
MARGARET GILMAN
RONALD S. CRANE

FOREWORD

THE READER, unless he is a student of ancient history, may need to know that this whole violent story is in part the story of a somber and terrible period in Roman history. A great civil disturbance had torn Rome and all Italian towns such as Larinum apart through the years from 95 to 80 B.C. approximately. This conflict, in its later phases concentrated between the senatorial-aristocratic party identified with the Dictator Sulla, and the popular party identified with Marius, had produced a long period of deadly disorders. These disorders form the setting of the early years of Cluentius' life, of Cicero's, of Julius Caesar's. Cluentius' trial takes place in 66 B.C.; but the private drama of that trial has its roots in the public tragedies of the Marius-Sulla years.

It may also be difficult for the contemporary American to understand the *formally* stratified nature of Roman society which plays a role in this story. The social classes in Rome were no vague affairs of status and symbolism; they were established, defined, and limited in their activities by law from earliest times, though the definitions and limitations were changed by historical urgencies from time to time. Thus a member of the aristocracy, or "nobility," or "senatorial order" — the upper class — possessed by law many privileges denied to a member of the upper-middle class, the *"equites,"* or "equestrian order," or "knights," and these in turn could engage in activities from which the senators were enjoined. These "knights" were not warriors or armor-bearers, as might be expected from their title; the military associations of the title are very antique at the time of our story. These "knights" were businessmen, who possessed a certain sizable fortune and had had no ancestors who held any major office in the government or membership in the Senate. We have decided to call this class "the businessmen" rather than "the knights" throughout our story, because of the misleading image summoned automatically to the modern mind by the latter term.

We owe many thanks to many people for help and patience with this book, above all to Mr. Peter Davison of the Atlantic Monthly Press, whose part in it has gone far beyond any ordinary standard of professional duty. Professors Agnes Kirsopp Lake Michels and T. R. S. Broughton of Bryn Mawr College gave generously of their time to answer certain small exacting questions; we thank them and do not wish them held responsible for anything. We want to express our special gratitude to the librarian of the University of Puget Sound, Mr. Warren Perry, for the interest, energies, and facilities he has placed at our disposal, and the pleasant time we have had in the last stages of the book, working in the new library of the University.

JOHN AND ESTHER WAGNER

Tacoma, Washington
1960

PRINCIPALS IN THE TRIAL OF CLUENTIUS

MARCUS TULLIUS CICERO,
Attorney for the Defense:

Praetor of the City (a judicial office which did not prevent the holder from appearing in courts other than his own as an advocate). Cicero is at this time forty years old, and aspiring to the topmost magistracy of Rome, the consulship, to which he will seek election in 64 B.C.

TITUS ACCIUS,
Attorney for the Prosecution:

It must be remembered that at this time in Rome murder cases were tried as civil suits. There was no district attorney, but a private lawyer briefed by a citizen who wished to bring the charge.

STATIUS ALBIUS OPPIANICUS THE YOUNGER,
Plaintiff:

the stepson of Sassia, Cluentius' mother; a youth in his late twenties.

AULUS CLUENTIUS HABITUS (CLUENTIUS),
Defendant:

businessman of the town of Larinum, son of Sassia, and stepson of Oppianicus the Elder, and stepbrother of the plaintiff. He is nearly forty at the time of this trial. His mother had married the elder Oppianicus when Cluentius was about twenty. The actions and relationships with which this trial is concerned cover the whole span of his life. Most vital of these actions, and the center of the whole case against him in 66, is another trial, eight years before, in 74 B.C. when he himself at the age of thirty-odd had brought a charge of attempted murder against his stepfather —

STATIUS ALBIUS OPPIANICUS THE ELDER:

Present throughout the story, though never appearing as a living person, is this elder Oppianicus, third husband of Sassia. He had been convicted of attempted murder in the trial of 74, in which Cluentius was the accuser. This conviction resulted later in the death of Oppianicus — indirectly, since there was no capital punishment save for one crime, treason. The conviction and the death of Oppianicus form the substance of the charge now brought against Cluentius.

Besides these major parties to the legal action, there figure prominently in the story:

SASSIA:

a gentlewoman of Larinum, moving force behind the prosecution and mother of Cluentius. Her three marriages were to:

(1) AULUS CLUENTIUS HABITUS THE ELDER:

father of the defendant and long dead at the time of the trial. She had by this marriage two children: the defendant, and his sister Cluentia.

(2) AURIUS MELINUS:

who when she married him had just divorced, at her instance, her young daughter Cluentia, his first wife. This young man was thus successively the brother-in-law and stepbrother of the defendant Cluentius. Sassia had by him a daughter, Auria.

(3) STATIUS ALBIUS OPPIANICUS THE ELDER:
by whom she had no children.

And:

MARCUS ASUVIUS:
a businessman of Larinum and old friend of Cluentius.

ASUVIA:
his young niece and ward.

TITUS POMPONIUS ATTICUS:
Roman businessman of great wealth, the close friend of Cicero at this time and all times. Expatriate by taste and temperament, he lived in Athens and came but rarely to Rome.

THE GIFT
OF ROME

I

Aulus Cluentius Habitus, son of Aulus Cluentius Habitus, sends greeting to Marcus Tullius Cicero, Praetor of the City.

IF YOU ARE WELL, then it is well; and to this conventional expression let me add one from the heart: if you are well disposed to my cause after reading this letter, then indeed I shall be able to add the last part of the ordinary salutation — "I too am well." At present, since I am so uncertain of your response, these words would be nothing but irony. I am in mortal danger. The peril which threatens me, and from which I feel that your particular talents are all that can save me, is of so personal a nature that I who cannot as yet claim friendship with you can bring myself to appeal to you only by thinking steadfastly, great Cicero, of your friendship to the businessmen of Rome and the businessmen of the municipalities, friendship shown in many instances of service and of understanding. More particularly I think of another friendship of yours; I think of it with hope, your long friendship with the claims of human decency.

You saw me once, in a Roman court eight years ago. I brought a civil action against my stepfather Statius Albius Oppianicus, of Larinum, charging that he had attempted

3

to murder me. Two agents of his were tried before he was tried, in this action. For one, the ex-slave Scamander, you appeared as a defender, among others. Our one encounter, then, has been as opponents in a legal action. Yet as the evidence unfolded and as that action drew to its gloomy close — the conviction of my stepfather, his sentence of exile from his estates and township — I saw you looking at me. You knew then, as did everybody, of the rumors which ran all through the court on that last day, that the jury had been bribed with a huge sum and a corrupt verdict reached. Yet as you looked at me I felt that you knew also that no matter what events had disfigured the ideal face of justice, the question of guilt, the question at issue, had been rightly decided. Furthermore, Cicero, I saw in that unforgotten look something which at the end of these eight years I hang to as to a line thrown to one sinking in a great bog. It was a look of recognition. I struggle in these days with the fear that no man knows me.

I knew of you only that you had been quaestor the year before in Sicily, and had so managed affairs that the provincials there had thought you honest. A Roman financial officer in a Roman province, thought honest by the provincials! My dear Cicero.

What you know of me I cannot know; I do not, however, forget that look. There was recognition in it.

I know that you must calculate with care in your year as Praetor of the City the number of cases and the kinds of cases which you plead in the courts. A judge at Rome may enter what cases he wishes, as a private attorney, it is true; but a judge who intends to be consul must be mindful. The elections which must precede your consulate must never be far from your mind. But I do not, Cicero, forget that look, and I dare to make my request.

The son of my late stepfather, Statius Albius Oppianicus the Younger, brings a charge against me, that I murdered

4

his father. His charge will include some vague talk of poison. But the real center of the case against me will be the attempt to make the jury believe that I murdered the elder Oppianicus through an unjust verdict obtained in a Roman court, at the trial you know of.

The attorney retained by the younger Oppianicus is Titus Accius of Pisaurum, a man of no mean ability in the prosecution of cases involving political prejudice. I know well that the recent juridical reforms, which have given back to the members of our *non*-aristocratic, businessman's order the places on Roman juries denied them under the Dictator Sulla, will be a point not in my favor, as one might think; but in Accius', for he will appeal to the prejudice of the businessmen on the jury, a prejudice they must humanly and naturally feel against one who *won* a verdict eight years ago in a time dominated by we know what vile scum of Sulla, reflecting all in Roman life most hostile to men of our class. I shall be made to look a master of juries under the Sullan regime at its lowest ebb; I shall be made to look like one, a businessman, who found real and vital advantage in the aristocratic, senatorial supremacy, and who could use that advantage to the lowest ends imaginable, to the securing of private revenge through the processes of public justice.

The case will thus, Cicero, be tried on political grounds even if the accusation be a civil one and politics seem far removed from the points in question. I know well how ill advised an undertaking the defense of such a case may seem to you at this moment which is as vital for you, in your political life, as for me, in my private life.

Yet this is my appeal: that you appear as my attorney in this case. Good men of my township of Larinum will be my witnesses of character, and witnesses also of the character of my late stepfather, my old enemy, if you should think this appropriate. I know that it is the custom to place the defense in the hands of a group of pleaders rather than a single one; yet there is no lawyer in Rome who can help me but you, Marcus Tullius Cicero; none but you; for there is none but you to care for my sort of man, and thus my sort of case.

I have no powerful claim upon you which I can now invoke. My father never was bound to yours by any reciprocal services or entertainments; though it is true that my friend's father, Lucius Asuvius, was many times a visitor to your father's home at Arpinum in the days of your youth. Many friends are ours in common, all through Apulia, Samnium, Falernum; many of the great businessmen of Rome will speak of me to you. Yet my life has been lived in shadow, in some ways, and I have not passed through any wide circles of acquaintance and of friendship. The claims which draw one man to another's side in our courts of law cannot be laid upon you.

Yet I make one great claim: my cause is just. I make another: it is difficult. It will call for the greatest of your abilities. In your mighty prosecution of the governor Verres four years ago your powers were great. But he was a vile scourge of Roman and provincial alike, and you could then invoke against him that anti-Sullan prejudice which will be invoked now against me.

My cause is just, Cicero. I am not guilty.

Marcus Tullius Cicero, Praetor of the City, sends greeting to Aulus Cluentius Habitus.

If you are well, it is well. What you tell me of your case is interesting, but not yet interesting enough. I remember you well; I looked at you eight years ago in that courtroom, as you say, and I believe I saw you.

I read your letter before I left my house this morning. In the Forum I spoke of you to Fonteius and to Axius whose

6

names you know; solid men. The rumor here is that there is much money in this case against you, not all of it belonging to your respected stepbrother; and that the instigator of the action is your mother, Sassia.

I not only looked at you eight years ago, but at your mother. You do not mention her in your letter to me. The case hangs in my mind; I have much to engage my attention, as you must know even in that quiet corner of the city where you are staying. You do well to remain in the house of your friend Asuvius. We shall meet, but not until later. I am taken up with the betrothal of my daughter and with the consequences of our debates in the Senate over the command of the war in the East. I do not even speak of my duties as chief judicial officer. But your case hangs in my mind, because of some old memories of eight years ago.

You will fail to interest me entirely, Aulus Cluentius, unless you tell me everything; and I do not mean "fail entirely," I mean just "fail to interest entirely" — that is what I must be, interested *entirely*.

Tell me the whole background of this case. Describe to me in detail, the greatest detail, and with absolute candor, your relations with your mother Sassia from the time of your boyhood. With the career of your late stepfather I am somewhat familiar; not without interest, Cluentius, I do confess. You are aware that I shall cut a ridiculous figure at this trial when Accius brings up my participation on the exslave's side in the other trial? I mean to say, Accius will *try* to make me cut a ridiculous figure. There are some amusing ways in which one can make this sort of attempt fall flat. I have had few amusements lately.

Your late stepfather was an amusing man, and Sassia your mother, Cluentius, NOT a dull woman.

I must know everything. Interest me, Cluentius. Engage my feelings. Liven up your style a little. Be your own advocate. The issue of my advocacy hangs in this balance.

7

I am not afraid of the political nature of this trial. I am not in a mood to fear, at present. I wish to dare. I am forty years old today, Cluentius, and it is long since I have tried a really difficult case. Should I take yours, I want no associates. Leave Accius to me. He is as you say: not without ability. Good.

But I must be entirely interested. You had better be entirely candid. What do you think of the relationship between your mother and your late stepfather? With your opinion of the younger Statius Albius Oppianicus we may dispense; this youth is a handle. He is no pothandle; he is the handle of a good sword or spear. We must gauge the workmanship of the blade. You are in a better position to do this than anyone else. Do it for me. Dissect your mother's motives. Simple greed is not enough. It would be easy enough for you, even at this late date, to forestall her attempts to lay hold of any fortune which might conceivably come to her in the event of your conviction.

I will undertake no case in which I cannot use my own methods. Prejudice will be the essence of the prosecution's case. A counter-prejudice must be the essence of the defense. The general tone will *not* be discreet. Since I know nothing of you save what I saw — your uprightness, Cluentius, your decency — I cannot know at this moment whether I shall have this absolute liberty I require. Your letter is dignified. Allow me to adopt the modes of our Roman comedians, and beat you over the head with a pig-bladder: what are the facts here?

I expect from you an answer of many words. Let them describe actions, persons, motives of persons for actions, and circumstances. Let me judge for myself the import of words like "guilty," "innocent," "just," "unjust."

Did you or did you not bribe the jury eight years ago? This is the crux of the case. I await your answer.

8

What sort of woman was your mother in past years? What sort of woman is she today? What shrewdnesses can we expect of her, and what follies?

I await your answer. Interest me entirely, Cluentius.

Aulus Cluentius Habitus sends greeting to Marcus Tullius Cicero, Praetor of the City.

I shall do as you ask. I shall tell you everything. This does not come easily to me. You are right. The heart of this case is my mother's heart. I had thought to appeal to your heart, Cicero, in the sense of this word which is popularly used: the seat of the deepest emotions. You are familiar with the old tradition which says that a long nerve runs from the third finger to the heart, and because of this nerve the marriage ring is placed on that finger. I shall not attempt to make any appeal to your heart in this sense. I shall try to interest you.

I shall begin by informing you that Sassia my mother is not to be understood unless by one who can see that the old myth of the marriage ring and the heart is in her case actual fact; discounting of course her first two marriages, to my father and to my cousin Aurius Melinus, and taking into account only her marriage of the heart, her third, to my stepfather Statius Albius Oppianicus the Elder.

My mother was the daughter of a patrician lady who had been born in Rome and early married to a member of our businessman's order, a distinguished citizen of Larinum. Early my mother, I believe, drank deep of our Roman history, hearing from her mother how that lady's great family, of the urban aristocracy, had lost fortune after fortune in the years which saw the birth of our two warring factions, the popular and the aristocratic, those which approach through every act of our contemporary history some new

9

phase of their long conflict. I heard my mother once telling my father that at the age of ten she knew her mother despised her husband, my grandfather; that gentleman, a banker grown rich from the very agitations which had brought my grandmother's family fortunes low, bought her, she felt, like a slave to improve his social standing. Her own august clan, she felt, had sold her like a slave to improve their failing fortunes.

My mother's mother, Cicero, had in her youth been one of the first of a new large class of Roman ladies, those who profited by a new tendency among certain aristocratic families, particularly those much influenced by the great Scipios. She had shared her brother's Greek tutor and been formidably educated. This education she passed on to my mother her daughter, tinging all its notions with a profound distaste for life and human beings, handing down the great precepts about the Roman Constitution, the Roman destiny, with a heavy seasoning of irony and scorn. My mother could early, and can still, Cicero, quote Euripides to the discredit of any human aspiration, or our old poet Ennius in any of his stern Roman moods in such a tone of voice as to make his verses a parody on all the pieties.

My mother saw her father Sassius the banker, my grandfather, with two pairs of eyes. She saw in him what her mother did, with scornful patrician eyes. But she saw also a dealer in realities, a sincere impassioned lover of the great games of marketplace, waterfront, and warehouse. He had no son. He walked with her often, late at night, she used to tell me, after dining with his friends. He told her what he had in mind in such and such an operation, exposed to her the complex, veiled motives which activated his associates in the same operation. He did not bother, with her, to conceal or to equivocate. At twelve years my mother, Cicero, in whom you interest yourself so readily, was already a product of a very curious double education.

She was married at the age of fourteen to my father, Aulus Cluentius of Larinum. He was a friend and business associate of her father's. I believe, Cicero, that my father had a special notion in connection with this marriage. I was his friend for a few years before his death, and though we did not speak openly of vital matters I knew him; he was a man who cultivated certain ideas, though he had not first-hand acquaintance with the philosophers.

The notion of taking such a young girl, heiress of the separate traditions of two great social orders, into his life, to spend his middle years in forming her, watching her grow perhaps into a new kind of Roman great lady, combining the stern graces of the old aristocracy with the energy and practical shrewdness of the new kind of businessman — this whole complicated notion appealed very strongly to him. He was a man of lively mind. He believed that in the small communities, the municipalities, like Larinum, the Roman world could exist in small, bound by strong ties to the mother city, yet possessed of a vigorous individual life.

He made with my mother's father a marriage settlement extremely advantageous to the latter, for he wished my mother to see that he was interested primarily in her, in making her the partner of the enterprise of his middle life.

My mother, I believe, thought then that money and local prestige were far more valuable than her aristocratic mother's old-fashioned notions of ancient blood.

I can see now why and to what extent this marriage was not a success for her. She found it too easy to direct my father; he must have been very soon the slave of her charm and her vitality. She directed the building of their new house, she presented him with two children, son and daughter. She was able to persuade him that this was all the family he wanted. The ease with which she in her late teens took command of this man and this household did not inspire in her any joy, except perhaps a limited one, I think now, in the recognition of her own powers, the knowledge that she was to be no one's slave and the prisoner of no circumstances. Do you recognize her, Cicero?

Cluentius my father was too easy; the society of Larinum too easy; to move to the center in that narrow circle too easy. She craved the difficult, the test of her capacities.

When war broke out between Italian and Roman, the war which at long last brought us our rights of citizenship and suffrage, she may have felt that life was beginning to take on new dimensions. My father, I now believe, saw that as this war and the other, larger war at Rome merged into one another and became our condition of life, our Roman world was to be something other than anything he had imagined: a world in which those would flourish who had a gift and a taste for conflict. A distaste touched his deepest being.

He turned from his family, except at the very end, when at the age of fourteen I was for a while his friend. He turned from municipal affairs and the whole business world. He saw the old friends of his family, no one else. At the age of fifty he felt old. I recall him as an old man. On his death-bed, in his fiftieth year, he made no fight for life.

Between my mother and me there had fallen a silence. You ask about early days: I answer. For the first years of the conscious mind, I lived in the fascinations of Sassia's company. She was already weary of our Larinum society, the society of the Cluentii and the Aurii clans. Of the company of her children she was prepared to make a diversion. She could amuse a small child for an entire afternoon with a sheaf of flowers, a live cricket in an indolently contrived cage of twisted reeds. A walk in an orchard with her was full of talk, tales, and the divine taste of fruit. She bit into your apple and handed it back to you. She plucked a particular grape from a trellis and pressed it against the roof of your mouth with the tip of her long, grape-smelling finger.

But I had to console my sister Cluentia for the banishments to which she was constantly subjected. My mother did not like the girl, once she ceased to play with her as with a monkey or a doll. I studied with a fine Greek tutor, my dear Apollodorus; you, Cicero, would have recognized the many voices with which he spoke. Cluentia was allowed one hour of these lessons every morning, while Apollodorus was instructing in Latin. My mother had early decided that my sister was capable of no Greek. When my sister was sent away at the end of this hour, my mother would often enter to share our remaining time; or she would have the two of us, Apollodorus and me, come to her summerhouse on fine mornings, where she could listen to the lessons as she wandered about among her birdcages and vines.

But when I was twelve she lost interest in me. How she could lose interest! — to a really extravagant degree.

My father now spent much leisure with me. New things, unheard of in the lessons with my tutor, were discussed; things for which my mother had no ears. Certain great shapes began to move in my mind: Rome, old Rome, the powers of the earth, some large idea of character and soul. I had no companions of my own age. Some of the young Aurii and Papii shared my exercise master and rode with me to the drill grounds; my life was without intimacies save that of my sister and my father. My great friend Marcus Asuvius did not know me well until I was fourteen. I had only myself to depend on.

The war between Romans and Italians ended, if you can call it an ending. There ensued the fiercer phases of the new conflict, already in some ways old even then — the conflict between Sulla and Marius. My father died. The temper of Sassia my mother shortened. Preparations were made for the marriage of my sister Cluentia, so dear to me, that laughing blue-eyed presence, to Aurius Melinus our cousin. There were a few whispered interviews between me and

Cluentia in the garden; I assured her, Cicero, that in such hands all would be well with her; at least, we *knew* him, I said.

Are you familiar with this story, I wonder, Cicero, once so celebrated in all the municipalities and in Rome itself? I weary at the thought of telling it you; yet you insist that I exclude nothing. Forgive me, then, if I retell something you already know.

My mother, once she had pulled off my sister's rich marriage, spoiled in Larinum for want of a center for her attentions. She moved back and forth, as in a cage.

My cousin, Aurius Melinus, had returned just before his betrothal and marriage from journeys to Alexandria and Athens. He had frequented a different type of woman from that represented by his mother, sisters, aunts, and their friends. He had dined at the tables of the great courtesans of Athens, the *hetaerae*, "companions," full of culture and savory graces. He had not since boyhood seen my mother Sassia, and he could look at her now with educated eyes.

I think that I can say with justice, Cicero, that my cousin Aurius Melinus was a young man of no particular distinction. I cannot know, nor can even you, what made my mother begin the flirtation with him which so soon grew into great scandal and passion, and which ended in so many deaths.

Within two years my sister Cluentia, now a mother, came back to live with me. Her husband had divorced her. He wished to marry our mother. My mother left our house forever, to move now in the fine rooms of the house where her daughter had lived so short a time with Aurius Melinus. My mother had not been his wife for a year before she most insolently bore him a daughter.

At home with me, my sister did not see nor concern herself with her children; she was but half herself, a shadow of the rosy girl who had grown up with me. She talked softly, Cicero, to me or to herself. Her hands made little endless gestures. Her blue eyes wandered, empty.

I read, I studied law with my uncle Numerius. I traveled to Rome with my cousins; not much, not often. I took my place in the religious ceremonies. I found that great interest of our class: business, banking, the deep unending fascination of trade. I bought acreage, I concerned myself with a model sheep farm, importing some expert shepherds and some new methods of feeding and of rearing lambs. My friend Marcus Asuvius and his associates taught me much. We learned in a hard school, I do not need to tell you; those were the years of Sulla's power, not easy for any business-man, for any provincial, for anyone whose family had ever been known as Sulla's foe.

Cluentia my sister died, gibbering gently, holding my hand and smiling vacantly from those blue eyes. My mother, bored now with her young son-in-law-husband, received the addresses of Statius Albius Oppianicus, home in Larinum as the deputy of Sulla; you declare yourself familiar in some degree with this life, this character; so I will be brief.

The Oppianici were a questionable lot; rich, unscrupulous, far more tied up with the senatorial aristocracy of Rome than was generally considered suitable for a family of our class. Statius Albius was by far the most vital of his gen-eration. He was the central figure of his household, though his brother was older and, through various peculiar lega-cies, much richer.

Statius Albius Oppianicus: He loved Greek poetry and the flute. He loved sport and week-long drinking bouts in the low taverns of the grubby outskirts of Rome. He liked to do everything himself. He wrote Greek verses and com-posed fantastic parodies on the nobler poets. He broke and trained his own horses, made his father's Greek secretary spend long writing hours teaching him all the modes of the

Athenian flute players. In the taverns he joined the professional dancers; in the salons of the racy young matrons of Rome he did not observe the reticence generally thought proper to young men up from the provinces.

He alternated his activities in the military campaigns which took him far afield — always with Sulla, always on the side where you did not *expect* to find a man of Larinum — with a series of projects in and around Larinum, projects which exercised to the limit his talents for audacious contrivance and the great bold stroke. His first wife had been a Cluentia, the sister of my father. He had spent five years of travel, wars, commerce, and this marriage; at the end of those years, Oppianicus was a master of the art of poisoning, and my aunt Cluentia was dead.

Three more family deaths, including that of his brother, and he was richer still. His subsequent marriages were as many subsequent scandals. And you will remember, I believe, from the testimony at the trial eight years ago, the story of his long plot to obtain the whole inheritance of the Aurii, the family of one of these wives, the family also of my mother's second husband, my once brother-in-law.

To any foreigner, the tale of his domestic crimes would seem like some crude fiction; where should he have found shelter from avengers, if not from justice? But you, Cicero, or any Roman, will know the sad old answer, remembering how easily in those years private horrors were lost in the successive waves of public disorder. In Arpinum and even in Rome you heard how when the Aurii threatened him at last with an accounting, he withdrew to the camp of Quintus Metellus Pius, that limb of Sulla and oppressor of our class, an old friend and comrade-in-arms of Oppianicus; how Oppianicus came back to Larinum with an order from Sulla himself, installing him as the Dictator's deputy, with unlimited power. Proscription! Those lists in the marketplace, entitling any citizen to murder any of the

16

proscribed — how few years, really, lie between them and us, great Praetor, and one wonders every day how many years, months, days may separate us from new ones like them.

My mother was long weary of her young husband; the *affair* had interested her, not the man. Statius Albius Oppianicus became her friend. Her husband was shortly after proscribed and killed. My infant nephews, Aurii heirs, died mysteriously. In the terror that followed the proscriptions, my mother came to my house, my father's house, "to seek refuge," she said. I was too young then to say at certain moments "No." It takes knowledge and experience, as you yourself have learned, great Praetor, to say at certain moments "No."

Curiously enough, I was put in a position to overhear the final negotiations between my mother and Oppianicus which led to their marriage. She saw to this, telling me she needed a witness, not telling me what the negotiations concerned. I thought they must have to do with family property. I need not tell you to what degree my mother at this time, as always, was indifferent to what I thought of her.

She walked in my small garden with him, holding herself very straight, and speaking rather loudly and clearly. She thanked him for removing the irksome presence of her second husband, Aurius Melinus. She was not likely to be ungenerous in rewarding him for this kindly surgery, she told him. I could from my place in my little study, though I could not see them except as they passed the small window, see in my mind's eye the frank look she gave him. There had been, since his return to Larinum and his approaches to her, no time for them to speak of the ultimate phases of love. She held herself in readiness. But he had written to her of marriage. She would not, she said, marry him.

I must speak to you now with that candor which you requested, Cicero, concerning the senior Oppianicus. With his various moves in the ever-narrowing circle of his close relatives you are already familiar. I must speak now of his central places.

For all his raffish singularity of mind, my late stepfather was beset by one general human weakness, an ordinary vulnerability: the longing, never allowed perhaps in his thinking mind, for a woman who would understand him. His wives had all been poultry, prey; these were not marriages but swoops. The great game of self-enrichment which he played through the time of war held deep absorption for him. He too, Cicero, in his mode, had a passion for technique. But I think that deep in his mind, perhaps for many years since his first acquaintance with my mother in the years when she was his sister-in-law, there had stirred the idea of a more natural mating: no wolf mates with a sheep, no hawk with a hen.

It is my conviction that in the pursuit of my mother he was but incidentally interested in her fortune. Naturally, it was a part of her spell. Its existence was for him a sign of her splendid competence. I think he apprehended dimly the possibility of a new type of campaign, with a new strange goal: the communion of two souls, a blending of his spirit with another's. He had no wish to match wills with my mother and conquer her. He wished to occupy the center of her attention, and to secure her further attention to common designs which they should outline together and work upon in profound collaboration. Perhaps his aim in courting her was not much different from the aim of my father Cluentius a generation earlier. My mother seems to have the gift of inspiring this desire for partnership with her. I need not say that the communion of spirits proffered by Oppianicus reposed on a much sounder understanding of her nature than that which my father had achieved.

As I reflect upon the mind of Oppianicus, Cicero, and upon his career following his marriage to my mother, I feel an odd excitement of understanding. I amuse myself with a vision of him amusing himself with a vision: the huge hurly-burlying world of Rome, the East, Spain, Africa, the great world, holding within itself like a small concentric sphere the world of Larinum, packed densely with the same shifting possibilities for extravagant action; within this, still concentric, held in a delicate balance, a minute but complete world, arrogant, private, shared by two.

I believe he was stunned with surprise when my mother said No to him in the summerhouse of my little garden. No woman whom he had approached had ever shown herself unwilling or even reluctant. Furthermore, his position in Larinum, with his mandate from Sulla, was such that it seemed unlikely that he would meet with any serious refusals of any sort.

He kept his temper and demanded an explanation. Was she afraid of him?

He held no terrors for her, she informed him. But he had too many children. The eldest, a boy of about twelve, the same who now is the seeming accuser in the case against me, she was willing to stomach; a great deal of Aurii property was settled directly on him, and entailed. The two younger, sons of other wives, must go. Provision which he might normally make for them could then be concentrated on her and on any children she might have by him. Though not in her first youth, she told him coolly, she was still quite capable of providing heirs.

The insane nerve of her refusal, knowing as she did the power he held in his hand, did something to Oppianicus. She had made a gesture of supreme impudence; it showed her worthy of him as he had not dared to hope. He could match that gesture with an arrogance not unworthy. I heard him call her She-wolf. I heard her cool laugh, and a long hot silence, Cicero.

The extermination of the children was soon accomplished, as all Larinum can tell you. The power of Sulla made all redress impossible. But in Larinum the feeling against Oppianicus was so strong that not even fear could make a respectable citizen address him, invite him, do business with him. No one was present at his wedding to my mother; but then, neither he nor she cared to have anyone present. My mother was no longer interested in the effect of anything she did on the townsfolk of Larinum, though she had once so much wished to inspire amazement and dread. The truth is, Cicero, that she was never again interested at all in anything not directly connected with Oppianicus, my stepfather. He became her Rome and her world, and she lives in him still.

She came back to Larinum, the location of their most substantial properties, with him after their first voyages. They settled in the house she still inhabits, once the estate of Oppianicus' murdered brother; they rebuilt and refurnished, magnificently of course. My mother began to make approaches to me. She wrote me about moneys. She sent her confidential slaves to me, proposing negotiations which seemed all in my favor. She sought my advice about gardens, investments, I do not know what. I kept my distance, though we remained on terms of civility. Sometimes I could hear her voice in my ears, my inward ears I mean; but never unaccompanied by other voices. There was the low soft babble of my sister Cluentia in her last hours, and there were the high voices of children I had never seen. There was also, Cicero, *to be candid*, a certain other voice, low also, cool; it seemed to say, *Look out, my boy*.

I believe I did not spend all my time in thoughts concerning my mother and her husband. These were for me the years of my full entry into the world. I had put on my man's toga early, for my father's will had freed me prematurely from all parental tutelage. But I had not, before now, truly practiced manhood in any recognizable sense; by which I mean, Cicero, the practice of one's full-grown powers in the world of action. I had learned a good deal about the processes of finance and the structure of trade which is made possible through those processes; these are the arts of our class, for not many of us choose the great world of the courts and of the public life which is made possible through the courts — the choice you have made, Praetor.

With my friends and kinsmen in Larinum I launched myself, even during those shady years of Sulla's abiding influence, on a sea of enterprise. Contracts and extensions, leases and purchases, the expansion of the designs I had but sketched in the first years when I was still learning, all these absorbed me as the practice of law absorbed you, in those early years after you emerged from your studies. You looked about you in the Forum; I did too, but I looked for other faces and listened to other voices. The rise in price of Sicilian grain, the new sources of timber and slaves, held my attention as the medium of my art. You have not cared for these things; nor I for power and the operations of power which you conduct through your friendships with senators and businessmen, your connections abroad, all leading to new influence or the shoring up of old influence. Yet you know that it is I and my friends who have enabled men like you, Cicero, to translate our Roman financial power into the political power which is the dream of your life.

When you were quaestor in Sicily, and had set your foot on the first step of the stair to the consulship, I was most of the year in Larinum. Of the life of my mother with Oppianicus no one spoke to me. I was fortunate in my friends and kinsmen, who did me the honor of obeying my wish that she not be discussed in my presence. But my friend Asuvius' brother, a sad youth, fell under the influence of Oppianicus, even though he and Marcus had been orphaned in the proscription directed by the creature. How this happened, who can say? There was a piece of human scum named Avillius, who made himself responsible for the poor youth's pleasures. This Avillius was the right hand of Oppianicus. Larinum is small; life is circumscribed; my friend Marcus much absent on business; and the company of Oppianicus an intoxication. In the spring of that year the young Asuvius was murdered in the brazen manner already becoming classic with Oppianicus; his will was forged; a scandal of the most abysmal squalor rose round the event. My friend tried to bring an action. The vile judge Manlius in Rome was bought off. My mother's communications to me began to exude a thin, faint, unmistakable aroma of threat.

I mortally offended my stepfather by bringing a successful action against him, in an affair of minor importance, which I undertook only at the urging of my friend Asuvius; you can imagine the various ways in which I felt bound and obligated to Asuvius.

In Larinum after that, I walked in immediate peril. My stepfather no longer could use the great tool of proscription. Sulla's constitution had been in force for long years now. The Dictator had wanted, in the end, to establish his own "rightful process of law," and "rightful process of law" was the mode. But there were other considerations. Oppianicus knew I had made no will, in accordance with my vow made long ago to private gods, Cicero, never to affront publicly the woman who was my mother. To disinherit her would be this sort of affront. This vow has been known in Larinum. I suspect that your friends Fonteius and Axius spoke of it to you, and that it is this which has prompted you to sound me out about my feelings for my mother.

Oppianicus, then, knew that upon my death Sassia and he would somehow be able to lay hands on the major part of my fortune. Prudence had restrained him; but the grip of prudence upon my stepfather was never firm.

Through the loyalty of a Greek doctor and the agency

of his slave, the plot against my life was revealed to me, that plot of which you heard so much in the other trial. I feigned illness to tempt Oppianicus; put my friends in places of concealment; the poison was passed from hand to hand, money changed hands, and in this exchange of packets of poison and packets of money, the agents of Oppianicus were caught and my accusation against my stepfather founded.

You ask about the bribing of the jury. Did not the actions brought against judge and jurymen following the trial demonstrate convincingly that Oppianicus had bribed, and failed in his object?

My concern for my personal future is less strong than you may think. Yet I have resolved that I must not lose this case. I will not lose it if you will plead for me.

May I have your voice in my cause, Cicero?

Marcus Tullius Cicero sends greeting to A. Cluentius Habitus.

If you are well, it is well, Cluentius. Though you interest me entirely, I have not yet decided to take your case.

How did your stepfather die?

The jury was bribed. Oppianicus dispensed money to the jurors, that is known. These two facts taken together do not constitute an answer to the question: did *you* bribe the jury?

What is to be expected of your mother? You answer much, but you evade.

Aulus Cluentius Habitus sends greeting to Marcus Tullius Cicero, Praetor of the City.

I write with my own hand, in haste; I shall not dictate this, not to the most loved of all slaves.

You ask about my stepfather and my mother. After the conviction, which of course meant much severe loss, Oppianicus nevertheless salvaged a good deal of his personal fortune, thanks to my mother's ingenuities and her own copious solvency. But he had to leave Larinum permanently and he could not take up stationary residence in Rome, naturally; so on a small, new estate in Falernum, near enough to the capital to allow him occasional excursions, he tried to retreat into his old diversions and into the private world he had always shared with my mother. It seems that nerves and exacerbations made this world no retreat at all.

A fierce jealousy took hold of her. In this little and restricted domain, hedged round with enforceable prohibitions, where they could not move from each other's sphere, she could not bear to share his attention nor could she bear its weight. He showed much affection, I am told, for his young slave Nicostratus, whom he had brought from the Islands in a happy year, just after their marriage. These two spent hours with flutes, wine, fishing nets, and avoided my mother's presence.

I know much about these days; I have kept myself informed, sure that on one day or another there would be some move against me.

My mother punished Oppianicus by demonstrating that she could still intoxicate and be intoxicated. The handsomest man in the district was the tenant farmer Sextus Attius. She began to ride past his fields, up to his house, send him small gifts, be seen walking along the hedgerows toward the spring where he was accustomed to drink wine at noon.

It was the slave Nicostratus' report of this that drove Oppianicus to his last lunge at fate. He shouted for horses and rode like a madman toward the outskirts of Rome, the scene of his bedraggled debauches, stopping only at taverns on the way. He fell from his horse outside the gates of the city, and died in a suburban inn. When my mother arrived with her doctor and a litter, his dark face was an even gray, his eyes closed, his breath coming hard. He died without moving or speaking.

Since my stepfather's death my mother has pursued me, with what implacable energy you already know. First she secured and tortured, in her search for evidence, two slaves, Nicostratus and another, called Strato; there were no results useful to her. Then she laid more careful plans, binding the younger Oppianicus, her stepson, to her by marriage with her young daughter Auria, the product of her short life with my sister's lost husband, Aurius Melinus. Finally she saw her chance when the slave Strato committed a burglary at her house. She seized him, got hold of Nicostratus again; tortured them both. Nicostratus has not been seen again. Strato was crucified after his torture and deposition; his tongue torn out. I think she feared that at the last he might retract and betray her somehow. Frenzy possesses my mother.

You ask what can be expected of her: let me tell you. The Furies which sit in her heart are a separate race, the Furies of love. She loved my stepfather. The affair with the tenant farmer in the last weeks of my stepfather's life was nothing but a clumsy attempt to bring Oppianicus back to her. Yet it was she herself who had driven him away, with her wild tempers and her moods.

The Greeks have told us that love is a poison, Cicero, a chain, a firebrand. You will remember the dark and terrible choruses of Euripides, you will think of raving Medea. The fate of Nicostratus I believe to have been a gesture of some Medean kind. I think my mother has always been persuaded that Nicostratus took her place in Oppianicus' heart, in his intimacies, in everything, in those last months, at Falernum. I think she is mistaken in this. My stepfather was as lashed by love as she. What he and Nicostratus did in their solitary hours I neither know nor care to imagine, but his heart was elsewhere. Whatever happened, it was again the same story as with the tenant farmer and Sassia.

When shall men speak in the Latin tongue, with Roman directness out of Roman experience, Cicero, of the savageries of poisoned love? I shall quote no Greeks. I wait for a poet who can find the great envenomed words for what I know. In the meantime, I intend to profit from what I know, and steer clear of this invading passion.

I am for my mother the murderer of love, for she never until the death of Oppianicus knew remorse or self-reproach. These feelings, I believe, have lashed her through unimaginable nights and days. She is filled with a kind of piety, Cicero! Fear her. As Oppianicus once offered her for wedding gift the murder of his children, so now she lives and breathes but for one object, to offer him as funeral gift the ruin of her son. My death is not enough. She wishes for me miserable life, the thing which poisoned the air between her and the one man who ever really existed for her.

What we can expect from my mother, then, is unparalleled intensity, inexhaustible energy; undeflectable singleness of purpose; *concentration* — these are her weapons. You said she was not a dull woman. You are right. Neither is she a stupid woman. All the resources of her fortune and all the resources of her experience — *her* experience, Cicero! — will be concentrated behind her attack on me.

But if she is single-minded and full-armed, she is also a woman in frenzy. Anyone of any real capacity, in her position, would use as primary weapon political prejudice, and try to show how I profited by the opportunities for corruption and crookedness offered by the Sullan courts of the time. However, I believe that this is the extent of her shrewdness. From here on, her follies are much in evidence. Her passion drives her and she has forged her instruments in its heat. But in the matter of detail, she is weak.

2 6

For example, I have it from good sources — good men of Larinum, called as witnesses by her to the interrogation of the slaves — that when she tortured these poor creatures and took the depositions, supposedly concerning the murders of her guards and the burglary of her strong room, supposedly revealing as if by accident the slaves' knowledge of her dead husband's "murder," she quite simply forgot to mention in the depositions anything concerning the burglary at all. These depositions are concerned entirely with the death of Oppianicus. Something rather serious was overlooked: the interrogations were supposedly dealing with another matter entirely. Her witnesses had come as all Roman citizens of our class will come when summoned to an inquisition concerning a slave's crime against his master; my mother's neighbors of Larinum were willing to forget their feelings about her in that common cause which all property owners feel upon such occasions. They were more than astonished to find the matter that had brought them there completely ignored in the investigation, and never mentioned in the deposition, although the whole countryside knew that the burglary actually had occurred.

For another example, she has allowed her feeling that she has got what she wanted to dominate her conduct. Once her evidence in hand and her attorney briefed, she has behaved as if she had won. She has waited long — four years since my stepfather died — she is not a woman gifted for waiting. She feels that the moment for self-discipline has passed.

She triumphs in Larinum like an accuser already victorious. She makes plans, openly, for celebrations attendant upon my conviction. She is so exultant that she has sent to her old favorite resort, Alexandria, for a crowd of musicians and priests of some formidable secret cult, whose rites are a perfect medium for unbridled exhilaration, and of which she and my stepfather were once initiates.

The effect of all these attitudes upon the citizens of our township has been quite lost on her; she has for such long years been indifferent to municipal opinion. For a very brief while, two years ago, she feigned concern with it, in order to accomplish the marriage of her stepson, an apparent reconciliation with me, a little circle of quiet from which to prepare her ambush. Now that her trap is sprung, she feels no further need for calculation. I am telling you of her follies, as you asked.

To write of her in this way, Cicero! For how many years has it been my consolation that I did not speak of her, save on one occasion to my closest friend, nor allow her to be spoken of to me, save as any mother might be spoken of. I have leaned upon this structure of decorum as long as I could.

Indeed, had she loved me, or perhaps Cluentia, as her one love . . . it has been known . . . she is a woman with a deep heart; she can love in such a way. . . . Are you aware, Cicero, of how potent, still, are her beauty and her charm? To enter her presence, as I did once, a few times, even, at the time of her daughter's wedding, in these long years of our estrangement, yes, is to feel oneself strangely at some source of life. The power of great love is a part of her enchantment. For many years, men and children moved round her never knowing but that any of them might suddenly be dowered with this treasure. She spent it all on Oppianicus; but the greatness of what she had to spend still lingers round her person and speaks in her voice, her voice not to be forgotten.

She cannot assess, she cannot calculate. She simply overwhelms — but when she is faced by a wealth of emotion equal to her own, and by a power of calculation truly expert, she will fail. I appeal to you, Praetor, defender and repository of man's justice.

Marcus Tullius Cicero sends greeting to Aulus Cluentius Habitus.

Whoever defends you must know your case. Did you bribe the jury?

Aulus Cluentius Habitus to Marcus Tullius Cicero, Praetor of the City: greeting.

I believe that you know the answer to your question. May I come to see you?

M. Tullius Cicero, greeting to A. Cluentius Habitus in haste.

Not until you have answered.

Aulus Cluentius Habitus to Marcus Tullius Cicero, Praetor of the City.

The answer is yes. I did. May I come to see you?

Cicero to Cluentius, greeting.

Three days from now at daybreak. The meeting will be short; I have much in hand for the day.

II

IN THE VIOLET LIGHT of evening, the Praetor of the
City turned in his cold pool, splashed and laughed. His
friend Pomponius Atticus sat at the tiled side of the
pool, a small fine-boned man, dark-eyed, wrapped in thin
wool, scowling as he held up sheets of papyrus to read by
the fading light the last page of Cluentius' last long letter.

"Your eyes are straining, Atticus? You're forever lecturing *me* about twilight reading. You're forever prescribing
that I have Cephisus or somebody hover around and read to
me. Allow me to summon a reader —"

"No. I'm finished."

"One likes to read with the *eyes*, I've always told you."

"Especially such documents as this. This man remembers
with the eyes. So do we all — with the eyes, the nose, a bit of
the ears; the fingers. But not all of us, not even you, good
Marcus, work so hard to get this part of the memory into
words. He's made a good thing here, back here, out of
'grape-smelling' — that grape against the palate, extraordinary."

"The evocative gifts of Aulus Cluentius, which I found,
like you, an unexpected source of pleasure and instruction,

are not our main interest here," said Cicero dryly. "Besides, he owes it all to me. I *told* him to liven up his style and make himself interesting." He stood in the pool and flicked water from eyes and eyebrows, rubbed his head absently. Atticus helped him from the water. They ministered to each other a bit. Each found sympathetic as always his friend's aversion to the clustering cloud of towel-flapping, phial-brandishing, rod-waving slaves which made the last phases of the Roman bath a scurry. Leisurely they ambled to a little room where Cicero's young Greek awaited them, ready with light oil, with short and unelaborated massage. As always, they did not speak until they walked again, dressed lightly in Greek over-garments, in the cooling paths. The violet deepened to gray. Atticus followed idly at his friend's elbow; they passed near a little garden in the rear of the villa, where the kitchen slaves scuttled about preparing outdoors the roast meat of dinner. Silver vessels gleamed softly in the remaining light; a few torches sputtered; Campanian tongues chattered, and a Greek one speaking with cold precision and a marked accent in Latin directed. The scent of crackling fowlskin, hot apples, a thin sharp herbal fragrance, drifted with the purple smoke into the air. As always in this man's company, Atticus felt his senses sharpen and his mind begin to move fast.

"The man seems somehow to know you," he said. "He knows how you are to be tempted. Notice how he talks of no legacies, no gifts of statues or books as one less well-informed might do. He talks of the difficulties of the case and the chance it will give you to display your powers."

" 'Display' — what an unkind word. Surely you mean 'exercise,' or 'put to a test.' But how beautifully impossible the thing looks, Atticus! O sacred, savory, herb-spiced impossibility, Atticus! How my mouth waters, Atticus, and how the scented garlands of the smoke —"

"Now just a moment. A couple of unsavory, flat-flavored

questions. *How* would you avoid looking a fool when the prosecutor mentions the entirely different view you took of this murder-plot story when you appeared for the freedman Scamander in the other trial — that *famous* trial, my friend, so very famous, which is sure to be the central issue in this case?"

"You insult me, Atticus. I shall arise, wearing the splendid new toga you have just brought me; I shall have spent some time with old Tiro and my little Tullia — very deft with the toga-drape, that girl of mine, little as she is — securing an extremely casual sort of effect. Graceful, easy; *bending*. I can't show you with this limp Greek thing. You'll have to make an appalling effort, Pomponius, and use your imagination." The Praetor struck a pose in the middle of the path, crook-elbowed, slope-shouldered, full of ease and dignity. "I shall then utilize a couple of points I've recently picked up from the cleverest of all our Greek mimes: a gesture indicating joy at the opportunity to be candid and free among people one trusts — and indicating also a sort of invitation to be *urbane* together — you know —" The fine forearm and beautiful hand moved in an even sweep, an expression of extreme smoothness and confidence established itself upon the broad mobile face, as Atticus, his face a few inches away from Cicero's, peered through the dusk. So close, he caught suddenly the wild excitement in the narrow blue eye, and felt sudden excitement surge in his own mind.

"Cicero —"

"You interrupt. I shall tell how when I returned from Lilybaeum after the hard public service of my quaestorship — duties performed with more than the usual scrupulousness, I shall remind them — rather ill-informed as to goings-on in the capital and in Italy, and all thirsty to get back into the splash of things, I was visited by a deputation of Alatrians, old friends of mine and neighbors. Their townsman Fabricius — agent of Oppianicus, you may remember — under such a cloud, Cicero! All odds so heavily against him, Cicero! Would I help? Would I speak for his ex-slave Scamander? But I know nothing of the case, I said. . . . Oh, quite sufficient could be learned in a very short time. . . . I need only appear briefly. . . . They themselves knew nothing of the case, they said, but township-patriotism and Fabricius' aging father . . . Well, Atticus, when they said they knew nothing of the case, I believed them, and I believe them now — but in the name of old friendships, the common interests of our class —" A glorious shrug, light but implying somehow the weight of the toga in all its amplitude, punctuated the discourse and broke up the pose. "Then I shall report, in my most inimitable manner, on how old P. Cannutius the prosecutor made a fool of me and contradicted me successfully on every single point —"

"Did he?"

"He did. There will be a fine chance for modesty here. To hear a city praetor accuse himself of having got stupidly on the wrong side of a case and made an ass of himself will put the whole jury in a good mood; they will be ripe then to believe that the side I was on *was* the wrong side."

"You keep saying 'will,' 'I will.' Cicero, have you resolved to take this —"

"No, certainly. I amuse myself with obstacle. Accius will then bring up the matter of the anti-Verres oration I published without delivering it — "

"Gods! I remember. You used the trial of Oppianicus as a major example of miscarriage of justice through corruption of the juries . . . you . . ."

"Calm yourself, my Atticus. Who is the Epicurean here, in quest of repose? Who is always telling everybody else to calm himself? Naturally, I shall be prepared to deal with Accius' no doubt sardonic allusions to my words upon that occasion. I plan already, and will deliver to you over some of that new Chian wine you sent ahead of you here, a charming essay on the crude inappropriateness of attitude, not to say rustic simplicity of mind, which sometimes drives an unwary attorney to allude in one trial to something another attorney said in another trial. I shall tell superb stories of the old Brutus and divine old Crassus, saying how they dealt with attempts to hold them responsible for remarks they had made only at the demands of occasion."

"Careful, Marcus! What your charming essay will really say is: No lawyer ever means what he says when pleading a case, so what he says should be regarded as air, for which he is not properly reponsible."

"I repeat, with the patience which marks all our mutual relation, my beloved friend, that you insult me. Just as the real import of my urbane and worldly little discourse will be dawning on my jury, I will straighten. My pose will change. My gesture will take on the old-Roman stiffness and jerkiness which indicate that a man is going to talk about Roman Justice. I shall say —" the light, quick voice deepened suddenly and atonishingly, a great grave organ note rolled into the new dark — "I knew nothing of the case when I appeared at that trial, misguided: I have learned I was wrong, gentlemen of the jury, as all Rome has been wrong! Full knowledge of the case leads to but one conclusion: that Oppianicus, so fortunately condemned and dead, was an enemy of gods, men, and Rome, a violator of all household gods in city, township, and province; that Cluentius my client was a just man then, rightfully protected by the blind goddess of justice and by the turning wheel of strange fortune; that he is a just man still, pursued by an injustice so monstrous that one fears impiety in even bringing it to the light of day —"

"Let's dine, before you get drunk right here."

"Cicero, the problems of the case are these. Not that you may lose — I know you can win, not easily, but you can win. But your supreme candidacy is at hand! Two years and you'll stand for the consulship! For eight years the case of Oppianicus has been used as you yourself used it in your published speech — as a symbol of the judiciary's total contamination, presided over by the senatorial supremacy, the work of Sulla. How often have we talked, and I approved, of your program of the harmony of the two upper orders — the peace-bringing, order-preserving, let us hope, collaboration between businessmen and senatorial aristocrats. It is neither necessary nor pleasant for me to recall to you the delicacies of maintaining and advancing relationships with the members of our august nobility. . . ."

The wavering light of sconced torches played above them. A fine Rhodian lampstand stood at Atticus' side. Cicero, in the act of pouring a last draught of the Chian wine into the carved cup Atticus held out, paused suddenly in his attitude of wine-server; slowly the vessel returned to upright, slowly the reclining form of the praetor straightened on the couch until he sat stiff and straight. He banged on the table with the vessel; his eyes blazed blue hot in the moving light. He rose and paced off to one side. The dining room was empty of all but one slave, the Greek youth, who stood in skillful inconspicuousness near the door, far enough away to hear no word, near enough to miss no summons. A gesture now dismissed him from the room. With joy, Atticus perceived that he had said a profoundly moving thing, in the mere introductory clause of a long sentence which he had thought to make moving only with its close. With prudence, he delayed, waiting until the nature and extent of the feeling he had aroused should be made plain.

"Delicacies. *Delicacies* of maintaining these relationships." The great broad face swung low over the back of a couch, as Cicero stooped to look into Atticus' eyes. He straightened, walked swiftly round the table, sat again, but did not recline, in his place.

"Indelicacies." Clawmarks, long lines, showed in his cheeks. He closed his eyes; opened them, and Atticus stirred and rose to a sitting position, roused by the long look of old pain in those blue eyes.

"Years now, Atticus. . . . 'Forgive me, gentlemen, GENTLEMEN, good men, DISTINGUISHED men, my lack of family tradition. No wax heads, no busts of consular ancestors in my courtyard! O Quintus Metellus, my good fortune in your friendship, such an honor. O Mucius Scaevola, your name with its memories of old Rome. I must be forever mindful of how little I deserve, of how much I owe.' You remember, Atticus, what my father was."

"A good man, Marcus; not a consul."

"Good, generous, and wise; successful too, and ambitious for me. But not a consul. Not a quaestor, aedile, praetor; an able man, but not any of these. So I must be humble. I must apologize and recognize the honors that are accorded me in the mere salute and company of *these others.* . . . "

"Cicero."

"*Good men,* in my speeches, Atticus, means those of senatorial rank and senatorial interest. Aristocrats. A locution, a phrase. Best men — this means those good men as a political group, it is their party. *Optimates.*

"The best man I know is you, Atticus; good, generous, and wise — learned even. Successful; not a consul. My father was a good man. The word has other meanings. In the company of words as of men we must be forever mindful, for they take on meanings according to what we are, what position we occupy, rather than according to what *they* are, and what their meaning has been. . . ."

"Cicero!"

"Cluentius, this Cluentius — you could see it, you can see what sort of good man —"

"Cicero, I interrupt you only because the spectacle of your pain is painful to me."

A short silence fell. The arm and long hand of the praetor shot out toward his friend. His forearm lay heavy on Atticus' forearm, the hand of each cradled and pressed gently the elbow of the other. The flushed face of Cicero broke suddenly into his most charming smile; his free hand reached for a grape, which with an extravagant flourish he popped into his mouth, squashing it against his palate with a little staccato sound.

"Mm! fragrant! oh, fragrant! oh, smell my finger, friend, grape-smelling! Remember your slavery, but smell my finger and think of us all as crickets in an indolently contrived cage of reeds" — a splendid, madly uninhibited leer twisted the Praetor's mouth upward.

"Your memory, Cicero — extraordinary. The words of Cluentius have found a voice."

"You are right. My memory is long, and my voice at its height *now*. Who knows whether I shall be in such good voice next year? To what man is it given, Atticus, to know in what month, what year, the sweet breath of Fortune . . . soft on his cheek, a vapor in the nostrils, will wrap him as in a cloud, guide and illustrate his life . . ." They began to murmur alternately short phrases in Greek words and meters. They had each had but two cups of Chian wine, heavily diluted with water. Their dinner had been delicate and light. But intoxication charged the air between them; they were men of thought and feeling.

"Cicero, the problems of the case are these (I start again)," said Atticus in the beginning of their late walk. "You have experienced every difficulty that it is possible to know, in cultivating and dealing with the senatorial faction. You need no longer concern yourself with the automatic opposition of the ultra-conservative — look at what happened to Catulus and Hortensius when they opposed you this year in those debates — and you know your friends. But you have never before risked alienating any large part of our order. The prejudice, for businessmen, that hangs around the mention of that trial —"

"It is possible to exaggerate that prejudice," said Cicero idly, sucking on a laurel leaf. "Cluentius' business career doesn't seem to have been much hampered by it. Fonteius and Axius told me he has the best credit of all their regulars in the *municipia;* that to deal with him is pleasant always and nearly always profitable; that he and his associates, mostly men of comparative youth like himself, were among the first to get their contracts and their ships for the renewing of trade with Asia, after the early unpleasantness had been settled there by the late L. Cornelius Sulla, dear man. The present unpleasantnesses, which our Pompey will shortly settle — when these are past, there will be another rise in Cluentius' fortunes. Ability is constant."

"*Marcus!* Business is different. We are speaking of the courts, of men's political emotions, *of your candidacy.* Who will be put off by your appearing for Cluentius? All the most respectable bankers, since they have worked so hard for the jury-reform that has put them back on the juries, and they have referred so many times to the trial of Oppianicus as the sort of thing that could happen only under Sulla. Then the tribunes — remember Quinctius brought that charge of bribery against the court after the verdict — remember that loud-mouthed Quinctius still lives and has a number of loud-mouthed friends. In the interest of your election and of the harmony of orders, the coalition government you dream of, let this case alone! To dabble with it and talk of your gestures and your voice is all right, an amusement, but to get *into* it is to stir up a storm of winged stings. It is not necessary! It is not necessary!"

"You excite yourself again, dear Atticus. That I should be railed at by the light of Athens, the priest of temperance

. . . Quinctius is not the only man with a loud-mouthed friend."

"Marcus!" But Atticus burst out laughing.

"Tomorrow, my Atticus, we will start for Rome. I am still drunk, of course, as I am drunk forever, from the beginning to the end of each of your visits. Visits so brief and so infrequent. That we should live so apart, you in your city — O that Athens! Only your adopted city, but how you insist on living in it! I shall never really love it — I in mine —"

"I shall never really love it."

"Cluentius talks of how love wastes lives. The love of Rome burns and chains, as does the love he speaks of; and the love of Rome is not some *notion*, such as you windbags of Athens propound. The love of Rome is not of *fatherland* — as philosopher I say those things myself, but philosophers are asses. It is the love of marketplace and court; part of it is Quinctius bawling in front of the benches, and the mad rush of words with which Hortensius tries to beat me into silence on the rostrum —"

"That *poor* Hortensius."

". . . it is the long face of Mucius Scaevola over his lawbooks, his fingers round the jars, scrolls falling from his lap . . . the yapping voices of our Populares, Champions of the People! The bald rake they love, Julius Caesar, smelling of Sicilian perfumes as he walks by you in the Forum on his way to the lady Volumnia at ten o'clock in the morning. Little glops of unguent on the ends of his scant hairs! But a man to watch. Ability! You can smell that on him too. I have known him long. It is dangerous to stop watching him. This watching — it is part of the love of Rome. The love of Rome is smells and talk, the clients streaming up the hill to your door in the morning, the schoolmasters yelling like maniacs in their doorways —"

"Cicero. We both have delicate stomachs."

3 9

"Ah. Sometimes I wish mine were as delicate as yours. But not often."

In the morning they left the suburb for Rome, a day's dawdling journey. For long intervals they descended from their litters and walked together, gossiping, laughing, returning always by some winding way to the one subject.

"I know when you've made up your mind, Marcus! You haven't quite made up your mind. You wait to see how you *feel* about Cluentius. Can't you calculate? Why must you always feel, and act, and feel again? Surely a little exercise of the reason . . ."

"Have you ever seen Cluentius?"

"No, I am not much in Rome, as you complain. He is as little in Rome, almost, and even less in Athens and Brundisium. I knew his father."

"*What?*"

"I don't want to talk about old Aulus Cluentius," said Atticus quickly.

"Why not?"

"You're too interested in this case already. There's nothing in it for you! Nothing but pain and conflict. Avoid pain!"

The blue eyes blazed in bright sunlight. The whole heavy face became so alert, so concentrated, so intensely settled on one thought, that Atticus shrugged his slight shoulders and gave up.

"I have blundered. I shall have to speak of old Cluentius."

"Well?"

"He knew my uncle and regarded him with humor when he was charging old friends and relatives twelve per cent a month as special discount. My uncle is terrible in his business, but he is not a beast. I honor him. The senior Cluentius was born between his generation and mine; yet he could win us both. The hard dealing at which my uncle was a master was strange to him; of the philosophy which enchanted my youth, he had but slight knowledge, nothing intimate. Yet he was a business friend of my uncle's, and a man whose name spoken in our courtyard could fill me with pleasure at an age when I thought all men barbarians who were not full of Greek."

"The husband of Sassia, of Cluentius' mother."

"That letter moved me."

"Ah. That letter moved you."

"Cicero! Don't take the case! The movements of the heart are no guide to action."

"Stop talking like a copybook, Atticus. You will be interested to share my hour with Cluentius tomorrow morning."

"What! You've agreed —"

"I've given him an appointment, daybreak. I explained that the interview would be short."

"Did you explain to him how crowded it would be? After three days of absence in Tusculum . . . O Marcus! In your absence the men of Rome begin to feel their boredom. What, no morning call on Cicero, no little exchange, no epigram, no little sharpness to season the day and provide the morning caller with his entrance line for all the occasions he is to be part of, later in the day?"

"Oh you Greeks — and greekified Roman too — curlicues, scrollwork!"

"We must stop joking. I have a feeling that tomorrow will be serious."

III

CLUENTIUS WAS TALL, and moved up the street that led to Cicero's house as if he had an ache in each long bone. How long since he had climbed a Roman hill! His habit was to move about as little as possible, when affairs brought him to the City. He had good agents, and a headquarters in the house of his friend Asuvius.

He had not wanted horse or litter for this occasion; he had wished to come unaccompanied, he had wanted to subject himself alone to the long narrow streets he hated; he had felt like exercising long-unused muscles in the early morning. But he hadn't quite realized what a distance and up what slopes he had to walk. As the streets began to fill, in the moment before sunrise, he had to pause often, and feel with displeasure the small facial spasm, mark of fatigue, which drew down one corner of his mouth in a little uncontrollable twitch.

He sat for a moment on a stone by a fountain in a little square. A child's ball whizzed past his foot; a small body hurtled after it, tripped, fell at his feet, just brushing his shin. He pulled back hard as if from some bruising contact; his dark eyebrows scowled over his dark eyes; the little girl stared up at him afraid, and saw his face change suddenly, as he bent toward her with a stiff motion, helped her up, smiled on and on at her, not speaking, for he could think of nothing but that she must lose that expression of numb fear. He knew enough not to *say* "Don't look scared!" but not enough to find something else. His smile was enough. She grinned impudently, asked him slangily why his mouth jerked around so. He still said nothing, until he saw that his no-voice was frightening her again; he spoke in his deep, grinding voice, which had always so much effort in it and so little ease; but he told her amiably she could mind her own business now, and she ran easily after her ball, able to dismiss him from her mind forever.

He sat for a moment longer, hunched up on the fountain's edge, his shoulders bowed, massaging absent-mindedly his sore leg, and worrying over the questions Cicero would ask. To think only of the next letter, the next interview, the next step, had been his careful policy since he had received, on business in Ephesus, the letter from Asuvius telling him of his mother's preparations for this suit.

What would this meeting be like, and what could he say? He had written too much. Cicero would expect him to be easy and quickly articulate. Those letters . . . how could any stranger know what departures they had involved? But the joy of those night hours in Asuvius' house, spent in dictating to his old loved slave, or in scratching, scratching with his pen, telling more than he had thought to tell, lit up his lean weary face. He tasted with care the few moments left to him in which he was not yet actually acquainted with Cicero. The demanding mind which had asked those questions, forced open those doors, *made* him tell and write and answer, this mind would assume a face with a voice. The lawyer of the other trial — eight years ago — across the courtroom, had a face and a voice, but

43

they belonged then to a man who knew nothing of Aulus Cluentius and had only guessed. How different was a man who had guessed at some things from this other man, who now knew so much! What else could he want to know, what other efforts must be made?

The press in the city streets of this important quarter was nothing to the press in Cicero's courtyard and reception rooms. The sun had just risen, the moment of the appointment just come; *this crowd!* Cluentius could not bring himself to plunge into it; but stood hovering outside it, feeling too tall, too heavy in the middle, too stiff in the joints; too old, too young. A young Greek standing near the door of an inner room, a step or two above the crowd, saw him, fixed him with a sudden intent bright gaze, and started toward him, moving nimbly around elbows; a murmur of names between them, and Cluentius found himself coolly guided through and around the crowd in some authoritative way, ushered, announced, and in the Praetor's presence before he had time to collect himself.

When he came into the little antechamber beside Cicero's bedroom, the Praetor was just shoving his broad feet into his sandals and reaching out his hand for his cloak. The air was chill. There were lines of weariness under the long blue eyes; but the Praetor's mouth was full of bread and he munched busily. A little plate of cheese, an apple in a bowl, stood on a low table. Only one other man stood in the room: no slave, a businessman of Rome, smiling from dark serious eyes, handing Cicero his cloak.

"Cicero will speak to you in a moment; he is occupied. I am Titus Pomponius Atticus of Athens." The smile broadened charmingly.

"Oh. Friend of my father," said Cluentius eagerly, stammering a little. A guarded look veiled the deep eyes of Atticus. Cicero munched and watched. Cluentius knew at once that they thought he was going to make use of this family connection in his appeal to Cicero. His deep voice ground to a quick stop.

"I had but slight acquaintance with your father, a much-respected man," said Atticus, in a light dry tone. Cluentius pulled himself together and spoke as quickly as his forever-hesitating vocal mechanism would let him.

"I know; you are not much older than I, after all, and he died when I was fifteen. I know of you only one personal thing — of course everyone knows of your interests — but in the old letters of my father, which I read many times after his death, he spoke always of this, that in entering the house of your uncle Caecilius he liked to find out immediately whether you were there. In the letters and the records that he kept, he always mentioned in the items dealing with Caecilius, whether or not you were there. This cannot have been for business reasons." The jaws of the Praetor stopped moving, but he did not swallow; he watched narrowly.

The guard dropped from the eyes of Atticus.

"This gives me pleasure," he said warmly. "Did your father ever get on with that plan he had about draining those low fields outside Larinum and running that new breed of sheep? There was a certain quality of wool he was interested in, very fine. My uncle disliked the idea from a financial point of view, but I could see that he was *thinking*. He talked often of the notion; thought it poetry, but he couldn't get it out of his head." Both men laughed pleasantly, and the stiff stance of Cluentius relaxed a little.

"My father was in many ways a man full of poetry. The sheep farm he thought of is in operation; I can't say it is one of my most resoundingly profitable ventures, but experts from Egypt and from your adopted country have

4 5

come to observe. A book will be written next year, if
. . . if all things remain in order."

"May I send my Tephiseus tomorrow? He will have a
particular interest."

The most gracious of short gestures answered him.

Cicero moved forward suddenly, and a quick silence fell.

" 'Aulus Cluentius Habitus from Marcus Tullius Cicero,
greeting,' " he said, his short, finely shaped mouth twisted
slightly. "I enjoyed our correspondence. I have thought of
you as a stylus, forever writing away, a real writing instrument; now I see you as a man."

"The honor is mine, Cicero."

The racket of voices outside the closed door rose suddenly as a slave half-opened the portal. Cicero made a swift
movement of the head, and the quick intelligent face of the
slave recorded the response. The door closed; the babble
was muted.

"You informed me of your crowded day. I could hardly
pass through your anterooms. You have admitted me first.
My thanks —"

"I have absolutely no intention, my good Cluentius, of
discussing that interminable affair with you here. It is possible that when I return to Tusculum in a week's time, after
my new hearings, I shall have the time to consider with
you. I shall let you know. In the meantime, I invite you to
accompany me to the Forum. I should like to ask you a
few, a very few questions. But I have so much in hand.
Here, give me a hand with this cloak; I shall carry it, after
all. Atticus is leaving, he goes by another street; he hates
the Forum. Be comfortable, Cluentius! Just follow along.
I'll be talking to a few of these people, but in between we
can chat a bit . . . well? Are you coming?"

"Of course, great Praetor: gladly."

"Pass before me. Now, Atticus, you!" As his friend

moved through the door, Cicero gave him a quick short punch in the ribs. Atticus coughed, and turned quickly; but the face of the Praetor was bland and smooth. The night's weariness seemed to have disappeared.

Ten grave businessmen of Rome, seven individuals of vague status, and the Praetor's two lictors, ceremonial attendants bearing rods and axes, symbols of authority, moved with them down the street. Slaves pattered before and behind, Cicero's and others'; schoolmasters shouted in doorways and messengers squeezed by, running, swearing under their breath. Cluentius walked on the fringe of Cicero's miniature crowd and knew nothing of where he was going or why.

At a narrow corner a procession barred their passage; as they all stood becalmed for long minutes, silenced by the clank of weapons and shields, the thud of feet and the bawl of directing voices, Cluentius moved inward from the outer edge of the group. More soldiers passed, three senators in litters; at the rear, a *legatus* and a military tribune, wearing the agedly haughty faces forever common among young officers, jounced by on their horses, looking down on the unmounted. As they passed, there was a short lull in the eternal clamor of the street. Cluentius caught the narrowed glance of Cicero, and heard the Praetor say to the fat banker on his right hand:
"Two Aemilii, a Catulus, and an adopted son of the Scipios! What a clutch, Papirius, of our young nobility! Happy omen for our little brotherhood of tradesmen here, to have our paths crossed by such eaglets! *Especially* that last, little Piso with his hand on the saddle-bow in the Numidian style — his poor splayed trembling hands hidden in those gloves, his crossed eyes under the visor, his

47

nose, Papirius, alone eloquent of the command for which I fear that small squeaky voice of his can never be a proper trumpet . . . though he does of course have the nose. . . ." Papirius laughed shortly.

"It's the nose of all the Pisos, Cicero; there must be something impressive in it, since you yourself will be related to it through your Tullia's marriage to that boy's cousin."

"Tullia is a child. She'll grow up, and she'll marry a Piso. But she —" The racket of the street closed about them, and Cluentius was spun against the wall by a passing runner. He lost Cicero's sentence, but the expression on that great mobile face, a look blended of pride, sarcasm, and tenderness, was not lost to his eyes.

The next quarter-hour was all noise, commotion, swift striding progress interrupted by maddening standstills. Cluentius concentrated grimly on survival and on keeping his balance. He heard a few snatches; the stout Papirius between puffs striving ably to interest Cicero in a case:

"— you know the friendships of my nephew, Cicero, and his former good services to many, in elections —"

"— in this year, with juries so intense, I've done very little with these extortion cases, you must have noticed, Papirius —"

"— such huge sums involved that it would be hard to put a limit to my nephew's gratitude when the elections —"

"— suggestion, my great friend Hortensius is still quite successful with these cases; last month, you remember that rather comic affair —"

"Hortensius! For four years now everybody knows he's . . . everybody wants Cicero somehow to —"

"You overestimate —"

"Impossible!"

"But Hortensius is just building his new house, and you underestimate —"

4 8

"Impossible, Cicero. He can't do anything without bribery, and this year the feeling about bribery —"

"Impossible! This alley has been impossible for four months now, ever since that edict about the wagons coming from the old gate — look OUT!" Cicero skipped nimbly to one side, switching his toga. The cart's mud missed him, but Papirius swore roundly.

"Why they can't pave . . . that damned aedile, with the votes we delivered — uh, Cicero! my nephew —"

But another banker strode at Cicero's side, gesticulating and talking about the taxes ruining the new grain markets.

"Vestorius! There's your house! Here comes another of those damned funerals — can't we get into your gardens for a moment?" The Praetor shouted at his lictors; the slaves caught the wave of his arms, and the whole little band trooped into a moment of sanctuary. Hushed and panting, they stood for a moment listening to silence, the street's racket muted by great walls and paved space; listening also to the cool splash of water in a pool. Rapid shiftings and regroupings took place. Suddenly Cluentius found himself with Cicero's hand on his elbow, pulled aside into a little study and business room; incredibly, he stood alone with the busiest man in Rome.

"Cluentius," said Cicero as if they had been talking in seclusion for hours, "you have heard gossip about the betrothal of my daughter?" Wearily Cluentius suppressed his astonishment and strove for ease.

"Why, nothing much, Cicero. I believe you yourself told me of the business in a letter. I heard Lucius Papirius just now speaking of the Pisos. She is betrothed to one of them?"

"Yes. But she is a child. Before she is married, I shall have been consul. This will change things for her in that family."

"I am sure — "

"Sure! What man is sure? But I swore long ago that she should marry one of them."

"The Pisos? I know nothing of them really — "

"No! I mean one of *them* — the good men: our *Roman nobility.*"

"Oh."

"You find this ignoble?"

"My father, great Cicero, allied himself by marriage with such a house; it was a part of his 'poetry,' as Atticus' uncle would have said."

"You suggest — one must infer — that in your experience such alliances make no great promises of happiness. Your mother was herself the daughter of just such an alliance; not a happy omen." A terrible stiffness paralyzed the countenance of Cluentius.

"I meant to suggest nothing about my mother." The tic drew down one side of his mouth. He could not continue. He forced himself to look squarely at Cicero.

"You persist, Habitus," said the Praetor in a very quick, low voice, hard-toned, edgy, "in maintaining this 'decorum' of which you spoke in your letter. You persist in being unwilling to turn at bay against your mother! You sought just now for words in which to tell me not to discuss your mother — *me!*" Red temper flamed in the heavy cheeks. A wave of exhaustion swept over Cluentius. *Temperament:* these temperaments.

"Have you not learned that 'happiness' is the idiotic concern of idiots, that one must settle on an end and then settle on the means best adapted to that end — "

"What if the end become adapted then, by the means?" said Cluentius swiftly, the habitual hesitations of his speech shaken loose. "It was not I who spoke of 'happiness' in connection with marriage, Cicero. I do not wish to offend you; may I speak to you of my case?"

"I am speaking of it to you. How do I know that I can afford your case, Cluentius, in this year of all years?"

A painful flush moved up Cluentius' long bony cheek.

50

"I know that the law which forbids advocates to take fees for pleading is easily circumvented, Cicero, and I am not unable — "

"Fees! Gifts! You babble. What I cannot afford is a lost cause."

"In this case, I can afford it even less."

"What I meant was this: If you obstruct me and dictate the terms of your defense, as you are capable of doing — O yes, my upright friend, honored of all! If you shrink from some slight mention of your mother, our opponent in this case — " A great light flamed in the eyes of Cluentius.

"You will take the case! 'Our,' you said!"

"Gods!" shouted Cicero angrily. "I misspoke, and you know it, and try to trip me with it! Listen to me, Cluentius, I shall build MY case on such an attack against your mother that the She-wolf will have strength left for not one howl, not even a snarl! There will be no cave in Italy lost enough so that she can slink to it! Don't speak! Silence! We will discuss nothing more. Watch me in the court today: I go to the Forum not as Praetor but as advocate. Listen to me. Leave the Forum when you have had enough. If you, my good squeamish briber of juries, feel yourself able to stomach the consequences of having me conduct your case, find yourself at Tusculum in three days' time, and we will then decide. *Now!*" He put out his hand to clutch Cluentius' elbow again. Something in the hard rigidity of the arm under the toga arrested the shoving motion he was beginning. He stared hard, at close range, into the deep eyes of the man from Larinum.

"Why, Cicero," said Cluentius in a voice low as the Praetor's had been loud, "do you propose to interest yourself at all? If you feel nothing for me, why take my case? No reason except, perhaps, a hysterical wish to involve yourself in some great sensation, even at some considerable risk; you seem to have a taste for hurly-burly — " suddenly, Cluentius found himself speaking through his teeth in a tone as tense and sharp as any he had heard — "for useless noise and bustle, and all men crowding round. Is it for this that you propose to consider my cause, provided that I let you make sensation enough of it?"

A heavy silence fell. Cluentius went on with his hard stare. The face of the Praetor suddenly broke up under his gaze; long deep lines showed on each side of his mouth, curved now in a smile of extraordinary sweetness. Warmth and charm and a kind of grave liveliness lit up the eyes so close to Cluentius' own; a long deep look held him, moved him, charged his mind with the memory of another such look, eight years ago, in a surging, howling courtroom under the high rostrum. The hard impatience of the hand on his arm changed in a moment.

"You speak the truth about me, Cluentius," said Cicero with great simplicity. Cluentius said nothing.

"But not the whole truth; not the only truth," added the Praetor. This time it was Cluentius who smiled.

Within three hours' time Cluentius stood aghast in a crowd of spectators ringing the benches of a tribunal in the Forum, while Cicero on the rostrum, the high platform towering over the benches, began the final section of a speech calculated to destroy all dignity, all tranquillity in the life of his client's accuser. The great voice rolled over the benches, over the rings of standing listeners, down the passageways and into the alleys: sober, ample, full of a splendid loathing:

". . . in what vile dens of the Subura, of all our low quarters, did he not disgrace before foreigners and slaves the name of Roman and of citizen? This one, this one, whose spirit wasted by disgusting loves — O gods! *loves!* what corruption! — now strives, still capable of its own disgust, to leave his body wasted by a disease so vile his own physicians will not, cannot speak of it. He is dying; his flesh prey to puddles of writhing maggots; yet with his last poisoned, poisoning breath, the breath of the whole sewer which is his being, he tries to accuse my friend here — " the tone changed abruptly; the Praetor's voice sank to a confidential tone, still mysteriously as audible as the sonorous shout; wrinkles of wit and pure laughter showed at the corners of the eyes just now burning somberly. "I'll tell you, gentlemen, a story, brought me just yesterday by someone I can only describe as *in a position to know* — " and in a swift-moving colloquial style, full of low puns and high exaggeration, he told a story so scandalous and so funny that its close was half-lost in the rolling roars of laughter. The story told baldly of some vices, hinted grotesquely at others. From the next court the spectators, already few, began to hurry over. The crowd deepened outside the benches. The prosecutor's face purpled and his mouth writhed.

Cluentius backed slowly through the press of elbows, extricating himself with care. Words, images, whole phrases bearing intolerable pictures, repeated themselves, wound sinuously through the ears of his imagination. He moved up one of the passageways; but he stopped in its entry, held in a surge of music, the music not only of a great voice but of mighty words. The Praetor spoke of the law of Rome. He spoke of order imposed by the minds of men upon the disorders of their own existence; an order forever the same in the shifting tides. Behind all flux, one permanence: the gift of Rome; a structure built out of men's many answers to the question: what is justice?

"Gentlemen, jurors," said Cicero softly. The court moved to his tune. His verdict lay in his hand. He perceived this, and fell silent.

53

IV

CLUENTIUS SAT in the darkened chamber on the second story of Asuvius' Roman house; a room set aside permanently for his use, bare and cool as he liked rooms to be, furnished with a few unornamented pieces which by now were as familiar to him as any furniture in his own house in Larinum. He had in this evening hour only a faint memory of the journey back from the Forum; exhausted beyond all his experience of exhaustion, he had hired a carter to drive him home. He had nodded fitfully and painfully in the undignified vehicle, his whole frame bruised anew by the grind of heavy wheels on cobblestones. He had kept his mind as empty, as bare and cool as he could. Now, after his bath and a rest, he let himself think.

His mind was full of pictures and his imagination full of voices. He could *hear* Cicero speaking of his client's enemy; he could hear the same terrible voice speaking of another client's enemy, that client's mother, Sassia of Larinum. That power of projecting verbal pictures! Scenes from the life of Sassia and Oppianicus, scenes in the marketplace of Larinum which could sum up in a hard visual form the hatred and

54

loathing of the whole township . . . scenes of intimacy, the walks with the tall tenant farmer by the wine-cooling spring . . . scenes of horror, the torturing of the slaves, the twisted crucified body of Strato the burglar-slave hanging on its cross, tongue torn from its hanging, gaping mouth. The words that Cicero would use, the tearing open of long-closed doors, merciless, merciless, the revelation of a life-time's buried truths — if only he, Cluentius, had not read so much, talked so much within himself, acquired such a vast wealth of words and experience of their sounds and shapes! Then he could spare himself until the day itself the knowledge of what that speech could do to his life.

Another thought suddenly possessed him, taking him suddenly in an access of surprise. He realized as if for the first time how entirely his private life was composed of his experiences with his mother.

How had it happened? No man was forced to live like this. The wide interests he had found in the world of business, the acquaintances; the one deep friendship, with Marcus Asuvius; the beauty he had known how to enjoy wherever he went, the delights of the mind — surely these should have in his mature years displaced at the center of his being that long-tormenting preoccupation. But they had not. They had become the skeletal structure of his life, but the vitals, the red central regions, were still the old conglomeration of mysteries, nightmare realizations, stern self-composings, stubborn hard-fought refusals, which made up the relationship with that woman.

After the affair of Cluentia and Sassia's marriage to young Aurius Melinus, his family and acquaintance in Larinum had at first kept silent upon the subject as a sort of automatic decency. But as the affairs of Sassia became the public affairs of Larinum and a part of Larinum's worst destiny, in the early years of Oppianicus, naturally Cluentius was addressed; deputations came to see him, his senior cousins wished to suggest courses of action. He discovered that he had lived on those early silences, on the cleared space around his vital concerns which that decency had afforded him. He could no longer do without it. He asked at first that all discussion of his mother's crimes be avoided, saying truthfully that he had agents who could keep him well informed and on guard. When attempts were made to breach the silence, he insisted a little, often he entreated. Then suddenly and with an immovable hardness, he demanded. Looking over these years now, he could see how in that silence his own injuries had festered.

The silence had been broken when Marcus Asuvius and some other old friends of the family came to him for help; for money and his voice and presence in a conflict. This was a small affair, an attempt on the part of the municipality to block with a legal action a move by Oppianicus toward further powers in the town. Cluentius had maintained through the first reports of the pending action his accustomed silence; now Asuvius said to him firmly that through this inaction he seemed to connive at the maneuver of his stepfather. His great reputation for honesty and for fanatical cleanliness in civic and financial affairs thus stood grotesquely as a silent ally of Oppianicus.

It was not a year since Asuvius' young brother had met his ignoble end at Oppianicus' hands. Deeply, painfully, Cluentius had felt himself involved in this cruel happening. How avoid the hard question: Could he have acted to save the poor young rake from his murder, knowing the affair as he did, in its early stages, through his agents? He had written letters to Asuvius abroad. This was all he had done, and Asuvius had arrived in Larinum too late to act.

All right, all right! He had put up money in this new affair between Larinum and Oppianicus. He had gone to Rome, appeared in a Roman court against his stepfather; now, remembering, he saw again the narrow whirling streets, the dark face of Oppianicus blackened with rage; heard the strangled shouts of threat, in that wild deep voice. His mind turned from following that memory; but he forced himself, for his will could open doors as relentlessly as it could close them.

Of that day which now seemed so long ago, the day after his return to Larinum from Rome, after this first engagement with his stepfather, he had spent the first hours in morning calls on two old bankers of Larinum. This was not Cluentius' ordinary practice, as it was the practice of many in his world and many more in the world of Rome. But he was just returned from the city and the savage struggle. He felt a bit skinned, much bruised, weary and nerve-torn after his first involvement in open conflict. His old need of solitude had seemed curiously secondary to him at this moment. He had gone in search of words, faces, outstretched hands of older men who had urged him to act and to speak.

Aged Gnaeus Aurius, whose brother had paid with his life five years ago for opposition to Oppianicus in the shadow of Sulla, had embraced him. Lucius Magius, whose grandson had been murdered as a wedding present for Sassia, had come out from his office chamber to welcome Cluentius, talk long with him. Both had emphasized to him one thing: although he had lost the case, and come as one offering apology and hoping for pardon — his action had had positive effect. Oppianicus had had to spend an enormous sum on his jury and even on his judge, just at a time when he did not wish any such outlay. Now he would walk carefully for a while, wishing no further involvement with any Roman court. Not that he feared verdicts, in that year of corruption, for all men knew they were to be purchased. But the price was rising, the uncertainties multiplying, the receiving of bribes becoming a complex, organized business necessitating the use of highly paid agents.

"You've put a crimp in the man, my boy! He's going to have to sell, do a lot of selling. . . ."

As he turned in at his own gate after these calls, absorbed in thought, he passed without looking at them a standing litter and group of slaves outside his wall. He heard, without quite yet really hearing it, an odd chatter from within his own courtyard. As he passed through the forecourt, sound struck his ears, no longer to be avoided: a cool, rippling voice, declaiming, chatting, laughing, while he stood there transfixed. A queer blubbering, glubbing sound interposed in the spaces of this speech. Cluentius moved past two small columns to look at the scene being acted in his further court, before his painted garden wall.

His tall, beautiful mother stood there, in an attitude, as so often with her, not ordinarily seen in any woman of Rome or Larinum. She had taken brushes and paint-tray from his old painter-slave Chrysippus. She daubed with swift strokes at the glistening designs on the figured wall at which Chrysippus had been working. The old Greek gesticulated, wept, and gobbled, for he could not speak. Cluentius had bought him in the worst time of the civil wars, because of his age and his lost tongue. He was fortunate in having lost only his tongue; he came from an estate that had known real massacre. Now he had done nothing for eight years but paint, and sketch for master and steward various designs for the decoration and enrichment of house and gardens. Sassia spoke to him over her shoulder, in quick huddling groups of words.

She wore a peculiar mantle, recognized by all Larinum. Oppianicus had brought it from Asia. It was striped and embroidered in the most un-Roman way, and he wore it as much as she. If you saw from the tail of your eye its strange green or its golden threads, you could not know immediately whether Oppianicus or Sassia walked, rode, stood in your neighborhood.

58

"Oh Chrysippus! Shush and listen to me telling you something worth while." A great somber line of tragic Euripides rolled from her tongue, decrying the low fate of the slave taken in war and led abroad. Around the Greek words, so full of pity and rage against man's fate, played her personal tone, altering, by her personal understanding and by her grim command of irony, the whole text into a hymn celebrating and rejoicing in the disgrace of men through crippling power. "Stop that capering," she said in Latin, and then changed it into the vulgar Greek of the Island sailors, twanging and insulting. "Gods, man, these daubs! Thank me! Thank me!" she said, and out came another set of verses, celebrating this time man's ingratitude and feeble failure to resign himself to superior will. She marred her effect slightly, as of old, by a burst of clear laughter, as she stood back from her work and saw how delicately she had deformed the grave face of golden Helen walking on the walls of Troy. The elders at the Skaian gate leered and goggled; she had done *something*, what? No crude defacement; just a line here, a blot there, a discoloration.

"Can't talk, can't paint, but I might *almost* say you could dance," she observed, and turned to face Cluentius, as she was made aware of the new presence by the sudden immobility of the slave. She threw down her instrument, stooped with arrogant bending grace to set her little tray of paint-pots carefully on the tiled floor. She strode toward Cluentius with color for once burning in her pale cheeks. She made no comment of any sort on what she had just been doing. She came within a pace of Cluentius, who stood rigid before her. A long look from her narrow blue eyes pierced him, but he outpaused her. She turned sharply from him, gestured with her head toward the little study that opened off the court, and moved into it, drawing him in her wake.

There she turned upon him and opened her mind to him. She informed him, in the long, precisely balanced sentences

59

which had always been the voice of her greatest rages, that she regarded the intervention in this trifling municipal affair as a stupidity of which only his poor simplicity was capable, and as an affront which only her full resources were capable of punishing. Was he aware of the inconvenience, the enormously unnecessary inconvenience, to which her husband had been put by this expense? Naturally, she knew that Cluentius was not shrewd enough to have calculated this; that he was quite capable of imagining, when the fat fools of Larinum came to him in the matter, that he could win a case against Oppianicus — *Oppianicus*. A stinging silence followed her repetition of the name. It was a very short silence.

The clumsiness of the maneuver had, she resumed, had an effect which could not have been more annoying to her had it been executed with the intelligence of which half his heredity and all his nature had so conspicuously deprived him. She was not prepared to see her husband again forced to renounce any plan on which hung his slightest pleasure — *slightest*. It so happened that the voyage which he had been planning with her and which they had now been obliged to give up, the other plans, the moneys they had had to divert, were of the first importance. Cluentius had refused her former approaches to him, she begged to remind him, her suggestions of a purely business relation — surely not even he could have imagined for an instant that she had in mind anything more personal. His reasons were naturally the same as the reasons which underlay all his decisions: his congenital inability to understand the simplest situation or perform the most uncomplicated action with effect.

She would, however, make one statement to him that she felt even he was capable of grasping, and upon which he was perhaps — *perhaps* — capable of acting. It was this. He would find any and all climates more suitable and healthy for him than the climate of Larinum. She would say no more. It was possible that he could understand. It was certainly desirable that he understand, desirable for *him*, since naturally for her his decisions, actions, and mental processes could have no possible interest other than their possible effect on her husband's comfort, even of an instant. Rather than endure for a moment the important — *important* — spectacle of Oppianicus' discomfort, she would consider it her duty and her pleasure to . . .

"Mother!" shouted Cluentius, using the word for the first time in many years. Her writhing lips closed in a long red line. Her eyes blazed cold and blue, a foot away from his.

"*Son?*" she inquired, in the low voice of her deepest hatred.

"Be quiet," he muttered. In the short silence she breathed hard. He drew himself together.

"You too must endure consequences," he said heavily. A faint look of astonishment altered for a moment her concentrated expression. "He has gone too far before, and that was when he had the Dictator Sulla. You speak," suddenly he found himself standing quite erect, facing her, looking evenly at her, answering her, "with your old eloquence about my failure to comprehend situations. May I suggest to you that your husband also has his moments of such failure?" A real surprise, open, genuine, dominated the face of Sassia. She was silent.

"The first," continued Cluentius rapidly, his hesitations forgotten in a tide of speech, "was when he disrupted the inquiry into the death of Publius Asuvius. My friend Marcus Asuvius is not the sort of man to submit to this. And, Mother, I must call to your attention the fact that those of us who were boys have since become men, while your eyes were elsewhere. I must point out to you also that the climate of Larinum like the climate of Rome is changing all the time, has changed since the death of the Dictator your husband's patron, five years ago. *I* can perceive this, though I was a young man then. I would suggest that you bring this fact to the attention of your husband, that attention which like yours has been elsewhere. He had small difficulty with the Asuvius inquiry, a great deal more with the one through which we have just passed. It's not hard to foresee that he will make further attempts. One could wish for his sake, were one his well-wisher as you are, that he could foresee increasing difficulties. I — "

"You!" said Sassia in the savage whisper she used instead of a shout. "You!" She made a sudden half-turn, so that her back was to Cluentius. The long green stripe of the Asian mantle glowed softly, the gold threads sparkled as her shoulders shook. Cluentius put up his hand across his eyes. A terrible trembling seized him. Like a sick man he half-turned, groped, sat down on a small bench.

"If I'd known your damned father was going to make that will," she whispered mournfully, talking half to herself, not caring at all whether Cluentius understood or even heard. "He never said he'd give you so much, leave you emancipated from guardianship" — she used here a precise legal term, as if it had been hurting her for many years — "of course I'd thought when he died it would be easy to get rid of you . . . marry off the girl, get rid of you . . . get rid of you somehow. But he got round me and fixed everything for you — he, I mean, your damned father. If not for that . . . *rid* of you . . . you'd just not be here to annoy him, my husband, my Oppianicus, contradict him, get in his way, make all these unnecessary things necessary . . . he's tired, bitterly tired and not over the accursed malaria — damn Sulla and those marshes — his fever goes up at sunset — so much better in Alexandria or the Islands and now I can't take him there." She stiffened as if to spring for another attack; thought again of it, reclined against a little mantel, wearily. She turned her head. The scornful mouth turned

6 2

down now, rich and crimson, unpainted, incredibly soft. The lovely line of jawbone and of neck was accentuated as she tilted back her head and put up her pale hand to flick with agile fingers at the tears in the corners of her eyes. Cluentius stared and stared.

"But Oppianicus," he said, and as if he also were not really interested in being heard or understood. "Oppianicus? Why him, why that one?" He just stopped, unable to go on. She turned toward him briskly and gave him her full attention. The tears were gone and her eyes hot and bright again, her tongue darting between her teeth.

"Who *is* he? What *is* he? You ask!" She hissed and stamped. "He is Oppianicus! What else, who else, fool . . ." She collected herself suddenly, gathered the mantle over her arm and turned toward the door. Very firmly and decisively she spoke her next words.

"*That* one," she said. "*Him!* Statius Albius Oppianicus." She stopped for a moment in the doorway, very brisk now.

"As you will have reason to understand, though not perhaps the capacity," she said. "Look out for yourself, Cluentius, and let your friend Asuvius look out for himself, and *good*-by, Cluentius!" And she was gone.

Cluentius went out from his study and soothed old gibbering Chrysippus before the wall. He sent a slave to tell Marcus Asuvius to expect him for dinner.

At dinner he mentioned a plan. Asuvius like Sassia stared at him in astonishment.

"You'd do that?"

"I'd do that."

V

AS THE WORDS of his mother's speech on that far-off day hissed and twisted through Cluentius' memory, he thought with relief of one fact: he had said nothing of this scene to Cicero in those letters, where he had spoken of so many others. This was still private property. He would never have to hear it presented, new-colored and given horrible new life, before a Roman crowd. Many scenes of which she was the center were available, if not through his own letters, then through the reports of others: he knew Cicero's habit of formidable thoroughness in gathering evidence.

The slaves, those inquisitions and tortures . . . much would be said, the eyes of many witnesses would be used. These scenes did not exist in Cluentius' memory, only in his imagination; but he could remember one scene in which the deaths were all implicit.

Two years after the death of Oppianicus, when Sassia's first savage, ineffective attempt to accuse her son of her husband's murder had already passed into uneasy oblivion in the mind of Larinum, Cluentius received a peculiar letter from her. She announced to him in graceful, formal phrases that his sister was to be married. His eyes closed nervously; he composed himself with an effort, saying "Auria, *Auria*," aloud to himself, forcing his attention to the fact that his mother spoke of his young half-sister, the daughter of ill-starred Aurius Melinus and his mother's second marriage, once so shocking, which now in retrospect and in comparison seemed rather bland, quite innocuous. He had never seen this girl. She was to be married, Sassia wrote, to her stepbrother, Statius Albius Oppianicus the Younger, who was her distant cousin, since his mother had been of the Aurii.

Remembering this letter now, so many years after receiving it, Cluentius could still feel like a physical sensation his intense wariness of its strange tone. His mother had made no move in his direction since the failure of her inquisitions with the slaves after Oppianicus' death. He had been aware of her only as an occasional glimpsed presence in a curtained litter; a face between curtains, a half-seen figure in a crowd outside some temple, in some square. She had made one voyage to her old favorite among cities, Alexandria; she had spent most of her time in what was for her an incredible quiet and immobility, on her estate. Yet in her silence and remoteness as much as in her words and gestures of other years, Cluentius had felt her hatred.

Now she wrote like any aging female relative, gossiping a little, preening herself on the wealth involved in her daughter's marriage, speaking in a matron's fussing tone of arrangements for the wedding. Her letters and messages to Cluentius were always dictated; he had got into the mental habit, in other years, of imagining her face and voice dictating the words he read. He simply could not imagine what face and voice of hers had dictated this.

"You must be sadly aware, as I am, of the lamentable divisions in our family," she wrote, like a dowager discussing some unfortunate old family quarrel over a will or a piece of property, "and must, I am sure, my dear Cluentius, wish as ardently as I that the harmony of this new *union* in our family should become a general thing. I have too long been at odds with all my own. Let us make this occasion one of a greater pleasantness. . . ." On and on she went. She who had always preferred the stiff rattle of papyrus had had this letter put on old-fashioned wax tablets, whose little wooden frames clacked oddly in her son's hands. She had sent it by an unknown slave, not one of her known household. She had been considerate enough to give him time, saying in her letter that her slave would leave this for his consideration, and return for his reply on the next day. Her desire was simply this: that he might be magnanimous enough, family-spirited and peace-minded enough, to forget the regrettable past and present himself at Auria's wedding. She was too humble, she wrote, to ask for any extensive rapprochement: his presence at the wedding . . . well, she would be most grateful, most appreciative if he could so honor her wish to enter once more into a more normal relationship with the community and her family. She made several references to her advancing age.

Cluentius had made his decisions about this extraordinary document and request quite unaided. His friend Marcus Asuvius was in Rome. There was no one to consult. He thought carefully, walking in his garden, sitting by his fountain, turning about his small bedroom. Cool reason warned him to steer clear. No part of his mind or heart had the slightest confidence. But a powerful subterranean current pulled him toward acceptance, speaking first in the name of shrewdness (better find out what she's up to), more convincingly without words at all, just a deep, quiet, irrational wish to stand once more in that presence.

In the morning he received her slave himself, and gave him an oral message: the Lady Sassia's invitation should be accepted, he accepted it in the spirit in which she offered it.

6 6

The slave departed; returned within an hour, bearing a letter written in Sassia's own strong sloping script, begging the immediate presence of Cluentius at her house, since she was emboldened by his most gracious granting of her request to ask him a further favor: would he look at her guest list, just cast a swift glance over it, and tell her which of the citizens of Larinum on it would be discommoded and embarrassed by her invitation, could not possibly accept, would be injured and damaged, as she truly did not wish, by her mere approach to them? On this delicate question he alone could advise her; she would abide by his decision.

Astonished anew, drawn by his secret tide, telling himself that at least he could save a few elderly friends from some bitter feelings, he sent Sassia's slave off with the message that he would come within an hour.

He took with him a real guard of three trusted slaves and his freedman steward. All four walked at his side through Sassia's gate and received together with him the word that he should stop by the trellised garden and kindly bring along with him to his mother's summerhouse the young bridegroom, whom he would find waiting there for his arrival.

In a pleached arbor in this little garden Statius Albius Oppianicus the Younger had been sitting, sucking an olive pit, sipping green country wine, reading Epicurus. He was drooling a bit, his tongue in confusion between pit and liquid. Cluentius stood a few feet away from him before he looked up, started nervously, knocking off his bench the little jar which had held the scroll he now dropped on the grass. Cluentius spoke kindly to him; apologized, picked up the scroll and looked at it.

"Aspiring to *ataraxia*, the mind's perfect peace?" he asked with a smile, unable to keep from his voice the hint of condescension, talking-down, head-patting, which tended to invade the voices of all men who found themselves in conversation with the younger Oppianicus. To associate this poor, pale visage and thin body with the bronzed face, great stature, blazing eyes and striding vitality of the senior Oppianicus was a futile exercise. It was hard enough to think of him as grown up, technically a man.

Even as he asked idly the question about *ataraxia*, Cluentius reflected that the mind's perfect peace for this youth must somehow involve dissociation from his stepmother Sassia, for too many years the center of his world. She had taken over his life when he was twelve. What kind of peace could be imaginable to a mind formed and nourished in Sassia's shadow?

The young man muttered a greeting, managed a polite little smile in the direction of Cluentius' steward. Suddenly Cluentius felt his wariness relax. Whatever Sassia had in mind, she could not be preparing any very complex program based on the employment of this hopeless instrument. Cluentius spoke kindly again to Oppianicus, laid his hand on his arm, and guided him toward the summerhouse, indicating with a gesture that the others could wait for him here.

They approached her small beloved summerhouse, half aviary and half indoor garden. Above the sound of twittering and of restless wings rose the thin, delicate, unbelievably sure sound of her flute, threading through a grave winding air. There she sat, as Cluentius or Oppianicus had seen no woman of Rome or Larinum sit, cross-legged on the ground and stiff-spined, her eyes glinting mirthfully over the reed, her lips curled up at the side in her peculiar flute player's grin. Nicostratus had taught her the flute — her late husband's favorite Greek slave — in the first summer after Oppianicus the Elder had brought him back from the Islands. She learned no new airs; the melodies she played were still the ones he had taught her ten years before, deepened and elaborated each year with her heightening skill. Where she had picked up her manner, the poise of her head, all the eccentric graces of her movements with the instrument, none could tell. Young Oppianicus leaned against a slim column to watch her, chin sagging slightly, head moving slowly in response to the slow measure. Cluentius stood still in the doorway. Her pale blue eyes under the black brows stared sweetly and blankly into his.

Her dark hair was striped with gray, for the cosmetician's art had never engaged her interest. All the unguents of Alexandria and the sharp herbs of old women's gardens near Larinum had kept her skin soft and clear, without flaw. The time she spent on the ruthless discipline of her body had been her husband Oppianicus' despair, in haste as he had been always, and unwilling to move without her. But the paintpots and blue powders of other dressing-tables, the cases full of little brushes and dainty receptacles for mixed colors, were not on hers. As her hair grizzled, she lost interest in its color, and had it dressed always more simply. But if for one day it lost luster and hung dull, her maid had ten lashes and was ill for a week.

These ins and outs of the Lady Sassia's boudoir were once well known to the boy Cluentius, and the man who stood before her now found his memory full of them. Her pale unpainted face, the wild eyes staring out unrimmed by conventional dark lines, her mouth of its own red, moving in its own outlines, had once been the basic fact of his life; how easily it could re-establish itself in his imagination. He noted dully, without wondering as did others, her abiding youthfulness, the strength and vivacity, the unimpaired physical magnificence of this woman who ought, by all the gods, to have a waist thickened and a face gored by these past years. She performed now the feat with which she used to amuse him long ago, rising slowly on one leg without putting her hands to floor or bench. Young Oppianicus smiled helplessly.

"How much longer will I be able to do that?" She fixed her gaze on Cluentius anew, piped shrilly into the flute and danced slowly over to him. Behind her the cage of indigo birds, housed all together for their harmonies of color, was silent. The flowers of the Egyptian vines she so loved breathed out their powerful yet delicate fragrance. Her stepson stood silent in his long trance. She brushed her cool cheek against his naked upper arm, pushed him gently to a bench, and gave to her own son a sweet and formal greeting. She began to talk to him in soft idle tones as she moved about amoung vines and potted shrubs, picking off dead leaves, collecting little sprays of blossom as she went.

"I've sent for Hirtius to come with the tablets and my lists," she said. "It is hard for me to tell you how gratefully I accept this favor you are doing me. You had always a talent for generosity; I am fortunate, and know it." She took care, skillfully, not to let any silence last long enough to make it necessary for him to speak any but the easiest short phrases of response. "You are unacquainted with your half-sister, my Auria. You shall meet before long. She is occupied now in the new wing we are establishing, for these young people." Her hand brushed young Oppianicus' shoulder lightly as she passed him to pick up a bowl and set it on the bench beside him. "My young Oppianicus has some tasteful ideas about the arrangement of columns and some new statues. Auria is learning. She argues a bit from time to time, but she will learn to do as her husband wishes. And of course *I* am giving her a whole course of instructions, very special instructions, on various ways of pleasing a husband." She drew a long breath from the flowers of Egypt. "Phases which may not have occurred to the ladies of Larinum, especially to those among them whom I especially hope to have at our reception." She grinned, her lip curled extravagantly at the corners, as over the flute. She looked hard and meaningly into the tube of a trumpet-shaped tawny blossom. *"Dear boy,"* she said, not to Cluentius, but to her stepson; she walked back to him, one hand clasping the sheaf of flowers, put one arm idly round his neck, and threw the blossoms into the great silver bowl. "There now," she said. "Here comes our Hirtius," and her steward entered with the tablets.

Gravely, sensibly she discussed the matter of the invitations with Cluentius. He remained standing, asking her permission to do so. From time to time she made some small courteous inquiry of young Oppianicus. At the close of the consultation, she thanked Cluentius with dignity and simplicity.

"Will Auria come?" asked Cluentius, stammering slightly.

"Oh, perhaps we'd best not cut into her deliberations this morning," said his mother coolly. "She does get so easily confused. You'll see her at the wedding, and before, for I shall count upon your presence at the family ceremony on the eve. She is fourteen. She has spent most of her life among women and children, living with the Aurii here and in the South. I've never had much chance to do anything for her," said Sassia with the most maternal of small grimaces, "until now: now, when I can give her for a husband this Oppianicus, give her life as the wife of a Statius Albius Oppianicus." The light voice grew deep. She stood straight and unmoving; her voice moved the bones in her son's body. "For my poor Auria, an Oppianicus," she repeated, and held out her hand to her stepson. "The treasure of a life," she whispered, and the sunlight fell green across her face through the broad leaf of a strange tree. Cluentius spoke the formal phrase of farewell.

He had just come from Sassia's little road, through her great gate into the street with his three companions, when they saw the Greek slave Nicostratus running toward them. Knowing of old the rear entrance to the estate and its weedy alley, Cluentius realized how fast he must have come. The young high-nosed, clean-boned face was white with strain; he could not speak for a minute, but stood gasping, blocking their way toward their horses which stood waiting with another slave.

"Aulus Cluentius," said the Greek youth painfully, "hear me for one minute. I beg you —" His face worked, his voice stuck in his throat. Cluentius took his arm and led him to one side, where a horse-trough stood in a little circle of thick green shrubs and in the shade of heavy oaks. The slave dashed water on his face, and raised his head to look at Cluentius with despair, a great claiming look of anguish.

"She means to reopen the case, Lord! She marries them only for that, to close her hand on him, that she may use him when her time comes, use him — she will have her case! You are deceived, Lord, by her looks and words; he knows nothing and can do nothing, though I have warned him and begged. But you are another one; you are one who can *do*, when he knows . . ."

"What is your reason for telling me this?" said Cluentius in a hard wary voice; he scowled, his eyebrows knotted over his piercing glance.

The Greek shrugged extravagantly. "For my life, I tell you," he said quietly. "She let us go, the other slave, Strato — you remember."

"I remember."

"She bought him, she has set him up in business here; she helps him, talking to him of his freedom every day."

"I know. There is little I do not know here, Nicostratus."

"You know then that she will have me again, now my master is in her hand — he tried to protect me then, three years ago when my master Oppianicus died; my young master; now when she marries him to her daughter, makes sure he won't move away as he had thought to do — stops him even from building his own house as he had thought to do, fixes him here — now she'll wait; the time will come, and she'll take me again. She does *not* forget! Strato is a fool and thinks she has forgotten," the young voice hurried frantically, though Cluentius stood stock-still, watching him, unmoving. "She does not forget!" Nicostratus finished lamely.

"This is your opinion, Nicostratus. What do you wish me to do?"

"Stop the marriage!"

"Impossible: you know how impossible."

"Don't let her have her reception, with the town all here, so that everyone will feel she has forgotten, and stop watching her, stop fearing her! They will come if you do as she asks, if you come. Lord, Lord! I know how I speak out of my rank, but —"

"You offer me no evidence, Nicostratus."

The Greek face froze suddenly in hysterical calm.

"It will come again — she will not give up, until she gets her case. Evidence, everybody wants evidence, Lord Cluentius; you, now; soon, it will be she. She will take us again, Strato and me; she will torture us again. Your Roman law!" The youth spoke still calmly with a queer quivering undertone; he spoke as no slave speaks to any Roman citizen, but as one man to another. "No slave's evidence is admissible unless given under torture. O Roman justice! Once my young master tried to give me freedom; she found out, and blocked him, stopped him, *persuaded* him. Persuasion! She'll enjoy herself on me — you think she's forgotten it was I who told my old master about her and the tenant farmer, those noons by the spring. Evidence!" And in one motion he collapsed on the grass, writhing.

"Oh, Greeks!" thought Cluentius with Roman impatience. But a hand closed round his ankles; he bent forward unwillingly, to stretch down his own hand, to offer what he could offer; a hand, only. Nicostratus raised himself with his other arm, let go his hold on Cluentius' ankle in order to tear off with a loud hysterical rip the upper half of his tunic. Sobbing, he twisted away, bent and squirming in the lush grass. Cluentius and his three companions had to look, had to see the long beastly scars, the little blue twisted lumps where the metal at the end of the lash had done something odd to the flesh. The knife's path — Sassia's own work, Cluentius recognized the facts reported in the record of the old investigation — raised its ridge of tissue below the shoulder blade. The long arm struck straight out, so they had to see the twisted, lumpy crippled fingers on that hand; three years since Nicostratus had fingered any flute.

"Nicostratus! What can I do?" The young slave heard the pity and the un-Roman feeling in the voice. He stopped his exhibition.

"Nothing, Lord. Nothing — there is no one. We must all of us do nothing."

Within two years of this day, Cluentius stood on a waterfront of Ephesus, weary from hours of argument with members of his syndicate over insurance rates and the necessity of resorting to Greek bankers; he held in his hand a tablet, a letter brought to him from Larinum by the confidential slave of his friend Marcus Asuvius. Silence settled around him and inside his mind, shutting out the never-ending chatter of Greek and Roman voices; he read:

Friend of all my life, I write in haste and anguish of mind. News has reached us from Rome. Your mother has reopened the case of what she calls the "murder" of Oppianicus. She will within two days bring her formal charge against you: as before, she will maintain that you were responsible for the death, by poison, of her husband. She has conducted two public inquiries upon slaves: one Strato, belonging to her, one Nicostratus, belonging to her stepson Oppianicus the Younger. She was enabled to do this because Strato, who has that shop at her place, remember, was stupid enough to commit a burglary upon her strong room. She used this crime as pretext to launch the inquiry. No one has seen the tablets upon which the investigation was recorded; we are not sure what is upon them, the deponents were respectable men, old Lucius Papius among others; I have not had a chance to talk to him. Strato has been crucified and his tongue torn out. Nicostratus has disappeared. She has briefed an attorney for her stepson — it is technically young Oppianicus who brings the charge, ostensibly seeking justice for the death of a father. His attorney is Titus Accius of Pisaurum. Beware. Your friends here are prepared to do what they can. I delay my departure for Rome, and have sent for my best agents there to join me here. Return without delay.

VI

EVENTS OF THE LAST ten years spoke in somber, painful voices in the mind of Cluentius as he paced his small room and waited for Asuvius. He thrust memory from him at last, by concentrating fiercely on his recollections of the morning and early afternoon: the virtuoso's voice of Cicero in the Forum, the blue warmth of the Praetor's fine eyes in the courtroom of Vestorius' house on the way to the Forum; before that, the dark gentle face of slight Atticus in Cicero's bedchamber; the climb up Roman hills, the little girl looking at him in terror and then in gaiety; after it all, the grind of a heavy cart's wheels on Roman cobblestones. Leaning against the wall by his window, he heard the opening of the front gate, the rush of slaves' sandaled feet in the main court, directions shouted, some small negotiation being accomplished with a maximum of fuss. Grateful for interruption, he looked from his window; leaning out, smiling, self-forgetful, to watch the spectacle of a traveling-litter being introduced into the front court itself. Knowing well that Asuvius would enter on foot, as he had left his house on horseback that morning, Cluentius knew who was in the litter and why Asuvius was having it brought so far into the house before its cargo could be discharged.

This was his friend's niece Asuvia, apple of her uncle's eye though rarely present in any of his households. He kept a small establishment for her in the South. In an old, unfashionable resort town she lived with her companion, an aging spinster of Larinum, and with an ever-changing group of tutors and preceptors of all sorts, over whose selection, transportation, duties, difficulties, and eventual removals Asuvius flapped and clucked continually, teased and called Mother by his friends, patiently endured by his steward and bailiff. The girl was the young daughter of that brother, Publius Asuvius, Oppianicus' victim in the old days when the great predator stalked Larinum, murdering, forging wills, evading prosecution, thoroughly enjoying his unimpeded advancement. Her mother, a thin fragile little daughter of a fat municipal clan, had died at her baby's birth, with the matrons of Larinum in a barnyard chorus proclaiming fulfillment of their predictions. When her father died his low death, her uncle became her guardian. He was at first occupied with preserving her from the further depredations of Oppianicus, who always liked to finish things up and leave as few potential heirs as possible in the families whose fortunes he managed to divert. When that threat was removed, Asuvius found himself ensnared in a deep, and deepening, concern for her education, her wellbeing, her future. She was coming from the Southern town now, to break her journey here with him; then she and her old chaperone would proceed to Asuvius' house in Larinum, for her first visit of several years, during which the female friends and connections of her uncle would begin negotiations for her marriage.

Cluentius had never seen her through all the years of Asuvius' talk about her. He knew that his friend thought her enormously and dangerously beautiful, that the elder

7 7

female members of the household thought she would just do, that her old Greek tutor thought her brilliant and her Roman cousins on her mother's side thought her a provincial little bore. Lost in the blessed release of curosity, he craned a bit.

She struggled to get out of the litter, awkward in her long traveling garment; Cluentius could see thrust out from the litter and reaching to the ground a remarkably long and bony young leg. She thrashed about for a moment and then half-jumped from the litter, struggling to reassemble her dress and mantle as she straightened up. She looked about her in the court, blinking, and walked around the little crowd of attendants and house-slaves, looking for her uncle, perhaps for the old lady who was in charge of her. The sight of this tall, gangly young thing, moving halfway between grace and awkwardness, attempting a hoity-toitiness in gait and expression for which she was obviously untalented, was so pleasing to Cluentius that he laughed; quietly, in his throat, but out loud. Asuvia looked up sharply, to see a lean-faced stranger bending from the window close above her, his face open and grinning, his eyes a little red, but lively. *Who?* Clearly not her uncle's melancholy and beleaguered friend Aulus Cluentius, whose story she knew and whose plight she had recently heard described among neighbors in her town. Her lips parted slightly in surprise, her eyes widened, and Cluentius found her gaze so blue and clear as to be somehow inhuman, somehow reminiscent of glass, gems, sea water, northern lakes, *things*. The whole girl was like an artifact: made by her uncle's concern for her, her strange isolated environment, her peculiar circumstances, her *age* — how could you *be* so young? And anyway how could anyone be human, just a girl, or just a man, in these generations? Cluentius came upon this thought in his mind just as he was about to speak civilly to her; he was so startled by its defined shape in his consciousness, by the articulateness with which it presented itself to him, that he forgot to speak. Asuvia saw the smile immobilized in an odd interrupted expression above her, saw the kind eyes glaze a little, was aware that the moment for salutation had come and passed; somehow she knew that this was Cluentius.

She pulled herself together, straightened, and spoke civilly to *him*, rising above the awkward silence.

"Greeting! Sir, are we guests together here? Are you my uncle's friend?" You weren't supposed to lapse from formality like that and to start peppering an unknown man with questions, asking him flat out who he was and what he was doing in the house. She knew it and looked sharply behind her to see if the old lady had heard; but the old lady wasn't even there, she had gone across the court to argue with the steward. She looked back at Cluentius, and saw him smiling again his warm and amused smile, finding her pleasant in some way she could not sense.

"I am Aulus Cluentius Habitus of Larinum, and I know very well who you are." His voice was very deep, seemed to move reluctantly. Asuvia saw so few people that she was an embarrassingly intent observer of the slightest gesture of expression of anyone new to her. She smiled, lifted her chin a little, tried to incline her head in a more formal bow.

"You are at a disadvantage," he said pleasantly, "having to talk up to me like this, while I can lean on the sill here and look down. I shall take no further advantage. Where is your uncle? I thought he was to return with you."

"He did, he's out there with the guard, and seeing about everything, *you* know. Oh! Not yet!" and she darted with sudden forgetful grace after the litter that the slaves were removing, to plunge her head and arms into it and come out again with a small squirming object: her pet, a little marmoset of startling coloring, with a miniature orange mane like a lion's, fierce bristling little tufts of white fur placed randomly about his anatomy. He squalled atrociously and stuck like a burr to the side of Asuvia's face, his hands in her hair, his cheek against her ear. Laughing, she moved off, unmindful of Cluentius, bickering with her young maid over who was going to have the marmoset. Full of a sense of life's small natural graces, Cluentius came down for his conference with his friend.

"You saw her? You'll see her at dinner, she's to dine with us. The old woman thinks it uncalled for, but the girl's sixteen and *could* be a matron, why split hairs? Look, Cluentius! I'm talking to distract you. I don't like the look on your face. Are you going to tell me Cicero refused?"

"No. He didn't refuse. He didn't accept. I'm to meet him at Tusculum, the day after tomorrow. I may not go."

"*What?*"

"Can't we go in the study?"

"First, you've got to read these. Reports from the legal codes on the use of the *Lex Cornelia*, in recent cases involving the crime of 'judicial murder' as it's called. There's a long report there of a case Accius conducted. I picked these up for you this morning on my way through the City."

At dinner young Asuvia sat charmingly erect while her uncle and his friend reclined. Cluentius leaned heavily on his elbow, his mind a maze of questions, his whole being full of a dull wish that the girl weren't there and that he could speak as he wished to speak.

"What memory can you bequeath posterity, Cluentius, of your first meeting with M. Tullius Cicero?" asked Asuvius, conversationally, gesturing with his cup, watching the girl out of the tail of his eyes like a schoolmaster.

Cluentius spoke, slowly at first; then forgetting all presences but his one friend's, everything but his need for words.

"So you see. It was a child's idea, a country idea of ours, to think of getting him for this case. He wants his great friends, he wants his consulship, he wants excitement. The more applause, the more people running around the benches to hear better, the more O-Cicero-Cicero-great-Cicero, the more he *wants*. Oh, he's tempted! Thinking of winning a case like mine, with everybody betting he'll never make it — oh, it makes him drool, all right! *Pulling it off!*

"He has changed, Asuvius. He's not the man we heard fourteen years ago when we and he were young; not the small-town man we've watched getting into the Senate past the patricians, getting past the arch-patrician Hortensius in the courts, speaking for our order, for us businessmen, when no one wanted to hear about us — the one man in public life you could look at and hear about without wishing you were blind and deaf —"

Silence fell while a course was removed, another served, cups refilled, basins and towels passed round.

"We of the Italian municipalities," resumed Cluentius slowly, "when the Romans did not want us as fellow citizens . . . we of the businessman's order when the ruling class wanted to use us as milch goats, as fetilizer; when the *populares* wanted to use us as clubs against the ruling class . . . we had a man from Apinum, from a provincial town, a man who became a great citizen of Rome, who spoke for us in the name of *justice*. There was heart in his words, and *mind*. Mind and heart which make animate, endurable, the lumbering, clay-wooden, animal life of man. . . ." A slave came round to light torches and set lamp-stands. An odd little chill had fallen into the warm evening, and Asuvius spoke in a low voice to an old slave, who brought in a little brazier and rattled it about, getting it going. The eyes of Asuvia darkened to violet in the dimming light. They never left the lean scored face of Cluentius as he thought, spoke, thought again, and fell silent.

"He did a good job, today," said Cluentius in a low, hard, vicious tone. "He knows his business. If he pleads for me, it will be the best show in Rome, that day." He leaned back and his face fell into shadow.

"Marcus Tullius Cicero," said Asuvius in a light, careful tone, mock-pedagogic, "was born, dear students, in Arpinum in Italy, forty years ago. His father knew modest success in agricultural enterprises, despite the time's great difficulties. In our world, roads lead to Rome. Marcus Tullius and his young brother Quintus, when their father saw that they had brains and spirit, were installed in Rome, that they might have the best education money and taste could provide for them. After the Greek rhetoric teachers, after the two years of reading law with great Mucius Scaevola and his son, after the military service —" (Cluentius looked up) "Oh yes, he fought in one campaign — Marcus Tullius began the pleader's career which is the prelude to public office."

"Don't forget that it is also the prelude to numerous legacies, loans of money, and assurances of financial backing, though the laws so laughably forbid advocates to accept fees," said Cluentius.

"Wealth and possessions, Cluentius!" Asuvius sat suddenly upright, impatient, snapping. "How very simple, my dear friend, to accuse a great lawyer of ambition! Is ambition so low a thing? And as for money, may I recall to you what many have said, many among *us* and Cicero himself, about our order's reluctance to enter the Forum as lawyers, to seek public office, to aspire to the Senate? Knowing their place, Cluentius? Sensitivity? Reluctance to expose themselves to the scorn of the great family office-holders? Or, dear Cluentius, simple love of money, simple abhorrence of the condition of senatorial office which rules with law that no senator may own a ship large enough to engage in foreign trade, no senator may bid for a state contract, those most lucrative state contracts, Cluentius? Love of money and fear of insult — which of these noble motives, or in what degrees both, hold most of us back from office-seeking? Cicero loves Greek sculpture and country houses. The sort of slave he has in his household comes high. His abilities — and they are his only stock in trade, for his father had few friends of influence — these abilities could have made him an Atticus."

"He didn't need to *be* an Atticus," rejoined Cluentius sulkily. "He *has* Atticus. That long purse is forever in his hand."

"*Why?*" snapped Asuvius. "You saw him with Atticus. I have seen him with Atticus. On Atticus' rare visits here he is forever in Cicero's company. You noticed how Atticus treats him? How he defers — not servilely, but with what grace and naturalness? As to a man richer than himself? With Atticus' long purse you mention, does that man have need of Cicero's political influence — never considerable anyway until this year — when there is no member of the Senate who would not gladly put Atticus in his debt? No man thinks Atticus a fool or a knave —" Suddenly he broke off. Cluentius' face came slowly into the ring of light shed by the tall oil-lamp, a steady light compared to the flicker of the torches. The friend of Asuvius moved stiffly to a sitting position, and raised his head. Asuvia caught her breath audibly. That naked, suffering face —

"What *is* it, Cluentius?" asked Asuvius, lowering and steadying his voice. "What *is* it you fear in Cicero?"

"This," said Cluentius: "that he will not, if he accepts the case, conduct it as I want him to. He could succeed in my way. . . . I think he will succeed, but in his way."

"You cannot know what will be his way. What is yours?"

"You know. I want to be acquitted as a just man. I want

it seen in a Roman court that the right which we hold incarnate in the law is in this case clearly, without question,
on my side."

"If you are acquitted at all, anyone will know —"

"No. It matters, in what way I am acquitted."

"Oh, Cluentius!"

"*No.*"

But Asuvius returned to the charge, as they walked alone
together, before retiring.

"Your difficulty is simpler than you think," he insisted,
gently. "Forget the character of Cicero as you imagine it,
and remember the character of your mother as you know it.
She has some evidence we don't know about; we've only the
vaguest reports of what is on those tablets she made her old
neighbors sign — the reports from the questionings of the
slaves. And what other evidence has she? There are things
to *find out*, Cluentius."

"I believe that *evidence*, as you see the word, will be important on neither side of the case." said Cluentius. "Yet it
could have been. There *is* evidence, on my side, that I did
not poison Oppianicus. Only — no one seems interested."

VII

ALL THE SAME, in two days Cluentius rode slowly north along the great Latin Way. One of Cicero's slaves had been sent to guide him, and rode beside him on a mule — probably, thought Cluentius, regretting the lively company which his master's small retinue would have provided.

As they first entered the main court of Cicero's villa, a small hurtling form came shooting out of the garden in the rear, shouting and gesticulating, hair bobbing out of its restraining bands. This was Cicero's Tullia, and when she saw that the new arrival was not her father, she stopped stock-still and allowed her disappointment to shout out of her sudden silence. But she gathered herself together, moved forward and managed a few of the conventional words of greeting; chattered to the slave about the hour of her father's coming, and ran off to circulate reports around the household. Terentia her mother was not at the moment in Tusculum, Cluentius was informed. She was in the north with her infant son; allowed her husband to keep the girl at Tusculum, where he felt she could pass a healthy, vegetable-eating, airy summer and still be where he could lay eyes on her at short notice. Like all Cicero's slaves, this one spoke well and had an expressive, feeling face. Cluentius grasped without effort the hint that Terentia viewed her husband's views on the girl's upbringing with a mixture of indulgence and impatience.

The ride had refreshed rather than wearied him. He decided to wait for his host before going to the baths, and to wait alone. Gently he dismissed the slave, gave a few directions about his effects, and passed through slender columns into a space at once open and part of the house.

For a long moment he paused, looking slowly about him, seeing how carefully statues, fountain, furniture had been placed not only in harmonious relation to each other, but so that the long light of advancing evening became a further ornament, a final element of beauty. A small statue, a nymph full of grace, stood at one side of the mosaic fountain; a low wall behind the fountain was covered with paintings, all human figures, standing, sitting, reclining. This panel was a discreet yet passionate tribute to the dignities possible in the human condition.

Cluentius passed on; a portrait bust, a little Hermes, some jars . . . a narrow green-edged pathway of tile led into a room, still darkened against summer sun, but showing in the half-light slanting through closed shutters the accuracy, the inevitability of its proportions. Shelves, jars with protruding scrolls, more tables: this was Cicero's library. Cluentius forebore to enter. A strange small wind of awe stirred in his mind; things seen long ago, things seen only in the imagination guided by his Greek tutor and fed by solitude . . . yet this house was no collection of mere objects. Somehow the whole place seemed the emblem of a mind, the expression, in infinitely varied and still unified form, of an individual nature. The house, the gardens, the faces of the slaves; the murmur of voices, and the new colors the painting showed in deepening rosy light — the whole thing spoke softly to his listening mind, and spoke of Cicero.

He stood unmoving, fixed in an attitude of combined repose and alertness, before a little portrait bust, looking into
deep eyes. He raised his hand and followed with two fingers
the clean-sweeping outline of a noble jaw. Steps came behind him unheard. A hand closed gently round his upper
arm, yet he did not start or turn. Deep and beautiful, the
most famous voice in Rome spoke in his ear.

"I don't know whose portrait that is," said Cicero softly,
as if they had stood there together for long minutes. "Neither does Atticus. He found it for me in an old house in
Brundisium, where he passed by chance on a day of auction.
All we know is that it's the head of a Roman; not more than
a century old, we think; done by a Greek, probably. Atticus
could have found out something about it, made some detailed inquiries round the house. We decided not to bother.
It's just this face: the face of what a man could be."

Cluentius turned his head to give his host a small bow
and a courteous glance. The blue eyes smiled mildly into
his.

"Could be . . . if?" rejoined Cluentius, smiling as gently
as the other.

"Oh, if," the fine mouth quirked upward, ". . . could be,
if he were different from what he really was, what we all
are. What we could be must live with what we are; the two
can look at each other," his voice quickened, picked up speed
as his thought began to amuse him, "can look at each other,
Cluentius, and perhaps when neither feels too much pain
at the contemplation, then we're over the steep place."
He paused, but before either could speak again sandals clat-
tered, hair flew, and Tullia was upon them. Her father
turned from Cluentius to swing her from her feet. "Tulliola,
Tulliola," he said, his face lost in the brown undisciplined
mass. When he straightened and set her down, he said to
Cluentius, "Done for! And just as I was going to get off

something rather good. The baths, friend, in half an hour's time."

Cicero liked to splash and paddle in the cold pool after the hot bath and the temperate one; Cluentius, like Atticus, preferred a quick plunge and quick withdrawal. So he too sat on the edge as Atticus had done, wrapped in cloth and grateful for it in the new delicious cool of the air, peering down at the Praetor and trying to follow his water-punctuated conversation.

"Pools! Blessed, damnable pools!" said Cicero, snorting. "They can ruin a man. Look at one half our greatest nobility, over there —" he gestured toward the Latin Way and the city — "sitting around, fooling with pool effects, delighting in pool effects, bath pools, garden pools, fixing their fishponds so their pet mullets will come up and eat bread out of their hands, inviting all their friends in to see them feed fish! Generals! *Ex-generals*! Fish-fanciers! Lost men!" He laughed, scrambled up, and let his young slave dry him while he gossiped about certain dwellers on the highest hill in Rome.

"Now, I don't say that *all* of them lack interest in serious matters," he said, as they paced along the tiled path to the library, the slave preceding them to open shutters and let in the last night before fetching torches. "Not all . . . but — ah, we'll wait here for word about dinner.

"In this room are books that you should read, Cluentius. Books on the nature of the orator's calling, specifically on the nature of legal oratory. Unfortunately, I have no time to remake your mind." An awkward little silence fell, and ended with Cicero's quick warm smile, his voice murmuring anew, his hand again on the guest's elbow piloting him about, guiding him, speaking of book after book with love and eagerness to make known that love and its reasons.

Dinner had but begun when a slave stained with the dust

8 8

of a hard ride was shown into the dining room by Cicero's
steward.

"From Pomponius Atticus, greeting," and a thin roll of
Egyptian paper was put in the master's hand. Excusing himself for inattention to his guest, Cicero read rapidly,
his scowl gathering and his mouth twisting as he read. Cluentius applied himself to dinner, courteously ignoring his
host's grimaces.

"The matter here," said Cicero suddenly, throwing down
the letter, "is one to interest you. Atticus writes, my dear
Cluentius, of matters we discussed before I left to join you
here. It is a question of bribery.

"For bribery will in two days be again the scandal of
Rome's day. You have been walking about with your head
in a cloud of private concern. You must have heard something, though, of the fact that the defeated candidates in
the late elections, those who were rightfully the winners,
my friends, move now to bring a suit against the so-called
winners. The charge will be substantiated. Read here what
Atticus writes." He shoved the paper along the table toward
Cluentius, and began to eat rapidly while the other read. His
mouth full, he leaned toward his guest and stabbed with his
finger toward the bottom of the last sheet. Cluentius read:

One last word. We shall be successful in this affair but
not without effort, vigilance, and time. Again I must urge
you, though with regret, not to involve yourself in the affair of Cluentius. Your famous voice against this scourge
of bribery. . . .

He read no more.

"You show me this," Cluentius said with difficulty. "I
commend your openness. You cannot take the case. . . ."
He kept his deep eyes from Cicero's face, fearful that the
sudden stirrings of relief in his mind would be legible. But

the Praetor was not looking at him. The Praetor was gazing with a strange, tight little smile and glinting eyes into a translucent cup. He said nothing at all.

"You show me, most honestly, why you must not take the case," said Cluentius.

"I do nothing of the kind. I have taken your case. I mean, only you, Cluentius, can prevent me from taking it. I show you the letter to illustrate the point I must make with you."

"The point?"

"This: that you must cease to be a man who does not know he is a political animal."

"*What*?"

"Oh, man! Man!" shouted Cicero, flinging his hand up over his head. "The affairs of men are only interesting when they are political! Your case is the most interesting that has come my way in many months, because, *because*, BECAUSE of political —"

"I beg your pardon," cut in Cluentius sharply. "The political considerations offer difficulties, as I said to you at first. But the case is a private one. Brought by one citizen against another, a matter of private interest —"

"I beg *your* pardon," snapped Cicero, "it's on a matter of such public interest that politics and nothing but politics will be the essence of the prosecution. You knew that, when you wrote me those letters — those letters, *misleading*, because of their intelligence!"

Cluentius' eyelids fell heavily over his aching eyes.

"What must I do," he asked in the deep grinding voice of his somber moments, "to give suitable recognition of the fact that I am a political animal?"

"Friend!" The Praetor's beautiful smile beamed upon him. "You must let me conduct the defense as I please."

"*How*?"

The Praetor leaned back, put his elbow on a cushion, and said in the most reasonable of voices, "Let's follow here the excellent pattern of the courts. You will speak first, I second; as usual, I shall get twice the time you get, for I shall be defending my position. You, however, will speak on one topic only."

"That is?"

"You will tell me in some detail, with the greatest frankness, the whole story of how you bribed that jury."

VIII

YOU WILL REMEMBER (said Cluentius) that there
was a short recess of the court, I believe it was one
day between the trial of Fabricius, my stepfather's
agent in the plot to murder me, and that hearing which,
after the verdicts against both your client Scamander and
this Fabricius, seemed inevitably destined to result in the
conviction of Oppianicus. In the evening of this recess,
shortly after dark, when I was alone in the house of Marcus
Asuvius — he was out for the evening, engaged in some of
the business meetings he had let slide for my sake during the
hearings — a visitor was announced for me: G. Aelius Staienus.

Concerning this Roman senator, candidate for high office,
and ornament of the courts, Asuvius and I had often joked
together. I do not know whether you are familiar with his
origins. He was of our businessman's order, but of a background so humble in rank and in fortune that when he was
elevated to senatorial rank as the Dictator Sulla was packing
the Senate in the first days of his new government, one could
only assume this gesture to be connected somehow with the
Dictator's memorable sense of humor. Staienus seemed to
represent a practical joke of the purest Sullan vintage, a

triumph of insult both to the patrician nobility at whose side he was to move in the Senate, and whose incompetences Sulla despised, and to the solid members of our order —what was left of us. His existence as a Senator and public man declared in a unique mode of expression Sulla's contempt for aristocrat and businessman alike.

There he sat before me, addressing me as "*Dear* Cluentius," "*his* Cluentius," and so on, that long nose of his dripping and twitching in the night air, his pitted face and dirty toga . . . but I spare you. He unfolded to me a remarkable story.

My stepfather had got his hands on an important sum. I recognized, of course, the intervention of my mother and the sale of some considerable properties. As I had warned her, Oppianicus had not been able to realize in time the change in court-climate in Rome, the rise in price, the added difficulties in negotiation. He had been thunderstruck by the swift convictions of Scamander and Fabricius, and had awakened, or been awakened, at last to the knowledge that this was a moment when all must be staked if all were not to be lost.

He had come to Staienus because of that beauty's status as professional juryman and jury-binding agent. He undertook quite simply — complex negotiation was not in his line — to give this enormous sum into Staienus' hands for distribution to the jurors. There were thirty-two members of that jury. A few were reputable men; others were uncertain; and still others, lice on the body of the law. But since a tied vote at the time of the verdict is interpreted as acquittal, Staienus needed to secure only sixteen votes. The amounts and means of distribution were to be left entirely to him.

Oppianicus was as usual moving too fast. He should have consulted more intimately with . . . but I wander. He had made his inquiries in great haste, and his informant had neglected to tell him that this Staienus, though undoubtedly a

93

performer of some virtuosity in these affairs, had just two years before accepted a huge bribe for the subversion of a jury and avoided distributing it by the simple device of keeping it all, allowing his client to lose the judgment, and then plaintively whining about how you couldn't rely on *anybody* these days.

Staienus, like many of Sulla's henchmen in the years after the great man's death, grew poorer every year. They had never realized that their master was serious about restoring law and order — of a sort, it is true, but even that sort was enough to disinherit them and drive them to scrabble in the dirt for their corn. The coup of that other trial gave my stepfather's chosen agent an idea: and it was not stupid, it was not petty, it had a certain scope. It was this: if I would match the amount and give it to him, he would distribute *my* money to the jurors, secure the verdict for *me*, and keep Oppianicus' bribe for himself. Oppianicus convicted, we should all be beyond the reach of his reprisal anyway.

How could I rely on him? I asked with some irony.

There are moments when a man like that looks at you as clear-eyed as any great gentleman of old Rome, and tells you the truth, and you can feel it. This was one of the moments. Staienus told me he could see too clearly that a verdict in favor of Oppianicus would be intensely unpopular. The moment for such knaves was passing. The time had come again when it was actually to a man's advantage to have a clean past and a lot of upright character witnesses.

I wish I could reproduce for you the honesty and the sincere regret for these facts in Staienus' gaze. How he would have enjoyed making this proposition in reverse circumstances, to Oppianicus!

He then listed to me the jurors whom he was to bribe and the procedure he was to follow. The arrangements were all quite canny and well constructed: notes of promise had already been issued, the disbursements would be made im-

94

mediately after the verdict. Only one hitch could possibly occur: if Staienus should himself change the course of events.

I could see he was uneasy about the current of feeling in my favor which ran so high in the courtroom as my attorney harped on the life and character of Oppianicus. But stronger than all else, he felt the grip of a great longing: for there in his poor vile house reposed that minor treasury, the thousands which Oppianicus had brought him, to be dispersed — ah, the agony of that dispersion!

There was nothing to do with Staienus except meet his terms. I had gambled, staked so much; not my life alone, though after this I knew well I would not live long, should Oppianicus move free and powerful through Larinum and Rome. There was the great wind of death that might blow on all who had helped me with this prosecution; helped me, out of their courage or their despair.

I made the arrangements with Staienus. I have nothing to complain of. He was in good faith. Without him, I should have lost. With his help, I won, and Oppianicus went to exile, to misery, to death.

I learned only after the trial that Staienus had bribed the judge as well as the jury. The rage of Oppianicus you remember — how he unleashed the tribune Quinctius against judge and jury alike, thundered and howled in Forum and basilica, and every howl a howl against the Senate, against his old Sullan friends, against his martyrdom. The indictments and trials that followed — no need to speak of them. All of them provided political capital for those who grasped at every means to strike against the senatorial party. It had just so very recently, then, become possible to strike against the senatorial party.

Facts, you said. You wanted the truth, the facts. I bribed a Roman court. That is the fact. The truth —

Cluentius' recital, begun so crisply, ended in a stammer.

95

IX

I HAVE ONE QUESTION," said Cicero. "What about the accounts?"

"*What?*"

"The accounts, man; stop goggling! Dɪᴅ *you keep your accounts in such a way that the withdrawal for the sum of the bribe was recorded?*" He rumbled this in the low snarling voice which had brought witnesses to a pitch of rage and revelation.

Cluentius lost his stammer and his wandering look, and snapped back to his normal self-possession.

"Certainly not," he said. "It was perfectly possible for me to make an arrangement with Marcus Asuvius, involving one of our common agencies, which dispersed the withdrawal and made it totally invisible. Do you take me for a fool?"

"Yes," said the Praetor incisively, "and no," he said with his glorious warm smile. He relaxed, the smile became a sort of grin; he leaned against the wall and rearranged his dining-garment. "*Dear* Cluentius," he said, and uncannily the whine of Staienus filled the room; "*my* Cluentius," he said, thrusting his nose to one side, sniffing, wiping the nose. "You relieve my mind," he said in his own voice, and burst into a happy laugh.

He called for wine, mixed and poured it himself, dismissed the slave, and settled back.

"My turn."

If you'd stayed just a bit longer (began Cicero) in the Forum two days ago, instead of running up that alley, you'd have seen something even more disquieting to one of your picky tastes, friend, than my speech that day. You'd have seen me in long, friendly, earnest conference with your mother's attorney, Titus Accius. Conversation with that really businesslike and able man proved most enlightening.

We have all heard, or at least all except probably you, about Section Six of the Cornelian Law Concerning Assasins and Poisoners. This section deals with the use of courts of law to entrap and convict the innocent; it sets forth the principle that a jury's verdict can be a murder weapon as surely as a club. I had heard that Accius was planning to use this section against you; but I was quite unable to believe that such an attorney would place full faith in it. As you may know, it applies only to men of senatorial rank. Now, a lawyer like Accius can still use it *in a way*, by appealing to our great Roman tradition that a jury is free to interpret a law according to its spirit, even if its letter inhibits such an interpretation. But Accius would know that any defense attorney would get up and say: Under this Sullan statute no businessman is attainable, for it applies only to patricians. *Everyone* knows that the statute is so limited because when it was passed there was no one on juries *except* patricians. Still, in the political weather these days, you could do something with a Sullan statute that was supposed to be insultingly exclusive of the businessmen, by manipulating it so that it could be protective of the businessmen. Juries are very odd bodies of men; even the best of juries, in the best of years.

Accius has not registered his charges yet, nor even applied for his *postulatio* — as you may remember from your experiences some years ago, the preliminary hearing where he must ask permission to present charges, and display some reasonable guarantee that they are well founded. Only a short time remains before the late-summer adjournment; the dockets are crowded; yet he delays. I wonder why.

I am convinced that the main charge will be some perfectly ordinary murder accusation: probably poison, since there seems to have been so much of this useful substance washing about the gullets of Larinum eight years ago and before. To bring a charge of poisoning will ensure that Accius will get past the *postulatio* and the other preliminaries without having his case dismissed. To use Section Six alone would be to tempt an able defense attorney — and I COULD do it, too — to get the judge to dismiss the charges in one of the preliminary stages, on the grounds of the technicality I just mentioned. Once before the jury, though, here is what will happen.

Accius will know perfectly well that the poison charge, the main substance of his indictment, can be disposed of with a minimum of effort by your attorney. He will, however, spend the whole first half of his speech and the last quarter of it in actually invoking Section Six, and calling you a murderer-by-juridical-conspiracy. He will harp and harp on the jury-bribing, and the offenses to justice enshrined in Roman memories of that trial. He will say, not once but many times, that a man who would so conduct himself with judge and jury must be recognized as a criminal to whom a mere poisoning would be a bagatelle.

Accius will not slaver and froth. He will use the principle — dear to all of us lawyers and deeply embedded in all our notions of evidence, but perhaps not known by name to you, Cluentius, with your other absorbing interests — the principle of *probabile ex vita*. That is, a man demonstrably of such and such character must, by extension, be judged *capable* of such and such an act, even where explicit proof may be lacking. It is *probable* that a briber of Sullan juries is also a murderer or could be, if other evidence is somehow available. Seems a trifle bald, put this way, but Accius won't put it this way. There will be some thick-maned, tufted oratory.

He will place his main hope on whipping up the prejudice which is always the aim of somebody arguing the *probabile ex vita*. Normally, the lack of other evidence would make this a ridiculous procedure; but not this year.

You read Atticus' letter concerning the elections, the bribery that was employed, the suits that are to be brought, the dangers the commonwealth is running. The Forum will for the remainder of this session be full of talk about bribery, oratory against bribery, *good men* going on record as to their feelings about bribery. An accident of history, entirely unconnected with your case, has come upon our scene to add to our difficulties. Your mother is having her usual good luck with her worst intentions.

However, everybody has left something out of their thoughts about this case. It is the thing which your mother, and her late husband too, consistently left out of their calculations. It is your *personal character*, Aulus Cluentius.

Once before this strange thing turned in their hands and bit them when they were not expecting it. Now it has happened again. The voice of your mind and heart have spoken to *me*, Marcus Tullius Cicero, Praetor of the City. I am not a modest man; we need not trifle with circumlocution. Because you are what you are, and I what I am, your mother is going to lose her case.

It is my firm belief that Accius himself does not know what those depositions taken from the slaves contain, and that he has a pretty good idea that he'd better not count too heavily on them. He was evasive; I asked him outright; he would not answer, and I could feel in my long lawyer's-ears the silence of a man who is concealing not what he knows but what he doesn't know.

I hate surprises. I want to know what's in those depositions. They must be still in your mother's hands. Your informant whom you mentioned in one of your letters knew that Sassia had forgotten to mention in these depositions the theft that was supposed to be the subject of the inquiry. Everything bore on the question of Oppianicus. But on *what?* On the "poisoning"? On jury-bribing? Very unlikely that she'd try to make it appear they had any knowledge of this — those slaves.

Well, we will have this information.

The Praetor stopped talking. He leaned his head on his hand, his body slanting across the couch; he seemed to see no one, hear no one's breathing, but to be listening to some far-off, unnamed and magnificent voice.

"You said," Cluentius remarked carefully, still tensely upright in his seat, "that you would take twice as long as I. You have been quite brief. Was there something further you had thought to tell me? Something about the nature of the defense?"

"Oh," said Cicero idly, sipping, "in the morning I'll have some more. We need rest. Look, Cluentius: you don't know what the organization of a speech for the defense *is*. You ought to refresh schoolboy memories, and vague recollections of your old attorney's spoutings in that last trial. I had this brought for you: take the jar: only two short scrolls, you'll see — my little essay on the aims of legal oratory. It is for you.

"We meet at daybreak and I shall spend an hour or so with you to finish our deliberations. I have not yet described to you . . . well, I must leave Tusculum by noon, and be in Rome by nightfall. In the meantime, read, and think! We must get hold of those depositions somehow. There is little time. I do not wish you to return to Larinum before the trial. Someone must go. I refuse to be surprised by the evidence in those tablets, and I want some time to think. Good night, and be mindful, Cluentius."

X

BE *MINDFUL*," Cluentius muttered to himself, pacing the cool chamber on the villa's second story, looking often through his unshuttered window on the moonlit tranquillities outside. One of Cicero's elder slaves came in, a man lost always in books and the arrangements for books; he set down beside the low bed, with a most courteous smile in the guest's direction, a lampstand with a large oil lamp. The guest looked admiringly at it, and gave back the old man's civil regard.

"Capuan," said the slave, with a little gesture of pride and delight.

"Of course," smiled Cluentius. "Very fine. I hope your master does not deprive himself."

The old man waved a hand and shook his head, in a gentle, touching mimicry of Cicero's characteristic not-at-all-dear-fellow gesture. "He said you would need it for your reading."

"Ah. My reading."

In the calm light from that excellent lamp he tasted the clarity of Cicero's exposition and the detachment of its tone. He forgot for a moment many things close to himself, as his mind stirred and moved in lively interest, responding to the crisp discussion of a technique unfamiliar to him, based on a set of principles with which he had been merely acquainted, as one makes acquaintance in student days with shadowy abstractions, called by one's tongue "ideas," though they cannot take on the flesh and bone of real idea until their outlines are filled in by experience. Lessons, treatises came back to him as he read, and as he conversed in his mind with the writer. He remembered descriptions of model cases; suddenly the memory of his old tutor Apollodorus disappeared, and another face shone in his mind with sudden soft brilliance: the face of his father, talking over with him some Greek essay on rhetoric, outlining to him its application to some far-off, famous old Roman trial. Sleep moved toward him softly. He felt that it would be sweet, that he would rest.

For Cicero had made no mention of Sassia's appearance in the speech for the defense. He had spoken of her, but as a presence in the prosecutor's case, not in the defendant's.

The light of dawn woke him, and the same slave who had ridden with him from Rome brought him some small refreshment and the news that Cicero waited for him in the little garden near the baths.

"My master told me to give you this letter, which arrived for you an hour ago from Rome. He said that you should read it, sir, before you join him. Since someone risked sending it by night, it may have importance for your discussion with him, he said for me to say."

> *Marcus Asuvius to Aulus Cluentius Habitus in haste.*

I send you Antiochus in spite of the danger of night travel, because a possibility has appeared which you may wish to consider at once, perhaps with Cicero.

In a conversation with my Asuvia at dinner last night, I learned that she had made the acquaintance of Auria, the poor girl your half-sister, now the wife of Oppianicus the Younger. You know she's hardly ever at home in Larinum; I didn't realize that she has for two seasons now made long visits to that old villa of the Aurii near Neapolis, not far from my Asuvia's little estate. During these visits the poor creature struck up acquaintance with my girl. I don't need to tell you I shouldn't have cared much for this, all charity notwithstanding, had I known — but perhaps this is why I haven't known. In any case, there's this possible link between that household and mine in Larinum. We spoke of the lack of important information about the prosecution's case. Naturally, there will be no question of Asuvia's visiting that household, but Auria might come to us just possibly, and some important information be obtained. We leave for Larinum almost immediately. Consult well with Cicero, Aulus, for in a few days, I hear, he will have small time for the preparation of your case, I fear. How can we profit from this connection with Auria? We shall consult in haste upon your return.

Cicero stood at the end of a walk, motionless, beside the small portrait bust which they had admired together the evening before. The Praetor's hand rested lightly on the edge of its little supporting column, as on the shoulder of a seated friend. Without word or gesture he watched the approach of Cluentius through the brightening light; feeling that scrutiny, the guest moved his long limbs a bit awkwardly, his shoulders hunched, his mind conscious of each stride.

"Greeting" — but he saw the grave face of his host still unmoving and voiceless, staring at him, with an expression only of extreme attentiveness. Cluentius, rather at a loss, put the scribbled wax tablet containing Asuvius' letter into his host's hand. The Praetor took his eyes from his guest's face with an effort, and seemed to take in the contents of the letter at a glance. His eyebrows moved upward slightly, a quick flash of approval crossed his face.

"You read, last night?" he said abruptly, letting the tablet fall from his hand into a miniature flowerbed full of little green shoots.

"I did, and I — "

"You paid particular attention, I trust, to the remarks on the beginning, the *exordium*, a subject on which I hold strong views," said the other in a quick, dry, lecturing voice. Cluentius opened his mouth, but was not allowed to speak.

"The beginning of the speech," said the lecturer — "who can tell how much is lost and won in those terrible first moments? Reason and passion alike must speak — never forget that in Rome our word for juryman is the same as the word for judge, most rightly so; for the verdict itself pronounces sentence, that having been decreed previously by law, to go automatically with the verdict. Each of those judges — each of the *seventy-odd*, in our case — must feel that this is a matter of his deepest interest, binding him to us on the one hand, to our opponents on the other, until the stones of Rome shall melt and vanish, in the Abyss.

"It shall be clear to our jury from the first word that what I say is truly an answer to what Accius has said, not some bleat out of nowhere such as they must listen to in nine causes out of ten. Each word in that introduction shall lead from what he has said into the defense that I shall make. There are two strands in this defense: one, the strand of the apparent charge; two, the strand of the real charge, based on the prejudice attaching to the earlier trial. I must clear you of this prejudice, I say to them, even though it may seem not proper to a court of law.

"This can be done with point and eloquence, briefly. It is, however, the false *exordium.*

"Any schoolboy knows that after the *exordium* comes the *narratio,* in which the facts of the case are set forth, the story told. Our events will speak for themselves. Yet our *narratio* proper cannot begin with Oppianicus. The man is dead. Reason can deal with him, and some emotion; but true passion does not find in him a suitable object, unless it spread to him from a truly suitable object, toward which it has been directed first." The dry voice passed suddenly into quivering silence. A heavy pause followed. Instants limped by while the careful abstractions of Cicero's last words took actual shape and meaning in the listener's mind.

"Listen!" said the light dry voice, and it was as if a third person spoke next. Beautiful and sonorous, carrying far into the clear morning air their burden of dark passion, words rolled out. Cluentius listened like a sleepwalker.

". . . MOTHER of my client Cluentius, yes, as a mother I must refer to her throughout this case — his mother, I must say, although she behaves towards him with the hatred and the cruelty of a mortal enemy: nor shall the recital of her monstrous crimes ever deprive her of the name which nature has bestowed upon her; for the more of love and tenderness the very name of MOTHER suggests, the greater will be the detestation which you will hold to befit this, the unheard-of outrage . . . that MOTHER who at this very moment, as for many years past, is longing for the destruction of her son — she, then, Cluentius' mother, conceived an unholy passion for the young Aurius Melinus her son-in-law . . . she did not quail before the night itself with its wedding torches, the threshold of the chamber, her daughter's bridal bed . . .

"In the whole life of Cluentius he has had nothing of disaster to face, no peril of death to meet, no evil to fear, save such as have been due to the contrivance and direction of his MOTHER . . . her effrontery, her money, her cruel heart . . . longing for his destruction, eager to shed every drop of her blood if only she may first see his poured out!"

Long silence, and Cluentius turned slowly aside, sick and shaking, to seat himself upon a marble bench. He raised his face, blinking, to the heavy profile of the Praetor; saw beneath it the lean, clean profile of the unknown Roman's head.

"Here begins the real narration," said Cicero quietly. "It is the end of the real *exordium*. I begin now to speak of Oppianicus. The courtroom is full of truth and hatred."

"You have pleaded," said Cluentius, stammering slightly, his mouth twitching, his hand writhing on his knee, "in your false *exordium*, for the abandonment of prejudice and the cleaving to principles of law and justice."

"I have kindled," said Cicero, "a fire in their minds." He turned his head to look into Cluentius' eyes, and the guest saw on his face, clear in the morning sun, a terrible sadness and a peculiar smile, bitter, yet not cold.

Cicero whirled about suddenly, took a quick step toward his client, turned away; turned back again, and loomed over him, swearing quietly under his breath.

"Ignorance of those who do not *act!* In ignorance, you say, you think — "

As suddenly, Cluentius leaped to his feet. His action brought him within a pace of his host. The Praetor stiffened and stepped back.

"Ignorance! Ignorant of action! It is you who are ignorant here, now, Cicero! You speak in your precious *exordium* as if I had sat weeping and sniveling through the years, afraid, as if I had not — " Anger passed in an instant from the mobile face so close to his, and was replaced by a leaping flame of interest.

"Had not *what?*" said the Praetor, fascinated. Cluentius' mouth writhed now, his tongue seemed stuck.

"Did *what?* What, man, say!" The heavy arm shot out from the light sleeve-fold of his garment; his hand gripped Cluentius' wrist. "*What* don't I know?"

"The plot was false." The client's voice was dull, and full of pain. "The evidence was false. I fabricated the evidence of Oppianicus' attempt to murder me. Conspiracy — he would have tried to murder me, but he never did. I concocted, and swore false."

"Conspiracy! What, old Baebius perjured, all those senators? Well, I'm — "

"No! Baebius spoke as he thought, he swore true. Not one of my witnesses was perjured! I deceived them all. Only my slave Diogenes, who could not testify, knew what was done. The others spoke truth in court, truth as to what they saw, did, believed."

"Truth in court. Cluentius, Cluentius, how entirely you interest me." The Praetor's eyes shone with an odd youthful happiness. "Sit down. I shall sit here. Tell me. I gape before you."

XI

EVERYBODY IN LARINUM (began Cluentius, very pale, and speaking with great discipline) knew that Gaius Fabricius had been for a long time the agent and creature of my stepfather. Diogenes was at first the slave of my doctor Cleophantus. I had known this slave since his boyhood; had helped Cleophantus to buy him, for he wished to learn for himself the arts of healing, and thus win to freedom and civil status.

After a certain interview with my mother, I became aware of dangers in store, not only for me — with those I felt quite prepared to deal in some less extravagant manner — but for others in Larinum, close to me and deeply concerned in all that concerned me. Oppianicus was like a sick wolf unleashed. I could feel that although certain of his difficulties were delaying an outbreak on his part, the outbreak would come, and the gods alone could know what suffering would follow. The breath of the Furies was on the neck of Oppianicus. We all could feel it, and he too. It seemed to me that I must now wait for the workings of Fate. I could not — I must — I worked out a plan.

I gave out that I was much bothered by illness and in

constant need of medicine. I made some arrangements with Diogenes.

I went to old Baebius the senator, my father's friend long years ago, and to Publius Quintus Varus, a name and a sure word both in Larinum and in Rome. I informed them that Diogenes had made known to his master and to me certain approaches to him on the part of Fabricius, agent of Oppianicus. Poison had been mentioned, I said, and a good sum of money. I lied, of course.

Baebius advised me well and just as I had surmised he would. He urged me to consult with Cleophantus the doctor, to tell him of this plot, and to ensure the loyalty of Diogenes by purchasing him. I negotiated with Cleophantus, and was happy to buy the slave: I assured him of freedom following the trial.

Diogenes now approached Fabricius. He spoke of a marvelous love philter which he had learned to make in the course of his studies, a thing of truly astonishing properties; everybody in the world of slaves and ex-slaves, it appeared, knew of certain disabilities which had lately been a source of real sadness to this poor swine Fabricius. Diogenes had no trouble in convincing Fabricius that the austerity and prudery practiced by me as his master, and the tedious cautions observed by Cleophantus as his instructor, made open dealing perilous for him. A rendezvous was suggested and a sum of money named. Fabricius, of course, sent your poor Scamander on that errand.

My friends, full of the poisoning plot I had painted to them in wild colors, were concealed in shrubbery close to the road near my rear gate. I lay on a pallet in my chamber, feigning illness, I told them, in order that Diogenes might believably be sent on an errand for medicine, and thus have an excuse to meet Scamander. Diogenes went out through the gate with a neat packet of the deadliest poison he could brew. Scamander placed a much larger packet, sealed, containing the money, in his hands. The transaction complete, my friends leaped from their hiding places. The ex-slave was seized, and the charges laid against him, against Fabricius, and against Oppianicus as the known patron of Fabricius and the only person conceivably interested enough and bold enough to contrive my death in such a manner. The love philter story seemed the clumsiest of lies.

I had allowed the report to circulate that my lack of testamentary deposition would make my mother my heiress in case of my death. As you know, there are various statutes available which can be invoked in the case of a death without testament: I had in fact left careful instructions with Asuvius my friend, to ensure that in the case of my death she would not inherit. But I had never wished this to be known. The general ignorance of my arrangements now served me well.

Oppianicus raved and raged, but Baebius and Varus took a firm hand in the proceedings. I believe that until the last desperate moment when the conviction of Fabricius was recorded, my stepfather believed that he would be saved without having to have recourse to bribery. He was, you see, not guilty. He had never known how powerless innocence can be.

"None knew of this but Diogenes?" asked Cicero quickly. "What became of Diogenes?"

"He was manumitted a year later; I waited that time so that his freedom would not have seemed too liberal a reward. I proceeded with Diogenes as I had promised; set him up in his art, let him practice and prove himself; then made it easy for him, in due course, to attain his freedom. He went south to Brundisium, where he had always wished to settle. He died there two years ago, of one of the fevers that so often enter those southern ports. I regret — he was a good man, and assiduous in his art."

"He left no —"

"No. I made sure."

"Oh, immortal gods," breathed Marcus Tullius Cicero softly, "this year of my good fortune! Praetor. Tullia betrothed as I wanted; the pieces falling into place, for the great work that will be my consulship and you, Aulus Cluentius!" He laughed, a low excited laugh. "Now tell me — Oh not of course if you don't wish to — but — well, what were your feelings, how did you —" But his voice stopped in his throat as he saw the darkened, twisting face turned toward him.

"I found myself exulting in my skill," said Cluentius harshly. "I found myself . . . it came easily. I felt, as not before, my mother's son."

"Your mother. Ah."

"She has been paid, she has paid a hundred times over for all her injuries to me. I saw that she should pay, that she should lose the one thing she ever wanted with her heart —"

"Your death? Your ruin?"

"No. The love and company of Oppianicus."

In the constrained pause which followed this speech, Cicero rose from his seat and stepped round the little bench. His large hand rested with great firmness and lightness on the shoulder of Cluentius. The many voices at his command seemed all forgotten; one remained, the voice of deep charity.

"You must forgive me, Cluentius, for some of the tones in which I have spoken to you. My friend, you love and hate and are of divided mind. But generosity and love of justice have guided your action. Oh yes! No matter what action you have taken, the springs of the well are clear. Do you think I did not know this? What I have understood of the jury-bribing has but been deepened and intensified by what you have told me this morning. You have feared — you have felt that my interest in this case has come purely from a wish to exercise my, ah, skill as you call it. You have been of divided mind about me.

"Cluentius, a moment comes, no man knows when it will come, but he must know when it is there. It is the moment when one must disregard the nature of an action in favor of its motive and its end: cast out the element of hate in some great love, the element of love in some great hate — that has not come to me yet as it has to you; and still, Cluentius, I know it will, for I am learning things each day that it would be easier not to know; yet know I must, and not by other men alone.

"You must be defended and saved, by me alone, for I have understood. You must yield to me in many ways; I shall yield to you also. You wish not just to be acquitted, but to be acquitted as a good man, wrongly accused. You wish to be purified by a verdict which shall clear you of that vileness which is the property and quality of your enemies, and through which you have moved, stained perhaps, but not in essence corrupted. It is an absolution that you seek. I shall bring it about."

He moved round again and sat beside his guest. They sat for a moment as each had sat in other gardens long ago, with a friend of boyhood; the Praetor's heavy arm encircled Cluentius' shoulders in a boyish attitude of comradeship and affection. He leaned forward suddenly, relaxing his hold, and shook off his sandal. "Damned little stones . . . of course I'm always paddling around outside the pathways," he said in a completely normal, idle tone. He got up and scrabbled about a bit with his sandal, turned to face the bench, set one foot on it while he reshod himself. His voice went on in a rich murmur.

"I have known something of you for these eight years. The stones of Rome, which I have loved, are made in part of the thoughts and words of men such as I; but the *spirit*, the breath of a man like you — this can animate our stones like

113

the music of Orpheus." The Praetor spoke gravely even with one foot on the bench. He looked deeply at his client. Down the lean face of Cluentius ran a few thick tears; he had not wept since the death of his father. Cicero cried every time he read Aeschylus or Sophocles, often in court even while he made his plea, and was relentlessly reproached by Atticus for weeping whenever Tullia had a fever or he heard of an untimely death. Yet now, in deep emotion, he only smiled his delicate warm smile, and reached out his hand.

"Come," he said, "brother. You did what you had to do."

"Can't sit sniveling and confessing here all day," he said briskly. "Gods, what a time of day for all this feeling! You're aging me, Cluentius. I can't afford it — not enough years left as it is. Let's talk about that letter you got. We'll walk up and down here; it always restores me to go here, and across here, and turn up here, and take deep breaths *here*. It's my exercise for firming up the wits. We've got to think fast.

"The best thing would be of course if this Asuvia of your friend's, niece or whatever she is, could introduce herself into the household at present presided over by Sassia. What is your opinion of her capabilities? How old is she, anyway?"

"She is a child!" said Cluentius decisively. He told the Praetor something of her history. "She is clever; Asuvius exaggerates her cleverness of course, but she has command of herself." In his mind he saw her again in his friend's courtyard, alighting with that personal blend of precipitousness and grace, that curious alloy of late-lasting childhood with precocious maturity. Was she young or old for her years? He could only remember her gait, the blue eyes wide open below his, her clear questions and quick answers.

"She will not be allowed, by Asuvius or by me, to visit

Auria at my mother's house," he said. "My mother knows everything that occurs at every moment on her estate. She would be placed immediately on her guard by the appearance of a member of Asuvius' household on the premises. Whatever her recklessness, I must remind you of her intelligence, and of her readiness to take decisive steps. I should most certainly refuse to permit that this girl should risk —"
Cicero gave him a sharp look.

"I understand. However, this Auria — well, we must use what instrument we have. Your girl must get out of this Auria what she can. This is what I need to know: I shall dictate these instructions before we leave, and you will have them by you. If these young women prove useless, other agents must be found.

"First: a *comprehensive* picture of the evidence taken in those investigations involving the slaves." Cluentius interrupted:

"Won't a general picture of that evidence have to be produced at the preliminary, the *postulatio*, and put on record, when Accius will be obliged to give the judge a notion of what base he has for action?"

"Yes, but I do not want a general picture. I want a detailed picture. Second, I am certain that there will be other charges: not legal charges that must be mentioned in the *postulatio*, but charges that Accius will bring against your character as supplementary indications of your rascality. He will not content himself with vague allegations of your untrustworthiness and general immorality. He will have chapter and verse. He must document this part of his speech from your mother alone. I have already ascertained that there is no citizen of Larinum, of any quality or standing whatsoever, who could possibly be brought against you as a character witness or would consent to depose. Some have witnessed, unwillingly, the depositions of the slaves: but they have refused to appear themselves on your mother's side." The Praetor gave Cluentius a long, admiring glance. "Unusual, my dear fellow. You are an extraordinary object: a man without public or private enemies. Save one," he added, somberly and quietly.

"Next, I want the names of all the witnesses to the torturing and examining of the two slaves. I have some; I need all. They must be interviewed. Your friend Asuvius will be the man for this task. And I wish to know the fate of the slave Nicostratus."

"Much detail is necessary here?"

"Yes. I respect Titus Accius, and I know him to be a close student of my methods. He is familiar with my taste for large quantities of corroborative detail. I must not disappoint him. This case, Cluentius, is going to be won. It will therefore be carefully prepared."

"You feel that the girl —" began Cluentius doubtfully.

"I feel about the girl what I see in your face as you speak of her. She is a gift from the gods. In our present impoverished condition, we can but be thankful. Make use of her. I shall send you, within two days' time, two excellent fellows, travelers, itinerant agents of the sort your lamented stepfather was so fond of using. Use them, in any way you can. They are strangers to Larinum. But make particular use of the girl."

Cluentius frowned and opened his mouth to speak.

"Ah!" interrupted the Praetor. "You are concerned. Nonsense. This is an opportunity for the child. Far better preparation," he added, grinning, "for *life*, my dear fellow, and marriage with some intelligent man, than any instruction she may have been getting from your friend's irreproachable female connection." They turned and moved toward the house.

"Educational," said the Praetor. "*Very* instructive."

XII

S HE'LL SEE YOU TOMORROW, if you really want
to," piped Auria as her slaves came up with her litter.
"Do you really want to?"

"Of course I want to," said Asuvia. "I told you . . . the
mysteries. I've got the book, sneaked it out of the library
right under old Philo's nose; both he and my uncle told me
I couldn't read it, so naturally I intend to. The Greek's
pretty peculiar though — not at all regular Greek; did you
tell her?"

"Yes. She wants to see it. She thinks she can read it, all
right."

"You have to know what it's about. Naturally I never
learned anything about the Egyptian stuff from *him*, or any
of the other tutors either. Can you see me asking anyone
here, showing them that book? I'd have it grabbed out of
my hands and I'd get clamped down on so fast . . . not a
chance. Not likely *she's* going to care about what my uncle
thinks."

"No. Not likely. I asked her, I told her. You can come
tomorrow."

What makes her look so idiotic? thought Asuvia about

young Auria for the tenth time in a single day. In the South, where they had walked together, strayed, idled, talked, while the old ladies babbled and fanned themselves in the garden, Auria had only looked simple, a little on the stupid side. Asuvia's furtive, darting curiosity had never been able to get much out of her. She giggled in a normal manner, though, and made a few mildly sarcastic remarks about her husband whenever Asuvia brought him up. She never mentioned him by name. She said things like "My mother has been there," "My mother bought some things," in a perfectly ordinary, tinkling little voice, without strange looks, so that no one in the world could ever have imagined the reality of that "mother." She did not mention her mother except when she and Asuvia were alone. This was the only clue. Her eyes were round and blue, her cheeks round and pink, her figure pretty and slightly plump. There simply wasn't anything to be done with her, no matter how much you applied yourself.

But here in Larinum she was different. You could handle her, get her to do things you wanted her to do, but she never said anything except in answer to some direct question. She just looked faintly feeble-minded, and her round eyes seemed colorless and blank. To work round to a discussion of any such subject as the approaching trial was so obviously out of the question that Asuvia made no attempt.

They had not been in Larinum a day before the stored-up talk of months, the news of Sassia, had flowed through every room in Asuvius' old house. Curiously enough, the matrons who came to visit Asuvia's old companion Axia talked far less about the accusation against Cluentius and the coming trial than they talked about the great burning subject of the town, the sacrifices, rituals, celebrations of the foreign cult apparently long practiced in privacy by Sassia and the senior Oppianicus since the early days of their marriage, but only now made known to Larinum in all its black open secrets.

When Asuvia had received her instructions as to what she was to pump the young Auria for and how she was to go about it, she had quickly made up her mind that she would not necessarily limit herself to these instructions. She had sat in an ivory-armed chair in her uncle's Roman office-room, her back straight against the chair's back and her feet neatly together, her arms disposed along the chair's arms, head up, eyes candidly upon her uncle's tense face: the attitude in which she had customarily been arranged for her chaperone's various lessons on deportment and the social disciplines. But her mind raced and one long finger moved restlessly, exploring the carved grooves at the end of the chair-arm, caressing, poking a bit, tapping.

She had gambled, though without recklessness, when she had told her uncle about the afternoons spent with Auria in the South, afternoons that her chaperone was gulled into sponsoring by a series of well-placed rambling conversations concerning the long relationship of the Aurii clan and the Asuvii. The old Axia had never been aware that her charge directed all her attention to the young matron so disastrously connected with the most disastrous of Larinum's families.

The Aurii women were numerous, and while Axia gossiped and nodded with the old in the gardens of afternoon, she imagined the young all together in some similar conclave, in a cool indoor chamber. By keeping out of sight during the visits, and by expert chatter about the other members of the household on the way home, Asuvia had disguised easily the intensity of her interest in the one out of all the numerous family whom she was instructed to avoid.

But her uncle presented her with quite different problems. She loved him. A world in which she should fail to love him was quite beyond her imagination. But she loved him oddly, for she had to deceive him constantly in order to have some freedom to exist.

She knew in a perfectly intellectual way as well as through intuition that he loved her dearly, and not just as a family relic. Growing up in her isolation, surrounded by the dull women who were her nurses and chaperones and the gifted, articulate men who had formed her series of tutors, she had learned to think. She had followed with quick interest her uncle's attachment to her, watching it, feeling it turn from an ordinary responsibility into a complex of strong personal responses. How he had stared, laughed, stared, slapped his knee, grinned, as her first old Greek tutor put her through her paces for the first time in his presence, and he could see that she had brains and nerve! She could remember always the new look on his face when he left her that time. The long letters addressed to her instead of the short ones to her governesses, the curious gifts from his returned trading vessels, the conversations in which he spoke to her with something almost like candor concerning her future — even without any basis of comparison, Asuvia knew what all this meant. Her uncle had been inspired by her to assume the vulnerabilities of real parenthood. She thought of this in these terms: he thinks about *me*, cares about *me*, it hurts him if something goes wrong; he worries. Yet by the time she was fourteen, she knew also that his Asuvia was not hers. He valued her out of all proportion, and he did not wish her to change, and he thought first, foremost, and continually of seeing to it that she should never have to fear, suffer, or act for herself.

When she had to deceive him in the interests of her own, separate Asuvia, she never lied. She failed to mention. One of her tutors, middle-aged and humpbacked Marsyas, in her fourteenth year had been vital to her because of the

voice in which he could read, the dark twisted face which
he turned on her to help her read between lines of somber
tragedies and cold lyrics on the mixed nature of human
love, human beauty, human joy. He drank hard, and a
rough popular accent occasionally marred — or illuminated
by its very commonness, according to what you felt —
his readings. He would not spend the proper hours on
mathematics, for he thought she was deaf to these tones,
and he had no patience. For what he considered her intelligences he had no patience either, but unstinted time.

When her uncle wrote her, as he did in these last two
years, about her lessons, she deceived by saying nothing he
would not like to hear. When he arrived and inquired and
discovered, she saw in the dark face how passionately Marsyas wished to remain in her household. She deceived, and
let him dictate to her in his most savage sub-voice. She
copied the answers he gave to the problems her uncle set,
and turned upon Asuvius' pleased smiling face her bluest
gaze from under brown arching brows.

And now the terrible old story whose shortest chapter
was her father's death filled her youthful life with its inti-
mations of what forms life and the world could take. She
was already worldly enough, through the trained operations of her imagination, to feel surely how her uncle's fear
for his friend Cluentius had moved to the center of his life,
overshadowing other concerns, dominating even his wish
to preserve forever her inexperience. So she had gambled,
told him frankly of her curiosities about Auria and her indulgence in those curiosities, during the hours in the stuffy
second-story chamber, the peripheral orchards of the old
Southern villa, while the other cousins walked in the courts
and the old matrons fanned themselves peacefully in the
cool gardens.

Her calculations were correct, and the two grave scowling men had trusted her, hedging round their trust with

prohibitions, limitations, insistences. But by the nature of the charge, they could not oversee her; old Axia was their only instrument of supervision. Asuvia smiled behind her submissive face, and resolved.

She moved in morning air through the streets of Lari-num, her maid at her elbow, her litter-bearers following, for she wished to clear her head and quicken her responses in her accustomed way, by physical exercise. She kept her mind off the encounter just ahead; she had thought it through, she would prepare for it now by detaching herself from it.

Still, its nearness lent intensity to her most casual observation. The old town, scarred at its heart by years of loss and conflict, lay serene in outward loveliness before her eyes. She passed the small municipal Forum, walking slowly, and saw a little group of grave-eyed men in counsel. One of them, the old banker Gnaeus Aurius, she knew; and she felt deep in her mind that she knew the names of the others, and the names of their fathers and cousins and relatives by marriage, names which were part of the stuff of her uncle's life, and of Cluentius', and hers. The talk was of business. A sharp-faced Greek steward stood by, with piles of tablets and accounting-rolls beside him ready to produce. Beyond this group, a young farmer stood grinning happily as his old shepherd fussed around a small group of beautiful little rams, apparently prize stock of some sort since they were so carefully groomed and roped together; anyway, you could see their beauty and their excellence, if you knew nothing of such things, in the lit-up face of their new owner.

For a long moment, Asuvia's detachment from her ap-proaching strenuous exercise became real. A deep, half-articulate delight took hold of her, delight in the morning of the old town of all her ancestors, interest, longing to know everybody's name and acreage, to be part of this as she was meant to be. She wished freakishly to rush up to the old banker, stick her head unforgivably into the little circle round him and ask: *what interest rate?* She would have dearly loved to be able to say something good about the rams, feel them in the right place and show her knowledge, share for a good tingling moment the joy and hope of their purchaser and the satisfactions of their breeder and seller. What life could be, what a day could be . . . she thought, and then: what life is, what this day must be.

The slave at Sassia's outer gate had orders, and Asuvia went in with her maid, leaving her four men standing wordless, unable as if by some law of Larinum to converse with the gatekeeper of the Oppianici. The young women moved up the long hedge-bordered approach to the house, Asuvia looking sharply about her, the maid close at her elbow muttering and mumbling, ". . . if the Lady Axia finds out . . . if the Lady Axia finds out . . . I know, I shall wait in the rear, mistress, but if this be found out . . ." Asuvia did not answer except by repeating brief instructions. She concentrated hard on her opening speeches, reviewing phrases, questions, attitudes.

The door of the main house was kept by an odd-looking dark man, bearded. He rose slowly from a little table where he worked with a small silver bowl and a set of engraver's tools; courteously he drew back the bar of the great door, gestured, smiled, bade them follow him, with the pantomime of an intelligent mute or of a foreigner who knows no language likely to be understood by his interlocutors. The beauties of Sassia's front court, famous in Larinum though familiar to so few, struck obliquely on the sharp senses of the girl as she passed through; in a blaze of subtle reds and intense blues, black marble, white marble, green and indigo of flowering plants in carved stone boxes, Asuvia crossed this space, her eyes steadily ahead of her on the arched doorway of the long wide room at the end of the court, once the office where Oppianicus the Elder met his associates and directed his operations, now the center of the administration presided over by Sassia alone.

The mother of Auria and of Cluentius stood in this doorway, very tall, very pale, her long eyes hard and narrow. She did not move forward to greet the girl, but spoke briefly to her dark doorkeeper in a language which Asuvia had never heard.

"Auria told me of your wish to visit here," she said without civil prelude, but standing aside courteously to motion Asuvia into the administration room. "You wish, I believe, to bring me some book of your uncle's library about which you are curious." Asuvia forced herself to look calmly and directly into the legendary face. She inclined her head gracefully as she had been taught, and uttered a conventional greeting in a low and perfectly disciplined voice.

"You are aware, of course," said Sassia in a light dry tone, "that your uncle and I do not exchange civilities. May I inquire whether the members of your household know that you are here this morning?"

"Lady," answered the girl, "as I told Auria, I am aware that this is not exactly a conventional visit. There is no one with us here at present who could help me with the book, but then even if all my tutors were here in a body, I couldn't ask them. I came across the book in the library the last time I was here, and was told that it was entirely unsuitable for my interest. I had to take it out of the library in secret, and I've had to come here in secret. Did Auria tell you what the book is about?" As she got through these sentences, planned with care, now sounding easy and sure in her ears, the tightness in her throat relaxed, her breath began to come naturally. As always, the discovery of her own competence exhilarated her and sharpened all her perceptions.

The deep line at the left of Sassia's long unrouged mouth, still red for all the pallor of the face, engaged her attention; the network of wrinkles about the eyes, the extravagant sharpness of the nose — was the woman so beautiful? There was a sort of yellowness at the base of her nose, in the morning light . . .

"Yes. It deals with the Egyptian mysteries?"

"With those and with other, Greek rites. It is in a Greek I cannot read, an odd script and I guess a dialect." The device of the book was Asuvia's invention exclusively. The instinct which she avoided recognizing as a talent for deception had made her keep, in her pretense, as many genuine ignorances as she could. In truth she knew nothing of the book's contents. In truth she had stolen it from the library, though for years she had known it was there and had felt no particular curiosity about it. She had asked about it once. The most austere of her old tutors had snorted contemptuously at her about the cheap mysteries of Egypt and the corrupted Greek of an ignorant priesthood whose two entrance requirements for their beggarly college were a capacity for hysteria and a distaste for decorum.

She took a small scroll from a linen wrapping and offered it to Sassia.

"Lady, the first book, the one dealing with Egypt."

The long white arm, the long white hand . . . Asuvia knew as if through dreams that swift gesture. Sassia motioned her to a chair, but remained standing, looking down at her with a small sardonic smile, still and unswervingly with a penetrating narrow blue gaze.

"Curious . . . really curious," she said with a little laugh to match the smile. "You, I mean. Do you know, I've never succeeded in getting your friend Auria to feel the slightest curiosity, about this or anything." The tone was not the tone of the dread practitioner. It was the voice of the eternally disappointed pedagogue, part sarcasm and part genuine regret. Asuvia had heard it many times from tutors, from her uncle himself, when they had been attempting to direct her attention toward unsympathetic studies.

"Tell me," said Sassia, seating herself with a sudden graceful movement, beginning to unroll the book, "are you interested in these practices for themselves, or simply because they are forbidden you by proper guardians, and perhaps, in Larinum, associated with other forbidden things?" The blue glance blazed at Asuvia. She widened her own eyes, hesitated, and chose.

"The forbidden, the secret and dangerous," she said; but as she saw that she had hit the right note, without having planned, she was unable to finish her sentence. Sassia watched her with lips parted. Obliquely, without the engagement of her conscious mind, Asuvia abandoned all question of the woman's beauty.

Sassia laughed, and this was as sweet a laugh as Asuvia had ever heard from any woman. The long eyes lightened, the grave tense poise of the head was changed as the lady of this house bent forward and drew her young guest into laughter with her.

"How *well* I understand, dear girl." The light dry voice was deep and lovely now, humor and a freakish sympathy flowed between the two. "Good of you not to giggle. It's hard to say 'The forbidden, the secret and dangerous,' like that without giggling, or feeling like it, but the gods know how big these words can be, to a young girl tired of her youth." A shrill squawking noise cut into the air. Sassia rose, crossed the wide room swiftly, and brought out from a little clump of plants a small ivory cage with a brilliant bird in it. Some sort of hawk — his beak and talons curved, sharp; but small, compact, fiercely green-and-tawny. "He's new," said Sassia in the most ordinary, pet-loving, house-wifely tone. "I keep him in here with me in the mornings.

He gets hungry, and *scrawk!*" Flawlessly she imitated the bird's wild grating call, and he flung it back to her. Sassia caressed him with a clever finger between ivory rods, murmured to him, fished out from behind the plants a brightly embroidered covering of dark cloth, which she dropped over the cage. "Forgive the interruption . . . a tiresome pastime, a foible," she said, smiling sweetly at the girl as she returned to her chair, picked up the scroll, unrolled it and held it with long-accustomed dexterity; reared her head back a bit, in a rather birdlike gesture, narrowing her eyes and peering to get a good look at the script. Asuvia watched her without thought of anything but watching her.

"Hum . . . not a very . . . Interesting, though, to see the words *written* in this country dialect; you hear it but not often read it. . . . I know this script, common. Bad copy. Well, it's a traveler's account. The man's just telling what he saw. Nothing in here you couldn't have seen your-self. He's a *visitor*. Not very intelligent. He knows the stories, and he's seen ceremonies outside the temple, nothing interior. Art critic, of a sort? Uh, not much in his language, but he can see paintings, care for the objects . . . well, *something* —" she murmured musically to herself, scanning, squinting. She lowered the scroll abruptly and fixed Asuvia with the piercing cerulean look again. The girl's heart thumped with obscure excitement.

"Do you know the stories?" asked Sassia.

"You mean those of the mysteries, of Serapis and Isis?" stammered Asuvia. She knew the names, everybody did. A picture stood in her mind, brilliantly remembered. She had walked with old Axia and a group of the older women of her little community, through the streets of gay Hercu-laneum on a day of festival visits. The strange temple stood on their way in the sunlight of early afternoon: a small crowd stood at the base of steps, an altar lay there open to the air, a perfume arising from it so sweet among low flames that Asuvia stopped, Axia dragging her by the arm, to draw in that penetrating delicate breath, a sweetness unknown and strange. Old Axia and the others stopped too, as if despite their wishes. There were among the worshipers near the steps the forms of Roman ladies of fashion beside Roman workmen and their women, slaves also. A shaven-headed priest held a tall vessel in one hand, a bizarre little singing rattle in the other. The rattle sang, the flames and the perfume breathed in the bright air, a rich beautiful voice spoke in Latin oddly accented but understandable, of sacred water, sacred fire, "O beauty, beauty of deathlessness, eternal and forever renewed . . ." A dark man crouched by the altar with a long flute, and a grave sweet air moved beneath the rattle and the incense. Asuvia's group moved on, muttering to each other of the shamelessness of ladies of Rome who would condescend to this slaves' cult, the scum of Egypt, low-priced merchandise of wandering foreigners.

"Serapis," said Sassia wearily. "One name — the most widely known. I prefer the old one of Egypt, *Osiris.*" And she smiled again sweetly, languidly, leaned back in her chair and quoted:

"Unto thee, O Osiris, lord of eternity . . . forms are many, attributes majestic, lord of the hidden place . . ."

Silence, and she closed her eyes — delicate, delicate veined lids.

"I know the story," said Asuvia.

"Isis embraceth thee in peace," said Sassia, eyes still closed. "She driveth away fiends from the mouth of thy paths . . . they breathe the air and they look upon thy face when the Disk rises on its horizon . . . their hearts are at peace in so far as they may look upon thee, O thou, Everlastingness."

In an ordinary, conversational voice she said, "Look at the

paintings behind the fountain, and that panel there over the carved chest; the statue by the brazier — this is the sort of thing your author describes. I make him out to be one more curious of the objects and appurtenances of the cult than of its words or living forms."

Asuvia got up obediently. She had scarcely looked at the room since her entry into it, her attention narrowed always to one small sphere within it. She saw now that its decorations and furniture were rich in allusion to Egypt and its gods. The painting Sassia mentioned showed a blue-green seascape, a black wharf, a long strange ship, a recumbent shrouded form, a frieze of mourning figures, one apart from the rest.

"Isis after the discovery of Osiris' body," said Sassia in her quick pedagogic tone. "You remember the death at the hands of the demon Seth, called also Typhon; the wandering, the search of Isis for the body; the reintegration of the God's form, his resurrection and return to life. Look there —" she indicated another painting, in a recess of the room, but intricately lit by an arrangement of perforations in the roof, which directed the high morning sun to the panel. In this picture dark priests crowned with lotos chanted and danced; flutes and rattles were everywhere, done in some strange iridescent paint which looked as if it must glow even in darkness. The God stood in the foreground, face raised to the sun over Sassia's house. A tall woman's form faced him, only the straight back covered with a striped mantle visible to the beholder. The head of Osiris was shaven, but his face was not priest-dark, not dark as those around him; he looked like a dark Roman, his eyes glaring from the painted surface with a truly resurrected vitality.

"Beautiful," said Asuvia, but with a kind of doubt. "Strange, wonderful," she said with clear certainty. Sassia gave her another of the quick narrow-eyed smiles, alive with unvoiced approval, sparkling with laughter, half sarcastic and half affectionate, the look Asuvia had associated all her life with her good teachers.

"Lady, whose skill in painting?" she began, and Sassia moved quickly aside, tossing her head, in an indolent, elegant gesture.

"Over there" (the seascape with the funeral boat) "a master of Alexandria, now dead. *Here*" (the resurrection tableau) "a she-master of Larinum, still alive." She cut a small piece of pomegranate from a plate of the fruit and handed it to Asuvia, speared on a little jewel-handled prong. Idly the girl took the fruit and ate, remembering even as her teeth nipped into the tart flesh her firm resolve never to eat or drink in the house of Sassia. That lady caught an expression on her visitor's face, and laughed.

"You remember Persephone in the house of Hades," she said. "You have the fabling, story-loving mind, my good girl." She speared two sections of Asuvia's fruit and ate them rapidly. "To be frank," she continued in her coolest voice, "it is long since I talked with one of our sex who had any sort of mind at *all*. Your uncle has seen to your upbringing. I congratulate him — tacitly, of course." Her eyes crinkled at the corners. "This room is not as it was," she said in the social tones of a hostess discussing conventional rearrangements. "It is not now and has not ever been, of course, everybody's taste. But I perceive that you yourself have not everybody's taste."

A steward came to the door and spoke with Sassia, while Asuvia's eyes roamed over this room, through its wide doorway into the court, while she listened in deep attentiveness to the cool ordering voice, the clear splash of water in fountain and tiled pool, the small curious clucking noises from the shrouded cage of the hawk.

"It is time for my consultation with the priests of Osiris, whose small college I have established here just recently.

You seem aware, through Auria I assume, of my interest in these matters," said Sassia, smiling suavely away all thoughts of the consuming interest of Larinum's daily gossip. "And I do not forget that you are curious of the strange. Your uncle's attentions to your education in this respect oddly miscarried," she continued. "He has forgotten, no doubt, how perilous a business it is to arouse and feed the spirit of inquiry." A lovely malicious gleam lit her eyes, seeming a small malice only, the sweet feline trickiness of any teasing, witty lady. "Nothing can give me more pleasure than to supplement — tacitly, of course, dear girl — the excellence of the general preparation he has provided for you." Asuvia laughed with her. "Come, and hear the plans for tomorrow's ceremonies, of which I somehow feel you have heard, and in which — correct me if I mistake — I somehow feel you more interested than in that feeble little book."

The dark men stood in a little ring, in an enclosed herb garden several minutes' walk from the main structure of the house. As they walked through two small courts, past the kitchen enclosure and stairs leading to the slaves' quarters (where Asuvia saw with a pulse of excitement her maid in earnest gossip with two young girls of Sassia's kitchen), the lady conversed with her young guest on the advantages of maintaining one's own private college of priests.
". . . can arrange things according to inner seasons rather than outer," she said. "The festivals of the cult move according to calendar and date. I prefer another sort of rhythm. Tomorrow's festival is in Alexandria an autumnal event, and the cycle it inaugurates finishes much later in the year. I wish my cycle finished long before —" she suddenly turned her head upon Asuvia, and the girl saw at close quarters her full face, bland now, stripped of all expression but a disciplined calm — ". . . before the courts close in Rome." She continued evenly. "Also, I can move

131

about, have some of the ceremonies here, others in the course of journeys . . . this year, perhaps some in the City." Again that bland look, behind which Asuvia could feel the ambiguous question: *You understand?*

They were walking so fast, the steward in their wake, that no response was necessary other than small interjections denoting interest. "*Here*," said Sassia, and began to speak rapidly in a Greek dialect. The first of the dark men muttered responses in a quiet, musical voice. The others listened. Sassia turned aside to translate.

"We speak of tomorrow's sacrifices," she said in her lecturing voice. "They are the beginning of our cycle which will end in the great drama of the painting, the resurrection of the God. There is the ram —" she pointed to a large woolly one tethered in an enclosure. "And my lovely hawk, he of the ivory cage. Maneros! Show to my guest the contents of the basket." A youth among the priests stepped gracefully among the group and drew back the lid of his reed basket. Asuvia forced composure upon herself; two great serpents reared up their heads, their throats swelling.

"Ah," said Sassia, and reached out her hand. She moved in a strange way, behind the snakes; she held now in her hand, taken from another priest, a bronze rattle like the silver one in Asuvia's memory of Herculaneum. Its oval frame shone dully, its four hooked rods shook softly. A carved cat's head at its top caught the girl's wandering eye. Sassia hummed in a soft plangent tone, strident yet subdued; the rattle gave out its metallic whistling, in a rhythm strongly marked; the youth put a flute to his lips. Music and voices filled the air, but subdued, calming, hypnotic. Transfixed, Asuvia watched Sassia's right hand moving over the serpents while her left shook the rattle. Their heads swayed, their mistress's head swayed. Gently, delicately, she touched their heads and necks. The rhythm slowed, the voices died. She drew her hand away, and turned upon Asuvia her pale face and empty eyes.

"The sacred serpents," she explained in her pedagogue's voice, "symbol of the deathless power of the God. They preside with me over the sacrifices tomorrow. Our temple, built in the time of the Dictator Sulla upon his return from the East, is an hour's slow walk from here. The walk will be a procession. You may ride in your litter, or in a pretty little oxcart which Auria prefers to the walk."

"I shall walk," said Asuvia coolly. "Lady, what part of the God's drama is the subject —"

"*Ah*. I cannot explain that now. I will tell you tonight, this afternoon I mean, for I shall enjoy dining with you, here, before sunset, and speaking to you at more length of our mysteries. At least," she added dryly, "those phases of them which do not demand initiation. I can satisfy your curiosity, short of initiation."

"*Tonight*," said Asuvia.

"Oh, there will be difficulties?" Asuvia looked into the hard eyes now shining with excitement, saw the small even teeth glint in a sort of grin.

"There will be difficulties," she said. "But I will come."

"*Dear* girl. How very pleasant for me. If the truth be known, I find the company of Auria and her husband . . . well. Tonight will be a diversion for me, and I hope for you; long, since I entertained one of your family."

Her heart rising in her throat as she deliberated on the difficulties, Asuvia stood quiet in the sharp-smelling garden, while Sassia directed and interrogated her priests. She looked about her, brought back by the consideration of the problems about the invitation to the consideration of her general problems.

She had not even as yet the clear idea of the establishment's geography which had been a principal object of her morning's visit. Knowing of Cicero's agent residing in an inn at the edge of town, full of her uncle's and Cluentius' commands to use him for any actual contact with the house of Oppianicus, she had thought to find enough, herself, here to give him orders more efficient and detailed than any of which her uncle or Cluentius would have imagined her capable. She sought now, and hoped her maid was seeking more effectively, an indication of some room or building apart from the others which might have a strong room air. She had heard much detail about the strong room robbery and murder which had given Sassia her claim to the inquisition on the slave Strato.

Asuvia had had to be cautious in her inquiries from Auria, but she had in their course strengthened her impression that in this room all secret things were kept, subject only to the keys and will of mistress and steward. The girl even in her youthful heart had small hope of ever holding in her hands or placing in any others the records of the depositions. Still, she thought, through familiarity with the household she could surely learn the nature of this evidence, gathered from slaves who had moved about here familiarly such a few short weeks ago.

"Come," said Sassia, and the cool white hand that had lately caressed the serpents closed lightly about Asuvia's upper arm. "You look about you. Let me guide you." As they walked through portico and court, she chattered idly. They moved along one side of the large structure. Asuvia saw a lovely small trellised arbor, a little garden full of fruit trees and white statues, a young man reading and drinking as he read.

"Oppianicus," said Sassia. "The *Younger*," she added, laughing. "I will not present you now. He is so *occupied*. He will be with us tonight, though he must fast." She shot

Asuvia another glance of that sweet-sour, playful malice. "He is an initiate, you know, and must sacrifice tomorrow."

"Is Auria?"

"No," said Sassia shortly. "Look! The *megarum*, my own *megarum*, converted of course. The sight of it never fails to move me." Something in the hard sudden excitement of her tone moved Asuvia too.

"The word is unknown to my ignorance, Lady."

"There." It was nothing but a crumbly little stucco-covered outbuilding, familiar to Asuvia as the type of structure which housed young fruit trees, or covered the entries of underground wine storehouses.

"In the days of my husband's forebears," said Sassia prosaically enough, but with her grasp now tight on Asuvia's arm, "there was a large wine cellar here. Part of the business of our estate. Roomy, beneath the surface, many-chambered: ideal. The *megarum* is the special chapel for initiation rites, where the most secret matters of our cult are contained. You see the painting on the stucco? Signs, mere signs, but full of power; for none may enter here, *none*, my girl. Death awaits the violator; none may enter. *Megarum*," she said softly, "and *purgatorium* both."

"*What?*" asked Asuvia, forgetting forms.

"Oh, there are two parts. One has a pool in it, you know. Very secret — you must humor us, dear girl; no one goes in," said her hostess. She let go the girl's arm, seemed to forget all the business of the morning, and began to talk fast and expertly about flowering shrubs. She told the steward to send for Asuvia's maid.

"Mistress, the strong room —"

"Did you let them know you were interested in it particularly? Did you remember —"

"Mistress! I asked as anyone would ask, because of the

murder, such a short time ago! Who wouldn't ask — two guards murdered and floating in a garden pool, and then the burglary, and Strato that we all knew —"

"What did you hear? Anything about the investigation?"

"They said nothing; I could see they couldn't say anything because they didn't know anything. They showed me the strong room, though; all her money and all the jewels, all the letters and account things are there, but only —"

"Never mind the strong room, now. You were good, Laetilla. I'll give you the marmoset as I promised, and the turquoises too. Come along."

The moment for maneuver had passed, and Asuvia told old Axia to her face that she intended dining with Sassia, Auria, and Oppianicus. She did not bother even to stress Auria and to obscure the others. The gray face and clucking voice of the aged woman as she took in the news . . . sorrow, terror, memory and fear in the old streaming eyes . . . but one must act, and delay feeling. Asuvia had never stood so arrogantly straight, spoken so harshly, thrown down between them this terrible obstinacy and determination; Axia looked now unrecognizingly at the young face, its eyes cold-blue and wide, its mouth straight and narrow.

"I shall send . . . I shall write . . . the messenger leaves this hour . . ."

"Send, write, let him go. I shall take four men for the litter and two others, and Laetilla will attend me also. Will you give the orders or shall I?"

"Oh, *you* give the orders, mistress! Naturally! And remember this: I told your uncle and I told your relatives, all of them, that it may be well for the men of Rome to bring their girls up in this way, but that in Larinum it would have no good end. The whole town will know what you have done, and it is I who will —"

"Quiet!" shouted Asuvia, in a voice she herself had never

heard. She stretched out her hand to the old fuming speechless woman, who struck it aside.

"Forgive me," muttered the girl, but her voice was still hard even in its undertone. "This is necessary. I do what I must. My uncle will know."

"Know he certainly will."

XIII

SASSIA STOOD ALONE to greet her young guest, in the front court, dressed in an astonishing long robe of some gauzy material. A great jeweled clasp held this garment at the shoulder; a necklace of many slender chains sprinkled with green gems clasped round her neck, draped out along her collarbone, clung to all the portions of her throat where age might have left clearest marks. Gold clashed delicately at her ankles as she moved forward. Asuvia, walking toward her, saw with the clarity of her strained alertness that large emeralds, rough-cut, were set in the very sandal straps. The light was just beginning to decline from afternoon brilliance, but Sassia's court was designed for morning brilliance and for afternoon shadow. Pearl-gray and green were in the light of the room, reflected from windows, roof-opening, through the leaves of trees and vines set all about the interior. Her eyes looked violet-dark. In the splendor of her toilette, one expected a blue ring of paint about them, but there was nothing but the deepening lavender shadows of her own skin, looking almost bruised just under the eye.

"Greeting. Ah! You brought your maid; good. She will

find companions — the stairway, there. Let us please ourselves tonight, my dear young friend. Look — dispose your people, send two of your littermen back to poor Axia to tell her they'll wait for you at the outer gate, and that their four fellows are here at my door, within your call. My dear," and a sweet, sharp, lemony perfume, light and full of tang, touched Asuvia's senses as Sassia bent forward with a welcoming smile as sweet and light, "our elders are, after all, our elders. You will feel lighter-hearted, having sent her some reassuring message. I know your presence here is not exactly a thing of no concern for her." Her laugh was untouched by any spite, just deprecating, sympathetic.

"You must overlook the extreme fashion of dress I've adopted," she said civilly, drawing Asuvia with her toward the rear court and its fountain-gardens behind the room where they had sat that morning. "But I must speak to you of our stories, show you a bit of the ceremony, instruct you and thus serve the God." She gestured toward the darkening interior of the room where the great glistening painting lay on the wall. "One must be properly dressed for such occasions. You are surprised that I can speak in such a light tone of serving the God? But the first thing to understand is this: that our cult is a cult of joy, grace, the forgotten sweetnesses of life."

Asuvia remembered the serpents in the basket. With her uncanny trick of seeming to move along the edges, if not at the center, of her interlocutor's mind, Sassia continued: "The, ah, seemingly less attractive forms of our worship, the sacrifices and the abstinences we enjoin upon priests and initiates — Oh yes, much fasting, but you will dine well, dear girl, don't worry — well, all this is designed to provide the contrast-note, the somber background for the gold thread. You noticed the high priest's robe? Dark, heavy, with the bright patterns embroidered? The dark is the mystery and the unknown — perhaps, who knows, even the terror-breathing Secret; the gay graceful signs woven in gold and blue, they are the forms which we can make known to all and the joy and grace which all can see even if only the initiate sees in true perspective, against its ground of pain and loss. But I anticipate. Auria awaits us, and Oppianicus."

Asuvia asked a question about the house, murmured with sudden spontaneous delight over a curious small shrine set into a stand of white marble; green mysterious leaves shaded and ornamented a black sculptured stone head of startling beauty. A flame burned in a niche in the marble. Sassia was silent. The girl walked to this statue and bent to look at the smooth planes of the face, the delicate hollows of the eyes. A slight shock ran through her: the face was the face of the God in the painting.

"Osiris?" she asked, hesitating, for the sculpture was Roman in aspect despite the exotic black stone.

"Oppianicus," said Sassia quietly. "The *Elder*," she added, "in deathless obsidian," and led the way toward an outdoor dining room, where Auria and her husband stood to greet the guest.

Idiotic, thought Asuvia to herself, snapping at Auria in her mind, unable to endure the passivity of the girl, who was not really after all *that* stupid. Remembering her perfectly normal prattle, the tinkling laughter over careless jokes, the normal if not sparkling run of anecdote and social exchange, one could not excuse this blank-eyed and phlegmatic silence. When Asuvia or her mother addressed her, she answered in a word, with the *feeblest* smile. Oppianicus was worse; he had *tics*, and said the most irrelevant things, knocked over his winecup, perspired in a quite unacceptable manner. The air of fidgety impatience with which Sassia regarded her stepson and daughter seemed no more than justified to Asuvia. *Really* . . . As the dinner drew to a close, Sassia gave Auria a few crisp instructions about wardrobe and punctuality for the ceremonies of the next day.

"You'll ride in the double litter with your new maid. Oppianicus of course walks with us. *No delays.* Curtains open — I want you seen. Now you may go."

Young Oppianicus reclined motionless, leaning heavily on heavy cushions. His eyes were fixed on Sassia as she leaned forward, sweeping him from her attention, freed of the limitations imposed by Auria's presence, to address Asuvia uninterrupted.

"You wish to know?" she asked. Her voice was low-pitched and slow, her eyelids drooped extravagantly over her extravagant eyes. She had eaten almost nothing and drunk only from a small special vessel brought her by the dark-bearded keeper of the door.

Asuvia spoke uneasily, but knowing she must speak. She described as enthusiastically as she could the scene at the temple of Herculaneum.

"Ah," said her hostess. "The ceremony of the sacred water. 'May Osiris give thee the water of refreshment.' Yes, that temple is the Goddess's temple. Here we concentrate on the worship of the God himself. Isis we see but as his handmaiden and instrument. Our *pastophori*, secular priests, and of course priestesses (though I myself am the sole one at present) are sacred to Isis; but our priestly order is Osiris' own, and the Goddess serves. You will see. I myself, in my curious capacity, dear girl, as priestess, celebrant, and directress, portray the role of Isis in the drama of resurrection which our ceremonies re-enact; a subordinate role, here. The ceremonies, which have taken on a peculiar local cast — all our cults of the God and Goddess are susceptible to local interest — are entirely directed toward the worship of the life-force of Osiris."

She leaned her head on the tall carven back of her chair. She had not cared to recline at dinner. . . .

You may recall (said Sassia) that Isis and Osiris of our story were brother and sister as well as husband and wife. There is even a most curious story that they had cohabited before their birth, swooning with pleasure in each other's company, in the long delight of the womb. There is no time in all history when they did not belong to one another.

When the evil god Typhon, of their same blood, achieved the death of Osiris, having woven a most admirable, most marvelous, most curiously fashioned web of deception round him, involving some truly athletic feats of false witness and hypocrisy, he sought to make death permanent by disgracing and scattering the body. Isis' long search for the lost body of her friend and brother, whose life and work she had shared as his inmost spirit, took her through years and lands. The ceremonies which we observe tomorrow commemorate her grief and suffering, in part; but their center is the affirmation of her joy and her certainty, the knowledge even in the pain of loss that the life of her friend is the heart of the world's life, and if it pass, will at length return.

In the sacrifice of the ram, in the sacrifice of the hawk, the coming of the Avenger is prepared symbolically; for the life of Osiris may not be renewed until the debt be paid, and Typhon suffer just fate, and take over the burden of death.

Our sacrifices here, in the little temple not far away, are rather genteel. Nothing out of the ordinary. You will enjoy the dancing, libation-pouring, and the like. You are perhaps fortunate to be an observer of the spectacle at this late period. The ceremonies have sweetened over the years, as all things go bland and palatable. In old times, a man was sacrificed. One was elect; chosen, and made to incarnate the Typhon-spirit. His hair was dyed red, the color of Typhon, and the same red smeared on beasts who accompanied him. There were in old times great battles of re-enactment at the end, when the forces of Typhon met, in the ritual, the forces of Osiris led by Isis. Now we do this with a sort of ballet. The final ceremony, in which the destruction of Typhon becomes the resurrection of Osiris, comes at a later season. Tomorrow we shall but glimpse it, and only delicately.

I dance the dance of mourning, but it ends with a prefiguring of the dance of joy. Oppianicus here, who will wear the Avenger's robe in the final ceremonies, has but a small part tomorrow. He appears in white, without the great mask of the hawk which he will wear over purple, later, when the enormous beautiful thing has been done, and the low Fiend brought low, and the way back to life prepared for our Master. . . .

She turned from Asuvia and leaned toward Oppianicus. His eyes were fixed on her face; a long look passed between them. She half-whispered something to him.

"My lord's son learns rapidly and well," said Sassia, speaking to Asuvia in a lucid conversational tone. "The litanies and long speeches aren't easy to remember. The boy has to speak them in Egyptian. I prefer it to the Greek forms."

"Egyptian is a difficult language, Lady?" said Asuvia, feeling very strongly the need to keep the conversation on ordinary social levels.

"Not really," said her hostess, idly drawing a finger round the top of her empty cup. "No structure at all, to compare with either Greek or Latin. Difficult sounds, rather. The boy's father," she added, fixing Asuvia with a grave sweet look, "and I, we studied it for pleasure, never thinking of anything hard or serious, for we visited Alexandria often in old times.

"He will sacrifice the hawk," she went on, "and speak the words — speak, dear boy, just the opening lines for our guest — these are not secret things, but accomplished in full view," she added. Her eyes rested in a soft indulgent glance upon the young man. He raised himself gracelessly upright at table. Halting and low, his voice came out, inexpert, in an odd babbling tongue. The voice of Sassia, rich and beautiful, tense with feeling, cut him short and took up the discourse.

"In Latin," she said, "the incantation of the Hawk:

"'O grant that I be feared, and make thou me to be terrible! May I be joined unto Isis the divine lady, may she protect me from him my enemy . . . but not anyone see me naked and helpless. . . . I shall rise up like the divine Hawk, Horus make for me a spiritual body containing his own soul, that I may take possession of all that belonged to Osiris. . . . Osiris . . . he hath established my heart through his own backbone, he hath established my heart through his own great strength, I shall not fall. My face is like that of the God-hawk, my strength like that of the God-hawk. I shall see Osiris. I have seen him dead. God-hawk, I shall see him live.' "

A charged silence fell. Asuvia drew in her breath sharply, angrily aware that she was trembling.

"It grows cold here," said her hostess, mechanically, as if in comment on the girl's shivering, but she never once took her eyes from the lost blind following eyes of the young Oppianicus. "Soon I shall take you to another room for some of our music." But she did not move, and spoke again, in her half-singing voice of incantation, to the youth:

"'Horus who wound bandages round Osiris, who has seen Seth-Typhon! Hail, thou who will return after smiting and destroying him before the mighty ones.'

"Go now, dear child." And she rose, walked lightly over to stand for a moment behind Oppianicus' chair, put her hands on his temples; caressed, with a softness and sureness that seemed tangible and actual to Asuvia across the room, his cheekbones and forehead. She brushed her cheek against his hair, straightened, gestured to Asuvia, and drew the girl slowly from the room. A young slave in the little vestibule outside went in to Oppianicus. It was quite dim now in the passages of the house.

"*Here*," Sassia's voice was still soft, caressing, delicately exploring, "the room of dancers — but we pass beyond. Here the little library he most favored — I never take anyone in. Here the *venereum*." Asuvia started and felt for the first time a sense of genuine and simple shock. These rooms designed and reserved for the pleasures of Venus, with their strange paintings, secret little doors to private lanes, low tables, soft couches, perfume-breathing lamps — she knew of their existence; what young girl does not hear, in the innocent company of her young friends both maid and matron, that these things exist and perhaps await? But to hear the *venereum* mentioned and indicated like any study or dining room . . . and with a new shock, and again for the first time, Asuvia thought that that room in the days of Oppianicus must have known the presence of her own father, drawn in, corrupted, ruined long before his murder, by the famous games of Oppianicus and his company.

"A simple bedchamber now," said Sassia, gliding past its half-open door, glancing casually at its dim interior. "I sleep there, when I sleep."

They came to a pretty little dining room whose simple couches and table had been pushed back against its rose-colored, silver-bordered walls. This was a room in which daylight must never have much part, Asuvia saw, since it had but one small high window, and the most elaborate articles of its furniture were the torch-sconces and lamps. These were full-lit and blazing now, though twilight had but approached. Three musicians who had stood that morning in the company of priests sat now on the floor of the

145

room, in a corner; motionless, just inside the door, stood the bearded man of the gate. When the women came in, he moved behind them softly, placed on the little low marble table a black obsidian cup quite unadorned, and poured into it from a small amphora.

"Ah. Yes. The other was emptied long ago. This is a draught which I shall not ask you to share — bitter to the unaccustomed taste, my dear. You would not, I fear, find it pleasant." Other vessels and another, more ordinary cup stood on the table. Sassia herself poured wine and water and held the cup out to Asuvia. Softly the girl declined. Sassia looked at her with the sweet grave glance, smiled with both humor and gentleness, and took a long drink herself from the proffered cup. Over the cup's rim her eyes met Asuvia's. They both burst out laughing.

"*Not* Persephone, any more," said the girl. "It is just that I do not wish to be drowsy, and miss something."

"Good. I had rather thought you were prepared to discount, temporarily at least, some of the old ladies' graver warnings," said Sassia good-humoredly. A father's murder, a family's disruption, the proscription of grandparents and a shadowed, exiled girlhood lay between them as if on the table: existent, unforgotten, real; but disregarded, in the potency of an occasion made up of intense moments. Asuvia understood as never before the nature of certain happenings in Larinum's past.

The musicians in response to their mistress's signal began to play softly, softly, subdued even in that small room. The flute, the small singing rattle, a curious little tambourine, combined a thin wandering melody with the assertion of a clear, emphatic rhythm. Sassia kept her eyes on Asuvia's face. They remained standing.

"Our cult is often despised as the resort of beggars, slaves, and those members of the upper classes who rejoice in anything not customary," she said, and as she spoke began to sway in a subtle rhythm, marked by the tapping of her finger on the table in time with the muted tambourine. "This view is, as I believe you begin to see, an ordinary manifestation of Roman ignorance, quite understandable, dear girl, in this so very understandable country. I confess that I myself regarded it rather as a diversion, an item of interest, a curiosity of travel, in earlier years. Initiation is in all truth only a beginning of understanding. Only very recently have I been able to see, with clear eyes, the greatness of its drama, its rich drama, its illumined tale of inevitable process."

"Process, Lady?" asked Asuvia timidly.

"*Process* from loss, despair, along the road, to joy and rebirth," said Sassia still more quietly. "The road is retribution, revenge if you wish to call it by that crude word — but it is not that, it is but a sacrifice, a sanctification of the Process, an opening of the passage. The slaying of Seth-Typhon, a bridge, a passage . . ." She stopped her swaying for a moment, and drank from her black cup.

"The dance of tomorrow, the dance of grief relieved only by resolution to follow the process, open the passage, this dance begins like this — I can show you, it is for any spectator to see; you will see it tomorrow, I shall wear on my head *this*," and she took from a carved chest a slender silver crescent, fixed it in her hair with a hooked clasp, so that it rested upright there, its ends curved up like horns.

"The crescent of the Goddess," she explained. "It forces one to move slowly and carefully, whatever the rhythm, always with back very straight; any undisciplined movement will make it lurch, fall, be ludicrous. Look! For you could do this. You walk as a girl should walk, you do not *patter*, you do not *amble*. You move with precision, and your legs are long. There are few so well equipped. Look!" She signaled to the musicians, and the music became louder, though still its movement was slow and gravely measured. Sassia

1 4 7

raised her long arms, sheathed in their gauzy drapery; she began to writhe slowly, head upright, her whole torso undulating in a series of intricate contortions.

"You think of the *cordax*," she whispered breathily as she moved, "the vile stomach-dance of the South — now practiced by our distinguished ladies of Rome, those who wish forever to try something *new* —" she paused for a moment. The music went on.

"No, Lady," said Asuvia simply and with truth, for she had seen the *cordax* in Herculaneum and Pompeii upon two well-remembered visits in festival time, and in a kitchen courtyard in the country, danced by traveling acrobats while the household's maids shouted and laughed and beat their hands. "The quality is different. The *cordax* is a wriggle and bounce, it is as vulgar as one's governess says it is, and therefore dull. I never found it in the least exciting. This is slow, and it looks more difficult. You couldn't keep that crescent on your head in the *cordax*. It enforces a dignity, the crescent, even when you're twisting about —" The brilliance of Sassia's smile sparkled in the light of the lamp flames. She whirled away in a series of swift half-turns; dropped to one knee and arched her long back, head thrown extravagantly backward, the crescent gleaming now in her hand. Asuvia saw that her feet were bare. The rhythm of the music quickened; Sassia moved only her hands and arms; then slowly straightened and rose. She whirled back toward the girl, and her eyes glinted in some new way, her lips compressed and tense.

" 'May my heart be with me in the House of Hearts!' " she said in a deep strident voice, the sibilance of the rattle following her like a low, sustained hiss. " 'May my heart be with me and may it rest there, else I shall not eat of the cakes of Osiris by the Lake of Flowers. . . . May that be done which I command, for I understand with my heart.' " She spoke in a Latin so precisely enunciated that Asuvia had to recognize the force of her will to be understood. Heart, heart, heart — forever and again, that word.

" 'This is the heart of Osiris triumphant, made new before the gods —' " and here the deep voice plunged to a deeper note, spoke in a guttural whisper, shorn of all feminine tones:

" 'My heart, my sister! My heart, my sister! My heart of my life upon earth! May none stand to oppose me in the judgment. May there be none against me in the presence of the sovereign princes . . . and may there be no parting of thee from me.' "

Fear rose in Asuvia's throat and she could neither speak nor move. The wild eyes so close to hers closed slowly, opened slowly, shone with heavy tears. The tears moved down the pale hollowed cheeks. A new wind seemed to the young girl to stir her hair and breathe in her ears, though the air in the close room was still, the dancer motionless. This was the wind of a half-sacred terror, the fear of madness. And in the middle of that wind of disquiet, in the middle of her own pale-faced fear, Asuvia heard a voice speaking quietly from within, recognizable completely to her as her own inner voice: *I am sound, I am sound; she is mad, and lost in madness.*

"Forgive me," said the cool dry social voice of Sassia. The writhing lips were composed though unsmiling, the wet trace of tears seemed but a trick of the light. "The music of our cult is a continual intoxication. You must go now, I know — useless to agitate this poor Axia further, keep her pacing the court and wringing those old hands. Return in the morning. I will send a guide. Bring as many of your people as you like. My doorkeeper will see to you now. Farewell."

Asuvia to Marcus Asuvius her uncle, greeting.

I write in haste, and send this by Philo himself, since I can trust no other. I follow, riding disguised with Ennius, within hours I hope, but send this so you may have it if I should meet delay.

I have disobeyed you, dear Uncle, and entered, myself, that house. I made progress in the confidence of Sassia. She thought me harmless, invited me to attend with her the Mysteries of Osiris. I went to her house this morning and told her I could not, despite my wish, attend the ceremonies, but begged leave to watch the departure of the procession. This she granted. I sent for Ennius the agent of Cicero, using the method you ordered. He went with me as one of my litter-bearers.

Sassia is so absorbed in these rituals, full of private meanings for her, that she is careless of all else. More of this when I come.

She gave me leave. I already knew that the greater part of her household goes with her on these journeys to the temple, since the ceremonies demand the presence of numbers not easily available to her. I could only hope for luck. You will not approve. Forgive me. I had to do this in this way.

I had seen among the outbuildings one which I felt certain was the place for what we sought — not the strong room, but a sort of secret chapel made out of an old underground storehouse.

No time to tell you all. Ennius and I managed to stay on the premises. Sassia was not watchful, did not care. He held the maids in talk while I got into the *megarum* as it's called — I knew how. I had a torch but did not need it. In the first section there is water but also daylight coming through chinks. Here I saw a great chest and many signs. I think it is the tomb of Oppianicus, and so does Ennius; he says it is this which keeps everybody on the estate out of the building; Sassia does not even bother with much locking. In the second chapel there is light, kept there all the time I believe. I saw the body of Nicostratus floating in a sort of tub, preserved in some strange way. His hair and all his head and shoulders are dyed red. He is a sacrifice to her God — if I can, I will tell you more about this, for I understand it. There are images all around, many of them in the likeness of Oppianicus, the dead one of course I mean. There is a pile of wax tablets, a table with piled rolls of paper. I worked fast. I looked at the tablets but had trouble in reading them in that light; also they seemed tampered with. One bears signatures, among them a Magius, a Baebius, a Lucius Naeva. I could read enough so that as I looked at the papyrus I could see that there she had written out a copy. A memorandum said *Copy of letters dispatched to Titus Accius in Rome*, and a date, scribbled, recent, which I could not fully make out.

The part made from the tablets said only that the slave Strato deposed that he knew Aulus Cluentius of Larinum to be the murderer of his late master Oppianicus the Elder. He deposed that he had always known this, but had feared to disclose it in the earlier investigation because his fear of Cluentius and death was greater than his fear of torture.

The slave Nicostratus apparently deposed in the same matter, but the tablets are much marked and smeared.

The papyri on the table instruct this Titus Accius in the attack to be made on the character of Cluentius. She uses the phrase, *probabile ex vita*. She talks of an attempt to poison the younger Oppianicus at his wedding banquet, by a cup of drugged mead which by mischance came to some young man of the company, Balbutius is the name I remember, and killed him instead. She talks of Cluentius as a profiteer of the proscriptions of Sulla, and speaks of some scandal that was caused when the ex-slave husband of some woman slave Cluentius bought up from a confiscated estate sued for the return of his wife. She talks of a legacy subverted. She says at the end: "So much for my son's conduct in private matters. The affair of the jury-bribing I leave to you." I remember these words.

Though I thought no one saw my going in or coming out,

Ennius is not sure. I was ill for a short while after coming out. He attended to me, but feared we were seen together there. I do not know the extent of Sassia's disregard of all opposition in her case. Ennius has talked much and heard much in the community. He fears her greatly. I am perhaps disarmed and put off by my experience of her company yesterday morning and evening. Ennius says that it is now time, since this much is done and known, that you, Uncle, come to Larinum and interview the witnesses of Sassia's inquisitions upon the slaves. He says "Numerius Magius and the senior Baebius." He fears that Sassia will find traces of my presence in the *megarum* and will make an attack on me to prevent my returning to you. Therefore we leave now, preparations being finished as I write. The return from the ceremonies must still be at least an hour away. Pray do not disquiet yourself, my dearest Uncle; I am in such good hands. I ride disguised as a boy. I have a cloak with a hood! Ennius has put on a dignified merchant's dress. We ride the two new Apulian horses — *very* fast, how exciting!

I too fear Sassia, I confess it. But I think she will wish to destroy me not because she fears any harm to her case, rather because I have gone uninitiated through the *purgatorium*, passed by the body of her husband who is her God, stood in the *megarum*, scene of her sacrifices — I, unconsecrated.

We go by back roads known to Ennius, and will pick up the Latin Way not at Aesernia but only at Fregellae. We shall go to the house of Cicero at Arpinum, Ennius says, for new horses. Uncle, dear friend and my real father, farewell.

XIV

ASUVIUS READ this letter aloud, in an uneven, rasp-
ing voice, to Cluentius and Cicero in the office-room
of the Praetor's house. He had come with it, upon
the moment of its being put into his hands at his own house
by the half-fainting weary old Greek, Asuvia's present di-
rector of studies. Cluentius had spent the forenoon at Cicero's house, working soberly and industriously upon the
preparation of the case.

"She has a cloak with a *hood*," he said painfully, and
threw down the rattling sheets upon the floor. "The two
new Apulian horses . . . fast, how exciting!" And his eyes
blind with tears blazed toward Cicero's, his face shook.

"Calm, friend!" said the Praetor. "The girl has done better
than well. You should be proud of her. She knows you will
be terrified for her. She puts in those childish bits on purpose, small attempts to cheer you up. They only show what
a low opinion she has of your feelings for her — she must
make these concessions to your will to see her still a child."

Asuvius covered his face with his hands.

"I assume," said Cicero crisply, "that you gave orders
that she and Ennius be met by a full escort at my house in

Arpinum." Asuvius nodded mutely. "Good. There is a reliable staff there already. She is probably there by now, since Ennius will have come up hill and down valley, partly across country and by hunters' roads; he knows fast riding — it is not the least valuable of his many skills."

"She keeps saying 'if I can,' and those farewells. She is afraid, my little one, my sweet care, my — Oh, apologies, great Praetor! I am immoderate. You would no doubt wish, were your Tullia some four years older, that she could have such superlative opportunities to display her good qualities, her resolve and resource, her Roman courage. You envy me, no doubt, my chance to rejoice."

The Praetor looked gray for a moment, then angry for a moment. Before the words of his reply came to his mind or mouth, he made an abrupt gesture toward Asuvius, with an outflung hand; his face lit up with its incomparable smile, the smile of the proud man admitting vulnerability. Cluentius, watching, knew this smile, and was moved by it now as upon his own occasions.

"Friend," said Cicero with simplicity, "I honor you. For I could not have done what you have done. You did it when you sent the letter to Cluentius at Tusculum, to let us know of this chance. You have shown love for your friend and, better, respect for your ward." He did not move, but his quiet voice filled the air with feeling. "You pay now in regret and anxiety the price of your openhandedness. Your friend and I, we shall not be so miserly as to grudge you a few harsh words for either or both of us," and his blue gaze drew Cluentius into the closed circle. Asuvius was still, though his hands again covered his face.

Cluentius followed as in a dream the currents of this exchange. Since Asuvius had read the passage in the girl's letter dealing with the discovery in the *megarum*, his mind had been caught up in an intricate movement of memory and imagination. As a traveler in the East, he had visited an ancient temple of Isis and Osiris. He knew the little local temple near Larinum, since its construction by veterans of Sulla while he was still a youth. But especially, with a scholarly friend of Ephesus, he had once penetrated in secret a *megarum* of the local cult, and indulged his traveler's curiosity and his wandering idle quest for the beautiful in many forms. His friend had drawn him to this *megarum* because of the beauty of its objects. He remembered the trace of ineffable fragrances, the jewel-encrusted adorable small image of the Goddess; but his constructing, figuring, uncontrollable imagination placed him at Asuvia's side in that obscure building he had never noticed, on either of his two visits to the home of his mother's heart.

The grotesque floating thing in the black stone tub, its red hair and shoulders crudely dyed; the effigies, the staring eyes, the sense of that other room behind her with its sarcophagus and deep pool; the guttering torches, and everywhere the breath of that strong presence which had made of this double charnelhouse its real home, its workroom, its resting-place, the point encompassing its past, present and future . . . He stood in imagination at Asuvia's side. No, not at her side; somewhere within her body and spirit, her youth, femaleness, otherness forgotten, her essence his essence in the moment of terror, revulsion, determination, and acceptance. Had she seen the livid scars on the back, just under or perhaps just above the surface of the water, had she seen that broken hand? He did not formulate the question, only saw these things with her eyes and his memory, and added other marks, from his knowledge of the later sufferings of Nicostratus.

He knew her illness as she came back into daylight and the upper world: the illness of divers brought too suddenly to the surface after an immersion too deep, rather than any girlish nausea. He knew her fear, the fear behind those "ifs" in her letter, knew it for the terror invoked not by Sassia's hatred and energy, but by her love and her despair — the hiss of the snake-whips of the Furies, the wind of their wings.

Cicero bent over to pick up the scattered sheets of Asuvia's letter. He unrolled with a slow hand, and searched for a particular passage. Asuvius sighed and sighed, puttered about the room, dashed water over his face from a copper bowl, shamelessly dabbed at his wet face with his tunic sleeve.

Cluentius came back from his voyages to this room. His deep eyes saw the Praetor's floor, the Praetor's sandal; his heavy lids lifted, and he saw the blue eyes of the Praetor fixed quietly upon him, the unrolled paper held off to one side.

"Now," said Cicero, "I recall my good Sosigenes. You are prepared to dictate, dear fellow? Let's see: collect our thoughts; this matter of the purchase of confiscated slaves, and that legacy . . . or shall we take the poison first?"

Asuvius poured himself a drink, stopped fidgeting, and suddenly began to laugh. "O Gods! poor little Balbutius and that seafood stew . . . remember?"

Cicero to Atticus, greeting.

Brundisium again, hurrah! you are off the seas. And you will return to Rome, my Atticus, though you deny it; you are wandering giddily up and down our hot roads like any Roman, and must return. All promises well for us. You write in such alarm of the imminent arrival of Lucius Sergius Catilina, with his gang and his debts and his extortion money from his rascally year in Africa, to align himself joyfully with the consuls-elect, that is to say, those of the bribed elections, not the real ones, our friends. O Atticus, have

156

faith! This whole action is not going to be hard. There was *too much of the bribery*. Excess, dear boy, has delivered the knaves into our hands, the hands of virtue. It will not be difficult, just strenuous.

You know how the businessmen hate Catilina and all that crowd, and of course the words "violence," "murder," and "bribery" are filling the Forum with synonymous sounds. Good, for the affair of the consuls; and good, also, that one of the false consuls bears the name of Sulla.

But bad too, Atticus. I never hide from you; I show you my heart, and you will be grieved though alas not astonished, indulgent friend, to see it so full of the cause of Aulus Cluentius.

What a cause, what a man, what a case! *Developments*, my Atticus. We know now in its main substance the nature of the prosecution's case — that is, the case which the woman Sassia wishes brought against her son in the name (and name only) of her husband's son. I have used to advantage my old hard-riding fast-talking long-nosed friend Caius Ennius, of such service to me in other interesting cases, you remember. But let me reveal to you one of the lively quirks in this quirky case: the real agent in the matter of finding out, *before* the preliminary hearing as I always like to do, what evidence is involved, has been a sixteen-year-old girl, the unmarried niece and ward of Cluentius' friend Asuvius, and the daughter of a victim of Oppianicus.

This girl has shown courage and skill, a talent for seizing moments with great hardihood; she is also a pleasure to the eye and ear. The lively ladies of our ever-new society often pall upon me as you know; how often, Atticus, we have mourned together — smiling discreetly of course, moderates that we are — the fact that the Greek ideal of constant female quiet, almost-constant female absence from men's presence, female simplicity of mind induced by firm non-education, has never succeeded as a Grecian graft on our Roman oak. But I feel grateful now for the existence of this young Asuvia.

The preliminary hearing is tomorrow. Our judge is old Voconius Naso — Quintus — remember him, squeak-voiced like all the Nasos, but a firm man in the judge's chair, a firm hand on the conduct of trials if the benches get out of hand, and a great lover of *detail* in all things. Not inflexible. It will be fun to be scrupulous and hair-splitting before him, this connoisseur. His political sympathies? Well — he wavers, like all of us in these wavering times; like you and me, Atticus, who have to swing back and forth a bit, things being what they are.

Well, Naso at the moment has sympathies like ours. This means that the name of Sulla and the term "corruption of juries" and the mention of court-bribing in general are going to have ready access to his ears. But Accius speaks first, I second — O Atticus, let him fill their ears with his "Sulla" and his "bribery," for I have a great song to sing.

Catilina will not come back from Africa for our affair of the consuls, until late in the year. He is too busy with his extortions there. The trial which will see the triumph of our friends and the disgrace of the false consuls will be delayed. You need not come to the city before two months have passed. But I hope that you will come at the beginning of next month, for the opening of Cluentius' trial. You will see me *at my best;* you know how you enjoy this spectacle.

I joke. You will see justice done, the greatest spectacle that Rome can offer.

"May I speak to Asuvia alone?" asked Cluentius astonishingly. Asuvius gaped at him. The girl was sitting in her chair and facing them, as on the occasion when, an incredibly short time ago, they had given her instructions. But she no longer sat so straight and prim as on that far-off day.

She leaned back in one corner of the chair, her long young body slanted sidewise in an attitude compounded of exhaustion, ease, and self-possession. There were blue shadows under her blue eyes, and her hair was carelessly arranged. Cluentius, watching her closely as she spoke and as she answered her uncle's questions, felt strongly that some grace had gone out of her. He had time to track down this thought. Whatever the cause, the girl of the marmoset was gone; it was the animal grace of childhood, prolonged past its usual point in the biography of a young Roman female, that no longer clothed her movements and her attitudes.

She looked at him now without astonishment. The contrast between her face, so young and so aware, and Asuvius', so adult and so popeyed and confused, struck Cluentius, and his grave face relaxed suddenly in a boyish smile.

"Forgive me," he said quickly to Asuvius. "Some questions about her impressions concerning my mother . . . you have humored me in these things before, please, now —" Asuvius muttered, made a jerky little *of-course-of-course* gesture, and withdrew, not without a scowling perplexed glance at his new niece.

"Don't worry about that scowl, Lady," said Cluentius, deliberately and meaningfully addressing her as the mistress of a house. "It was just more surprise. I needn't tell you that he is a man of strong affections. He has been buffeted between alarms and surprises, all concerned with those dear to him, for the last weeks —"

"It's just that I hate worrying him so, it's just that I *wish* he wouldn't —" said Asuvia in a tired little murmur. But she straightened in her chair now, and all her look of intense and concentrated awareness was back upon her face.

"I felt while you were speaking to us both," said Cluentius, "that you . . . had much more to say concerning my mother's state of mind. That you most courteously, most graciously, in my behalf, wished not to be too candid, that you . . . Your uncle has told you, I am sure, how slow I have been in wanting ever to discuss the matter of my mother's disposition in the case. You can believe me when I tell you that I have been brought recently to change myself, at least to adopt the beginnings of a more reasoned attitude." The formality of his speech and his dark considering eyes in that long lean face gave Asuvia the poise she needed.

"It is this that I must tell you then," she answered. "The Lady Sassia's obsession with these religious things *isn't* with the religious things really. She sees in the whole Osiris story — *she* keeps calling it a story — a kind of imitation of her own history, the whole affair, you know, her husband and the other trial, his death."

Cluentius was genuinely startled, and looked it.

"I know it's so *very* strange," she said quickly. "How can you believe — but I'll tell you, anyway. I must tell you. I think she is acting out to herself that story — that for her, Oppianicus is Osiris, that you are the evil kinsman-god, remember, Seth-Typhon or whatever his name is, who kills Osiris through guile; that the revenge she seeks through this trial is like the triumph of Osiris' devotees, led by his wife or sister, over Seth. The real purpose of that fight and victory being not just to *pay back*, but to resurrect and restore the life of the husband-brother."

She made this speech in such a dry, careful, lip-moistening, eye-avoiding manner that Cluentius felt more strongly than anything else the strength of her consideration for him, her deep involvement in the whole affair. He remained silent for a moment, quite unable to speak. But he saw the trembling of her hands, the nervous fluttering at the corner of her mouth; so always, in old times, did his own nerves betray him when he feared for his private truths.

"Are you telling me, Asuvia, that you believe my mother to be entirely insane?" he asked in the calmest of older-brother voices.

"No!" said the girl, quickly, without reflection. "At least, not really that. She certainly isn't reasonable or practical or shrewd at *all*, about the case itself." Cluentius thought with faint excitement of his own remarks to Cicero on this subject, in the early stages of the correspondence. "The evidence stuff I found, well, I guess Cicero just wanted to find out as much as he could as soon as he could, but there really isn't anything important there. Those old stories aren't going to *be* anything. Stories about you, I mean."

"How do you know that, may I ask?" he smiled. She did not even notice the smile; her mind was working on something else.

"Oh, everybody knows you weren't, you never, you couldn't — Oh, nobody has even to be told," she said impatiently. "But I think it's this: the way she is about the Mysteries is simply part of the way she is about Oppianicus. She's using your stepbrother in the prosecution not for any practical reason at all, just because he can figure as this Horus or whatever it is, the son of the God, who is the means of revenge. She despises him, that little minor Oppianicus, I mean, for being little and minor and so forth, but she loves him too, for being really an Oppianicus, of the name and blood. She's tied him to her in a hundred ways, but for this, his name and blood, *not* just his usefulness to her. She doesn't think of any of it that way — what's *useful* — she can't, any more. She's acting out the whole thing because it's the only way she can still feel close to Oppianicus."

Cluentius rose stiffly and went to the window, to look out on Asuvius' little inner court. Asuvia spoke again, very low, but insisting.

"Her life goes on where no one can see it. I thought once she was mad, but it's not that. I guess it's what the Greeks talk about all the time when they go on and on about Madness of Love, Disease of Love, and all those things." She spoke as if to herself, and yet as if she had to be heard. Awkwardly Cluentius turned from his window. At the sight of his twisting face, Asuvia rose swiftly, in one long lovely certain movement, from her chair.

"O Aulus Cluentius," she said, and tears came into her eyes, "it is I who am mad, talking to you now and here, in this way —" But he smiled, with difficulty, and spoke kindly, in a low, grinding voice.

"We have all, my dear, been much impressed with your intelligence and your wonderful activity in this matter. I must thank —" but she jerked away from him.

"Oh, don't! The *worst* thing is, the very *worst*, you mustn't thank, the worst —"

"Well?" he said, moving so that he stood at her shoulder. She could feel if not see the gentleness of his look.

"I had such a good *time*," she said like a schoolgirl, but with a sharp irony, a woman's irony, in the schoolgirl words. She turned about and faced him. "The Lady Sassia isn't like any woman I've ever known. She's . . . she's . . . she liked me because she saw what I was like. She is wonderful. Yes! Wonderful! How she looked and talked, the things she knew and the things she could do! I had good luck; she wasn't on her guard at all, for the reasons I've told you. I can't take credit; until the very end when I profaned her chapel I knew I wasn't in any danger. I felt all the time I was there that I should be glad and grateful — I could see her and be with her and get an idea of her, without having to be hurt at all, without having to pay — that little Oppianicus and poor Auria —" She stopped suddenly.

"I forgot. You — I forgot. Of all men." She was quite pale, and her young blue eyes were wide and hopeless. But he smiled again, and took her hand in his for a warm moment.

"You're right in all this," he said simply. "And of more value than you can know, to me and to all my case. So — do not pity me. It's no longer necessary. And now, most

162

gracious Lady, I feel we must join your august uncle. What will he think? What will he say to me?"

"Wait — just one more thing." She licked her dry lips childishly to compose herself, then spoke gravely and sweetly.

"I can thank you for something else. In these days I learned to look at Larinum. It is beautiful. I thought I saw, I thought I learned — well, the old Forum on one morning, and sometimes just listening to the steward talking with old Philo about your farms there and the things you and my uncle have thought of and planned . . . I won't pity you, if you won't *thank* me," and she was suddenly able to smile again, for he was smiling at her; his eyes were deep as his deep voice, his hand closed over hers.

"Thank *you*," she said.

XV

THE PRAETOR of the City greets you, Aulus Cluentius, and invites you to ride with him to the Forum," said Asuvius' doorkeeper and announcer, in ringing tones, to his master's guest. It was clear that he was impressed. Cluentius himself felt a bit awed. It was so early that the sun could not be said to be really up. He knew that Cicero wished him to be present at the *postulatio*, the hearing where the magistrate would give permission for the prosecution; but the presence of the Praetor himself before the gate was unexpected.

As Cluentius came through Asuvius' main door, his surprise became real astonishment. In the brightening light he saw a crowd of people, not one litter but three, and the two praetorian lictors standing stiff and solemn, axes and rods in their hands as if they escorted the great magistrate to some high ceremony.

Cicero half-sat, half-reclined, motioning Cluentius to the seat beside him. Stammering a greeting, Cluentius did as he was directed. His own slaves joined the hurly-burly, and with much shouting, arm-waving, signaling of all sorts, the procession got under way.

Cicero leaned back in the litter, twitched the curtains even wider open, and grinned at his client's look.

"Ah, you marvel at the size, unwieldiness, and luxury of this litter," he said smoothly. "A gift of Atticus, especially made. On the rare occasions when we can make some journey about Rome together, we dislike walking, and dislike moving out of each other's earshot; hence this rather effeminate mode of transport." He leaned forward as if to demonstrate some accessory.

"I wondered rather," said Cluentius quickly, for his old slowness of speech was being rapidly modified these days, "at the size, inconvenience, and magnificence of —"

"Oh yes, our entourage. An elementary device. I forebore to discuss this sort of thing with you in our conferences, out of respect for your, ah, obsession with *essentials*, my dear Cluentius. Look — your friend's house is oddly located; it will take us some time to arrive at the Forum. But we will arrive toward the end of the first hour of full daylight, and the place will be jammed with everybody preparing his business of the day. I intend to proceed through this press with you and my crowd. Those litters there contain two portly friends of mine, whom you will recognize when they stop snoring behind their curtains and open up as we enter the Forum. Businessmen of Rome, substantial in their fortunes, weighty in their connections, heavy in their respectability — see how their bearers lumber and groan — and above all, burdened with obligation to me, for certain negligible but fortunately effective interferences in legal affairs which might have gone badly for them. I wish you to appear, Cluentius, on the way to the *postulatio*, which you are not even obliged to attend, as all men know, surrounded with men, heralded with ceremony" — he gestured toward the lictors — "and, especially, flanked by solid citizens of the businessman's order, whose prejudice against you poor Accius is counting on."

"But these men," stammered Cluentius, his new quickness forgotten again, "Cicero, not *my* friends, men who know little of me —"

"Bah, friend. In affairs of this sort, appearance *is* reality. Your own friend, Asuvius, he is still in Larinum?"

"His letter arrived last night. He leaves there this morning, and rides fast, so will not write again. In a few days' time we shall have all the information that Larinum holds for our cause. He tells only that his interviews with the witnesses of the inquisitions are complete, that as you thought we have nothing to fear there — details later — and that the young Oppianicus left the town, unattended by any of his family, some days ago. He will undoubtedly be present this morning."

"This we already knew," said Cicero negligently. "He has to be, he really has to be. What else — how, unattended by any of his family?"

"My mother," said Cluentius evenly, "will not depart until she hears that the day of the trial has been set."

"But she is coming! She is coming!" said Cicero, excitement glittering in his eyes.

"Yes. Asuvius says that she waits to hear of the second hearing, the formal registration of the charge."

"The *nominis delatio*. The setting of your name on the roster of defendants."

"When that news arrives, she will prepare to set out. Then there is the third hearing, and the setting of date for trial; then the interval, ten days' minimum I believe, between setting of date and beginning of trial — you see I rehearse these things I had forgotten, and hoped to forget forever — this will give her ample time. She means to travel with a large suite, and at a leisurely pace."

Immense satisfaction radiated from the Praetor, though he said nothing of it.

"We must try now to hurry everything," he said. "Show no surprise today, if I try to hustle our judge a little, about the next two hearings. It can be done, *if* one is deft in the matter of magistrate-persuasion." He smiled happily. "The two next hearings, the *nominis delatio* and the regular inscription and setting of the trial date, can be partly combined in one. The purpose of the longer intervals and the multiple hearings is, dear student of Roman justice, to give everybody all opportunity for the gathering of evidence. Accius will not dare let it be thought that he needs this time. He too has his appearances to consider, which are realities so far as public opinion goes, and he relies so heavily, poor man, on this public opinion. The case has been in the public ear for many weeks now; he must play the role of a man bursting with certainties."

"You say 'poor man.' You think public opinion not much of an asset? Yet you have told me that this opinion, made up of political air, is the heaviest weapon in our enemy's hand."

"Heavy, yes, formidable, all-conquering; but how two-edged! How likely to turn in one's hand! How very probable that poor Accius will suddenly see the handle in our hand, its blade facing him! I mean, of course," said the Praetor dryly, his eyes wandering aside, "his client."

On the high platform of the tribunal the senior judge Voconius Naso sat in his magisterial chair. On a heavy table at his side, moved up alongside his own table, were a pile of paper scrolls and a few battered-looking wax tablets. Titus Accius gestured above these, standing before the magistrate. Tall and wiry, quick-moving, a specialist of the low, intense, hurrying voice, he jerked his head from time to time, pointing, so to speak, at the figure of his young client sitting on a bench below the platform. His hands were continually busy over the papers and tablets. He gave the judge many a deep, meaning glance, pausing and straightening as if in communication of a certain indignation, disciplined but deep.

Cluentius sat on another bench below the tribunal platform, with Cicero's friends and retainers filling places beside and behind him. After the first glance and nod of recognition, an obscure sense of delicacy kept him from looking once at the pale exhausted face of his stepbrother slumped on his bench, blinking nervously as the subordinates of Accius constantly whispered comments and instructions to him. Cluentius watched Accius' back, watched the judge's face, for brief instants; but his eyes and mind were directed for the most part to the figure of Cicero, and on his face rested his old look of weary astonishment.

For Cicero acted, with a perfection made largely of understatements, the part of a bored man. He directed little looks of incredulity toward Accius at regular intervals, as if he had been recalled from absent-minded musings by some inanity so startling that it became almost interesting. For the rest, he stifled yawns, fidgeted, looked around at the other courts. He sat alone.

". . . these the copies, these the tablets, depositions to be entered in evidence of course . . ." said Accius, watching Cicero from the corner of his eye. The judge pawed among the sheets of paper, rattled the wooden frames of the tablets.

"Really, Accius," he said in a gentle, complaining voice, "it *really* doesn't seem that these are going to — the signatures aren't —"

"— properly affixed? Quintus Naso, I agree," said Accius very quickly and smoothly. Cluentius could feel that his neighbors were straining to hear this, that something was going on. About Cicero he could feel nothing.

". . . *standing* of the witnesses seems very ambiguous," complained the judge. "Not at all the same as the signatories in the first investigation, the one with negative results. Surely you are aware that Cicero will point out —" and he turned toward the isolated figure of the Praetor, now deeply engaged in an examination of an inkstain on his hand. "Cicero!" called the judge. Cicero looked up, nodded rapidly, waved his hand dismissingly. He seemed to say: "All this is of no account." Yet the witnesses of the depositions, solid citizens of Larinum as one had heard — Cluentius' mind strained after the mind of his counsel.

"Naturally," said Accius suddenly, "I do *not* plan to rest my case on the testimony of slaves, witnessed in any fashion whatsoever." Silence fell, a listening silence.

"I have been discussing the accusation stemming from the *fifth* section of the Cornelian Law Concerning Assassins and Poisoners," continued Accius. "Now, we are all acquainted with the *sixth* section of the same law, which relates to judicial murder, 'the encompassing of a citizen's ruin through false conviction in a court of law.' We are all aware that this section technically applies only to members of the senatorial order; we are equally aware that the reason for this limitation — the fact that formerly only members of this order were active in the courts and thus subject to these temptations — has now passed into history."

"But had not so passed, eight years ago, at the trial where my client was prosecutor!" said Cicero suddenly, jumping up, all boredom gone, face aflame with concern.

"Ah!" said Accius. "My great opponent in this case at last feels some interest! He seems to feel that *here* there is ground for conflict! So you see, distinguished magistrate, that an argument is in order —"

"You are asking for dismissal on the grounds of this technicality?" inquired Voconius Naso formally of Cicero.

"Decidedly not! Which is not to say," added the Praetor, hitching up his toga in the famed casual-elegant drape which all admired as a part of his distinctive presence on the platform, "that I do not mean to argue the point. For Quintus Voconius Naso knows as well as I, Accius, that you will fight the case on the grounds of prejudice against my client, and that in order to beat up the prejudice you will do a great deal of talking about Section Six of the Cornelian Law. Decidedly not to be dismissed, this accusation! Honored judge, my client and I, far from wishing to have this case dismissed, wish to have it *tried,* in full and open court, and as rapidly as possible! We are willing, yes, *eager* to argue this point of the applicability of Section Six to members of our businessman's order!" A faint pomposity crept subtly into Cicero's manner. "It is long since I have had a chance to argue a legal point like this in any detail," he said, bridling a little, gesticulating amiably toward the judge. "I look forward to it as to a pleasant adventure. Let me urge you, my dear Voconius, to press the next two hearings as much as possible into one, for the sake of speed. Accius here is of course full of evidence and argument; it's all coming out of his ears, it's spilling out of his mouth right here, when he doesn't need to do anything but rattle his wax tablets and go! And I have already consulted my old friends from student days, on the aspects of jurisprudence here to be examined. It will be an *interesting* assignment, an *interesting* case, to which I shall look forward the more, Voconius," and the Praetor made a graceful half-bow, "because it will involve you as spectator and participant, you with your distinguished knowledge of all subtleties of the law, *and* not less" — a dazzling smile — "because it will engage me with a truly stimulating opponent.

"We leave then," he said abruptly, "we take for granted the good-faith oath of the prosecutor," and he shot a courteous, forbearing glance at the young Oppianicus. "We leave, and urge all speed in this matter." Fussing with his scrolls, plucking at his toga, calling to his attendants, the Praetor made his way from the platform. Accius watched him with a veiled smile. Voconius scowled a little, gnawed at his lip; then gestured to Oppianicus, and prepared to administer the ancient ceremonial oath which calls the deities of Rome to witness that only the sacred need of justice has motivated the prosecutor in making his charge against the accused.

Racked with confusion, pale with weariness, Cluentius sank silently into his place beside the Praetor. As they passed up the aisle and into an open part of the Forum, the Praetor, in a flurry of nods and gestures of greeting directed at passing citizens of prominence, gripped his client's arm firmly above the elbow and muttered in his ear. "Cheer up, friend! All went merrily! In a few minutes, I'll tell—" but he stopped the litter to lean out and speak warmly, still holding Cluentius' arm, to a group of three bankers.

In an alley off the Forum he at last turned from his bowing, drew the curtains in a swift gesture, and bent his whole attention on the glum, long face of Cluentius.

"You reproach me in your mind, friend! As your innocence continually allows you to do. But I shall take pleasure in explaining to that innocence. Look: long ago I discovered that this *postulatio* is a heaven-sent chance for the defense. A little play-acting, a little shrewdness, and the course of the prosecution's case can be altered, subtly, at the will of the defense! I tell you this in *confidence*," and he gave his rich savoring chuckle, "for the students of my method haven't yet taken it up. They only go to the *trial*, you see.

"Now, the great thing for the defense is that the prosecution must speak first. If the prosecuting lawyer at the *postulatio* can be given a false impression of the line the defense plans to take — Oh, it's not necessary, legally, for the defense to give any impression at all, but that's my method; I always *do* just that! Now Accius in *his* brand of innocence, so very different from yours, thinks that I intend to make a great deal of that legal technicality which you have urged me to ignore. Accius thinks — I should be honest and say Accius *knows* — that the knowledge of law, the scholarship of law, is far from my strong point. He thinks — Oh, he knows — I am a vain man. He thinks I want to win this case on lawyer's virtuosity, on point of law, so that I can profess to have outgrown my early deficiencies! He will spend a lot of time on this big argument over Section Six!" The Praetor lay back suddenly and began to laugh, shaken with delight, his shoulders heaving. But he sobered.

"I shall brush Section Six aside. Juries hate a man who knows a lot of law and tries to make it count. I've kept myself ignorant on purpose. I shall admit frankly, since it's the truth, that you *are* being tried under that section, whether it's legal or not, because of the prejudice. So I shall defend you under that section; I shall clear you of the charge implied in Accius' using that section."

"Of the charge . . . judicial murder?"

"I shall clear you of the charge of having bribed the jury."

"*What?* Oh! You mean you will justify —"

"*No!* Justify! You talk like a schoolboy. I shall prove that *you did not bribe the jury.*"

"Cicero! *Cicero!*"

"Stop gobbling. I shall clear you in this trial on the strength of your character, as a just man. It is this upon which we agreed. We both know what I must do. I alone know how I must do it."

Within two weeks the formalities of the second and third preliminary hearings were encompassed, the date for the trial set with the ten-day minimum interval, and Asuvius back in Rome. Cicero had had to be absent briefly from the City on another matter; as he came back, even before returning to his own house, he stopped at Asuvius', impatient for first-hand report.

Before he could ask any question, Asuvius began to interrogate him.

"Cluentius tells me, great Praetor," he said, after hurrying through courtesies, excusing his friend's absence, "that there are names on that jury-list . . . that Voconius was good enough to show you the list at the last hearing, you saw those names — Attilius, Manius, Marullus among others — these are men who must be recognized as hostile to our cause! They are small businessmen, anxious to become greater; they are in the hand of a man, you must know, Cicero, who is in the hand of your enemy Catilina, who is in the hand of your enemies the false consuls. Why did you not object to these names? Cluentius has his right of rejection, within proper limits of course —"

"Calm yourself, friend — Oh, why must I who enjoy excitement myself be forever urging various peace-loving citizens to *calm!*" said Cicero humorously. "And I still not out of the travel-dust!"

"Forgive me!" muttered Asuvius in shame, and set in motion the scurryings of slaves bringing water, linen, fruit, cheese.

Refreshed, Cicero wiped his fingers and began to speak.

"Remember, I am Praetor of the City. Remember, it was I who drew up those lists of qualified jurors for this year! Remember, if I object to any as unqualified because of low connections or disposition to prejudice, and go into long explanations, Accius will enjoy himself greatly, inquiring why men so easily disqualified were put on the qualified list as capable of dispensing justice. Jury-challenge must go, for this year, friend: many things are to be kept in mind," he added mildly, selecting a final grape. Asuvius murmured, abashed.

"Come," said the Praetor. "Larinum? *Details!*"

"Most extraordinary of all," said Asuvius, cheering up, "are the reports about those depositions. You know we heard they'd been signed by solid citizens of the town, of the same stamp as those who witnessed the earlier inquisition years ago? Well, we've been away; nobody asked, but nobody dared hope this information was entirely false.

"Yet, Cicero, it *is* entirely false! Old Naevius told me they'd been summoned, and gone with every intention of signing — for you know how terrified those old fellows get whenever a slave is taken in crime; they all feel murder and theft at their own elbows in these cases. But when they got there and saw the inquisition had been already conducted, one slave dead and another disappeared without trace, and the very depositions unconcerned with theft or murder committed by any slave, they refused to sign. Sassia has some signatures, though no one can tell whether they're false or forged — but they're from scum-citizens, sub-citizens, all men over whom she has some hold of hope or fear. None would dare say anything if the signatures *were* forged. But if they aren't, they're still not worth much. The respectable names Asuvia saw in the chapel must have been on the tablets saved from the other time; Sassia has kept everything, as some kind of sacred relic."

"Good, but unimportant," said Cicero. "Those depositions haven't worried me since we had the girl's letter. But with Sassia, one wishes to be certain."

"She is *mad*," said Asuvius.

"Titus Accius is *sane*," said Cicero sharply. "No false safety, friend! Titus Accius is *clever*. Titus Accius is *ambitious*."

Asuvius nodded, accepting correction.

"Titus Accius is *worried*, too," he said, grinning. "I heard in Larinum that he sends two messengers a day over there to plead with Sassia, begging her not to come to the trial."

"She answers?"

"No. She sends instructions. But all know that she will come."

Cicero smiled.

"Oh welcome, thrice welcome, She-wolf!" he breathed. "It's for her sake I've rushed things so. Cluentius keeps asking why — I forbear to dwell upon the point — but you must realize, Asuvius, how very *suitable* it will be for us if she arrives in Rome, and at the Forum, *after* our proceedings have begun."

"This can count for much?"

"One can never know for sure, what small or great thing will count for much," said Cicero soberly. "But I think it might. All the City will talk of nothing else but our case, once the trial opens. I should like her approach to the City and her entry into it to be accomplished under the eye of that concentrated attention."

Asuvius watched him speculatively, thinking of Cluentius and his harsh exclamation: "When he defends me, it will be the best show in Rome, that day!" Cicero's glance crossed his.

"You think I concentrate my own attention on these entrances and exits, this element of spectacle?" he asked idly, tilting his head to rest against the chair-back. "Well, friend . . . I hardly blame you."

"Great Cicero," said Asuvius hastily, "it is not for me —"

"Oh, come," grinned Cicero. "We're all friends here, and can approve or disapprove." Asuvius sank wordlessly into the spell of the famous charm. "Remember this, though," said the Paetor. "I concentrate in reality on one thing alone."

"Victory!" said Asuvius warmly.

"In this case, justice. Tell me, did you make the other arrangements in Larinum which I asked of you?"

"Yes, and in neighboring towns. My letters will have

been all delivered by now — written just as you asked."

"Cluentius knows nothing of this?"

"Nothing."

"Good. If our hopes of these things fail, I do not wish him to know what we hoped. But I believe with all my heart that we have cherished here no empty hope."

XVI

"THE PRAETOR of the City greets you, Aulus Cluentius, and requests . . ." said Asuvius' doorkeeper as before, but in a voice heavier with sleep than on the earlier day, for the hour was gray dawn only. Cluentius had been in the business-room for an hour, since his night had been sleepless, and he had come down, dressed for the long day of the opening of his trial, to pace and muse in his friend's office which was half library and half account-room, to compose in his own hand a few letters, while his loved old slave sat drowsing in an armchair beside a dying lamp.

He had heard the knocking at the gate and the scrabbling of the doorkeeper with bars and bolts. Now as he stood in the dim light in Asuvius' front court, he saw the slave interrupted and shoved aside in mid-announcement, as Marcus Tullius Cicero himself, splendid in praetorian robes, strode up to Cluentius, squinting and scowling.

"I *knew* it!" growled the Praetor in a low savage tone. "Thank the gods I *knew* it and came early! Those clothes! You dare! But I knew you would dare. Oh, *curse* you for a damned dignified fool, Cluentius!" and Cicero actually grasped the fold of Cluentius' toga, wrapped closely around him in the chill, and ripped, jerked, tugged. Beside himself, he thrust his face into the gaping, speechless face of his client.

"You imagine this to be the correct dress for a defendant on trial, on a capital charge! You *idiot!* Don't dare plead ignorance — you may have made no specialty of the courts and be proud of it, but *you have been in a court*, Cluentius! You know the custom!" and the Praetor swore, at the top of his voice. Asuvius, nearly dressed, came running up the side of the court from the stairway. Doors were opening and closing all over the house.

"Calm yourself, Cicero!" said Cluentius at last, though breathlessly. Cicero paused at this remark, staring.

"I am perfectly acquainted with the custom of appearing in court in mourning, and in ragged clothes, with ash-marks on forehead and shoulders," said Cluentius. "Asuvius and I have discussed this. You know as well as I that there is feeling in many quarters that the custom is outmoded and undignified —"

"I do not see *you*, Aulus Cluentius, of little lost Larinum, coming up to Rome to teach the senators, businessmen and people of the City how to mend their manners and modernize their customs," snapped Cicero.

"I do not see myself as a suppliant, begging for mercy —" ground Cluentius. They glared and glowered. Suddenly the tension slacked. Cicero stood back and began to laugh.

"Schoolboys!" he said. "And he tells me 'calm myself.' You make progress, friend; most certainly you make progress!" But he sobered. "Let us be serious. Asuvius, Cluentius: it is my plan to conduct this trial in the old mode. I plan to emphasize as heavily as possible your qualities of outmoded virtue, dignity, adherence to the spirit and forms of ancient notions of character. I defend you without associates, in the old manner now outmoded, staking unaided my reputation, alone, on your character and its bearing on your case. You must do your part. You must appear in the traditional, if outmoded, garb and guise of a Roman defendant. *Not* as a suppliant and victim, I do not ask for that; but as a respectful observer of the ancient manners of our ancestors." There was no cynicism in the Praetor's look, nothing but a kind of connoisseur's fanaticism. Cluentius looked long and hard at the heavy face. The light was pearly gray.

"I see your point," he said.

"I give you thanks," said Cicero in an old and formal phrase. "*Now,*" he said, and gestured to Cluentius' old slave, who stood goggling between the doors of the business-room. Cicero spoke to him in rapid Greek, smiling charmingly; Asuvius stepped forward, smiling also; the slave brought little knives from a stylus-cabinet, and they all began with great seriousness and care to make rents and rips in Cluentius' clothes. The old Greek pattered out to the outer court, where a row of little trees stood in boxes filled with earth. He brought handfuls of this earth and some ashes from a cold brazier, and began gently, artistically, to daub at his master's face, and to mark the arms, now visible through long ragged apertures.

"Ah, just so," said Cicero gravely. "Asuvius, for you not so much of this, but mourning dress, please." Asuvius looked a bit shocked; he and Cluentius exchanged a brief glance.

"All the way, with the old mode," said Cicero. "Summon the girl."

"The *girl!*" exploded Cluentius and Asuvius with one voice. Drawing in his breath sharply, making the face of one who prays for patience, the Praetor said:

"Your progress to the Forum is to be that of a family in mourning. Cluentius is to embody the old principle, dear to our forebears, of the man accused as a man who is to be saved from death and worse than death, a man who stands in death's jaws while the charge remains against him. His family mourns. His friends beseech the dispensers of justice to rescue him. This is a grave old part of our ritual of law," said the Praetor gravely, in his deepest and most beautiful voice. "I love it; I have always loved it. Never as in this case, my friends, have I seen the ritual so clearly as an outward sign of inward truth. Such visions rejoice the heart.

"Cluentius has no family, no wife, no brother, and no sister. But he has you, Asuvius, and yours, bound to him by no law of blood but by the excellences of his own character. The girl is beautiful, but she is more; in the dignity of her bearing and the candor of her look, she represents, she incarnates. She is both young and old. She has innocence, but a kind of high intelligence; her maturity has come to meet her, so young. To see such a woman walking as a family mourner in Cluentius' train is already a deposition about his character, for all men of sense and honor. I have not asked you to hire or to bribe mourners, as I have commanded in various ways a suite of worthy Romans to walk with *me*. Where Cluentius' private life is concerned, we keep to truth. The truth is *for* us, and is sufficient. The girl has done much. It will both please and honor her to do more."

Cluentius stood silent before the Praetor's unmoving form, his mouth working a little, his head inclined. Asuvius left the room silently. Within a quarter of an hour he came again, his white garments replaced by the dark dress of mourning, and accompanied by Asuvia, tall and pale, her light-brown hair on her shoulders, unbound according to the ancient custom, yet in calm and order. She wore white, since women did not change the color of their dress for mourning; in the absence of all color, any simple jewel, any ornamental scarf or delicate veil, the little shadows under her high cheekbones seemed of some rare violet shade;

the strong clear blue of her eyes seemed no blue of any sea or sky or flower, but color so quintessentially human as to render any poet's comparison powerless.

The journey to the Forum passed as in a dream. Tall and stiff, Cluentius walked through many narrow streets, and the Praetor strode at his side, never speaking, never looking at him, eyes turning neither to one side nor another; greeting no friend, giving no smile, never, for all the crowding, allowing himself to be separated from Cluentius' side by more than an arm's length. Forms and faces blurred in Cluentius' field of vision. He felt hot, felt his stained forehead damp and gritty, though the air of sunrise was still cold. He heard the walking behind him. With the vision of dreams which gives one eyes where there are no eyes, he saw Asuvius and his niece walking in his wake. Ahead walked a dozen distinguished businessmen of Rome, friends and associates of Cicero, very much with Cicero, but speaking never to him or to Cluentius, only among themselves. The tribunal platform loomed up before Cluentius suddenly, as if from a sea of dark, though he knew coldly that it was now full daylight. He knew, coldly also, that it had been a long walk, especially for a young woman; yet with another knowledge, as if in his own bones he felt the athletic young strength of Asuviua, her long legs and her whole body exercised, through years of country life, as no ordinary girl's could be.

Cicero stood aside for a moment, pushed him into a row of benches and made him sit down. Dimly he remained aware of settlings and dispositions of limbs and togas, all around. Then Cicero was on the platform, where Titus Accius stood already. Cluentius, so close under the structure, could not see clearly but could yet be clearly conscious of the large shuffling crowd of men at the rear of the platform. Voconius Naso sat in his tall chair, his hands full of scrolls; a slave read names to him from various lists. From the crowd, a jury was in process of selection.

Accius and Cicero came and went, from one side to the other of the platform, speaking quietly to the judge or to each other. Accius conferred often with the cluster of five men who sat on his bench, his own associates in the case. Of these, one man older than the others, older even than the judge, wore the broad wine-red border of the senatorial aristocracy, and charged the air all about him with the heavy authority of the Senator, optimate, ex-holder of potent senior magistracies. Cluentius, for all his strangeness in the Forum, recognized this man. Eight years ago he had sat on the jury benches at Oppianicus' trial; his name was Sextus Claudius Niger, and he had been one of the five jurors who voted for the acquittal of Oppianicus. He was the only one out of all the five who had even in the vilifying, mudslinging corruption trials after the main trial not ever been the target of any accusation. He was a puritan member of a famed old family of Rome.

He had deposed after the trial that he had voted for Oppianicus' acquittal, though knowing the man guilty, because the whole jury knew of the bribery of some of its members. He, a Claudius Niger, was not prone to ally himself with victors in bribed courts. A higher question, he had said, was here at stake than the mere guilt or innocence of any defendant. The scum-ridden justice of the day was standing its trial, and he, Claudius Niger, scornful alike of the late Dictator's degenerate heirs and of the creeping, crawling life which attempted to displace the blood of old Rome while professing to attack Sulla's spawn, had voted to acquit Oppianicus as a gesture of protest. He sat now as associate counsel on Accius' bench. The harsh lines of purist fanaticism on his face were deeper by eight years.

The process of impaneling and swearing went on, on,

on; no recess at noon, as for all the rest of the Forum; only the courts continued their scurryings, murmurings, shoutings, under the merciless sun. His face streaked with earth, ashes, and sweat, his torn woolen garment heavy as a load on his back, Cluentius sat without rising until the jury was complete: seventy-two citizens of Rome; twenty-four of the senatorial order, twenty-four of the businessmen's order, twenty-four of the *tribuni aerarii*, or businessmen of lesser substance. Should thirty-seven of these men pronounce him guilty, in the same spirit as that in which Claudius Niger had pronounced Oppianicus innocent, Cluentius must go into "voluntary" exile, stripped of all citizenship and status, dishonored, a man without country, a man who could never afterward engage in any contract, conduct with reputable men any reputable business; a man no longer alive, as surely as if he had been condemned to physical death. Verdict and sentence were one. These men were his judges.

Surely the impaneling of this huge jury would be considered the day's business, and further proceedings be postponed until the next day. But — Cluentius saw the little huddle around the judge's chair break up, Accius stride to his bench looking annoyed, Cicero to his with a bland look on his composed, unwearied countenance. The jurors, sitting in various sketchy attitudes on their rows of benches behind the judge's chair, stopped talking as the judge turned to address them, then settled, with astonished faces and many shrugs exchanged, into poses as comfortable as possible. The heralds came up to the edge of the platform, looking sleepy and ruffled, and went through the ceremonial stages of opening the pleadings.

In the drone of the voices of judge and herald, in the heat of the sun, in the weariness of his long immobility, and in the simple suffering of thirst and hunger, Cluentius felt himself swaying on his seat dizzily. The most honored of Cicero's Greek slaves sat beside him. This man now gave him water from a little covered vessel, and hitched himself expertly near, so that Cluentius might feel himself supported. Gratefully, Cluentius let himself sag a bit. An interval of semiconsciousness passed. When he straightened, his eyes clear, he saw Accius standing at the platform's edge, half-turned in the classic attitude of the pleader, so that while seeming to concentrate alone on judge and jury, his speech might yet be heard on the last bench of the seats below the platform, and beyond, where stood those of the public who could not find seats.

". . . Aulus CLUENTIUS Habitus," said Accius, gesturing, sweat pouring down his face, "as you know, jurymen. I have associated with me in this case various upright men, but notably the Senator Sextus Claudius Niger, whom I have implored to speak for us in the matter of that other trial, the trial at which he was present in so lamentable but admirable a capacity, the trial . . ." He paused in his swift clear speech; said slowly, heavily, "The *murderous* trial; the *weapon* trial; that trial, instrument of death."

Heat and thirst and weariness forgotten, the whole court listened in a straining silence. Cluentius closed his eyes, but could not close his ears.

"I must now speak to you, at some length, gentlemen, forgive me and bear with me, on the subject of Section Six of the Cornelian Law Concerning Assassins and Poisoners."

The Praetor of the City sat fanning himself with a shrewdly folded sheet of papyrus. He inclined his head toward the speaker, in an attitude of grave, listening courtesy. Upon his face, so often legible, there could be read nothing at all.

XVII

HALFWAY THROUGH the time allowed for his speech, Accius professed great weariness and obtained, after many courteous and considerate remarks from Cicero, the recessing of proceedings until the following morning. It was still full afternoon as the party traced its footsteps through the Forum. Again, though many approached as if to greet him, the Praetor paid no attention to anyone. He walked with his face set in a cool, impassive mask. The stones of the Sacred Way were hot and rough underfoot, the jostle appalling; yet the head of Cicero did not turn and did not bow, seemed wrapped in some veil of passionately guarded silence. Even in the small street where theirs was, for a while, the only large party, he kept silent.

At Asuvius' door he stopped and faced his client.

"You look faint, you look much worn, my Cluentius," he said in the gentlest of all his voices. "Refresh yourself."

"How . . . how . . ." panted Asuvius, coming up to his friend's elbow.

"It's going well, I think," said Cicero without pride or anxiety.

"Keeping them there, making him begin today, in the heat!" said Asuvius jubilantly, his eyes all alight. But Cicero shook his head.

"It cannot be known," he said, very low. "Perhaps this was the worst that could have been done. Perhaps the prejudice he has set afire in their minds will be nourished by what he gave them, so that it will be stronger than he could have hoped, before he even begins tomorrow's pleading. We cannot know. We cannot know. We can only do what we have decided upon. We can only use our resources; *all* our resources, all." He smiled at last, as Asuvia stood before him.

"The Lady has a sunburn," he said. "Right across the forehead, there, look. See that your maid gives it attention. The sun of the Roman Forum, on a young unveiled brow, it has a special intensity. We others, we are tougher, and we're not used to head covering anyway. But you must look out." The girl smiled back at him coolly, self-possessed. She shook back her hair in a slow little gesture, and said nothing.

"Inexhaustible," said Cicero, smiling still, delightedly. "The *inexhaustible* women of Rome." He turned from the door, uttered his farewells, made his appointments, and moved off.

". . . and I repeat, but yes, I must," said Accius rapidly, scowling fiercely, foot advanced, head thrown back, "for they cannot be said too often, the words that my associate here has used in his too-short speech to you; indeed, indeed, the whole of Claudius Niger's speech, and most of mine, is in these words: 'The perdition of Rome was in the perdition of those courts, and made poisonous by the poison-breath of vile gold, the gilded fangs of vile serpents.' We know all, here, what was lost in those courts, and at what cost to businessmen of Rome, and at what gain to the henchmen of Sulla, already, then, maggots on a dead body ever since their strong master's death. We know that the men who with their money and their cynicism made it impossible for any Roman to find justice are no longer masters of our justice; that our reconstituted juries, our tribunals swept clean of that filth, stand now as living monuments of hope. Let us in our new good fortune have pity," and he bent forward graciously, in an eloquent pose, hand outflung toward the bent figure of young Oppianicus, who sat with his elbows on his knees and his face in his hands. "Let us have pity on the memory of those who lost their sacred honor and their lives, through these hideous crimes against justice, crimes of which the very processes of justice were made the deadly weapons. Let us, above all, have pity on these victims' sons, the living children of their blood and name, who after so many years still mourn; let us place in the hands of these poor sufferers of their fathers' dishonor, the means of purifying their fathers' shrines, sweeping clean their fathers' names of filth that was not of their fathers' making, and the means of bringing at long last the slayers, who wielded false justice as a murderous weapon, under the clean avenging blade of justice that is not forsworn, but true and Roman."

Five hours had passed in the pleadings of Accius and his chief associate. Of the whole flood of words, Cluentius had been able to follow in detail only one part, an hour's worth of close and powerful argument concerning the spirit of the law as distinct from its letter. Accius had called splendidly to mind the ancient Roman tradition in favor of the spirit. He had dismissed as niggling the legal technicality which would make the laws against "judicial murder" applicable, through historical accident, only to one class. This part of his speech Cluentius had followed with a curious detached pleasure, as of old he had followed demonstrations in mathematics.

There was a brief informal recess at noon. In the shadowy interior of an old banker's office in the Forum, where he had formerly passed always, on his infrequent but crowded business visits to the City, Cluentius stood sipping wine, eating bread, with Cicero's Greek slave. He had come to this place as to a refuge. The old banker was absent at some cool resort. His clerks were napping in the rear of the little booth-like structure. His nephew had greeted Cluentius guardedly, given orders for his comfort, and then sagely withdrawn. All through the Forum, wherever he passed, Cluentius in his mourner's dress felt exposed like some unshelled crustacean, felt harsh on his mind's surfaces the grating touch of unfavorable opinion. None knew him! None knew him! After Accius' speech he had plunged up a little side alley, seeking to avoid the consolations of Asuvius, the blue searching eyes of Asuvia. The banker's nephew knew his name alone, and turned from him because of the credit of that name. He had not had to avoid the eyes of these strangers; theirs were avoiding his.

The Greek spoke low and courteously, distracting the surface of his attention.

"In a half-hour he will be speaking. He likes the afternoon hours; likes the hearings to go on till nearly sunset if he can manage it so. He could have ten hours for this speech if he wanted! But I know it will be shorter. He plans to divide it into two parts, following what he calls the 'rhythm' of Accius' speech. I thought he might ask for recess until tomorrow, knowing how he likes the cumulative effect of a long plea. But he says this weather is wrong for such effects."

"He means the heat?"

"That," said the slave with a quick intelligent smile, "and

perhaps the inner weather of the jury. Who can ever quite tell, with him?"

"Ah. Who, indeed?"

"Master, you will see me scribbling on wax and shielding my tablets from the sun. Do not be disturbed if I stir about a good deal. I have read the speech as it has been prepared —"

"You *have?*"

"Yes. But there are always changes as it is delivered, always. I try to get down the new passages as they come; my memory holds fast the ones I have read, and tells me when I am hearing something new. It is an absorbing task, and I am likely to shuffle."

"You will not disturb me."

"Ah! a little breeze. The wind is changing. He thought it might cool off a little. He went in the recess to dash his face with cold water, in the temple of Janus. He likes the old statue there, Etruscan you know; always his taste for old things gets stronger when he's in a case that really interests him." Before Cluentius could quite take in this curious remark, the cultivated soft voice went on, as they left the row of small offices and started back toward the tribunal. "He never rests at midday, even in summer, even at Tusculum, even in the South, at the Bay . . ." Talking of details of his master's life, of procedures followed in the composition of speeches and essays, the slave interposed a thin delicate protecting gauze between Cluentius' raw spirit and the eyes and voices of men.

A heavy silence fell as Cicero stepped to the edge of the platform and assumed the pleader's sidelong stance. But his opening words were no thunder of eloquence. He spoke in a calm, conversational voice.

"Gentlemen, let me repeat the prosecutor's last words. We have all been sipping and gossiping, the weather is not suitable for long memories, and the speech too good to let slip from your minds. Its last words will recall its quality to you: '. . . justice that is not forsworn, but true and Roman.'

"Now, gentlemen, I noticed that the prosecutor's entire speech was divided into two parts, in one of which he seemed to be relying with all confidence upon the now time-honored prejudice attached to the earlier trial; while in the other part he seemed to approach in a reluctant, even timid sort of way, as if for form's sake only, the question of the charge of poisoning, the charge with which this court must deal exclusively, in accordance with its establishment by law." He paused. He had spoken slowly, with no particular emphasis, but every word fell into the silence and was heard. He drew breath, and looked about him, at Accius, at the judge, at the benches below him where sat Cluentius and young Oppianicus. He raised his eyes, over the heads of the standing spectators who were ranged in a triple ring outside the farthest benches. He straightened, drew himself up from his casual pose, as if to gather himself for a great and powerful attack upon the idea of prejudice, as if to claim in the name of inalterable law and right that his client be tried on the one charge alone. But even as the words he would use were suggesting themselves to his hearers, he used others. In the same informal, talking voice he went on:

"Now, I propose to follow Accius' example. I shall divide my speech between the question of prejudice and the actual charge. Alas, when I think of how to go about this — here I take you into my confidence — I must face the fact that the defense against the true charge, with which this tribunal is rightly appointed to deal, is so easily put forth that it will require small time, no effort; it's the easiest task I've ever had. But the other charge, the prejudice-charge, quite alien in its very nature from the atmosphere of this court or of any court, fit only for the disorder and hurly-burly of a common political meeting — to defend my friend on this charge is going to be most difficult, most laborious. I see this ironical fact; I tell you of it frankly.

"But there are consolations. In the poisoning charge, only my client's interests are at stake. But in the other, the question of prejudice — ah, there is involved the self-interest of each one of us. So in the one part of my speech I shall use the language of demonstration; in the other, the language of entreaty — for I must there implore your good will —" His voice was deep and sweet, he seemed to have forgotten all hearers but those on the platform — "for no man can hope to withstand prejudice without your support, and that of men like you."

Another long pause. He turned slowly sideways, so that the crowd below the platform could see his brow creased, his whole heavy face weighted with question.

"I confess," he said, still low, still full of dignified humility, "I don't know just where to turn."

A little whisper ran from place to place among the hearers.

"It is beyond my power," continued Cicero sweetly, "to deny that the terrible scandal we know of did exist. It is beyond *my* power." His voice gained volume suddenly, picked up speed. "But it is *yours*, gentlemen, the power to help my client, this innocent man, your power to come to his rescue in the flames of this fire of false report, a fire which threatens us all, and equally." On and on he went, reasoning, requesting, imploring attention, "that you may listen carefully — and with kindness in your hearts."

His tone became dry and brisk.

"Aulus Cluentius Habitus is charged with having bribed the court in order to secure the conviction of his enemy,

Statius Albius Oppianicus the Elder, an 'innocent man,'"
said the Praetor matter-of-factly, as if repeating the terms of
the formal indictment.

"I shall show you," he went on, lingering carefully on
each word, still in his dryest lawyer's-voice, "that my client
is innocent of this bribery."

Astonishment filled the air like a wind, a scent, a noise.

"First," said Cicero, as if merely saying what all might
have expected him to say, "I shall show how *innocent* was
Oppianicus. Then I shall show that the judges who condemned that man had to condemn him — they had no
choice — for they had given previous verdicts on his two
agents, verdicts so compromising to Oppianicus himself as
to make it impossible for them or any other jurors to acquit
him. Then, I will proceed to a point on which I know you
are all most anxious for enlightenment. I shall show that in
that trial bribery was indeed attempted — Oh yes! Attempted, but not in my client's interest! No! *Against* his
interest! Against him! But wait."

And in a swift, lively, narrator's tone he began to tell a
story. Cluentius sat transfixed, pierced by an occasional darting glance from the wandering blue eyes, bound in the
net of words and pictures, as he had so long foreknown that
he must be.

"Aulus Cluentius Habitus, gentlemen, father of my client,
was a man who, in character, reputation, and nobility was
far the most pre-eminent not only in the township of Larinum, but in that whole district . . ." Two more very swift
sentences disposed of Cluentius' boyhood, his father's death,
his sister's marriage; then at last came the name of Sassia,
her face, her voice, her hatred and her rage: ". . . passion
undeterred by considerations of a son's indignation, a
daughter's tears. The young husband's heart, which lacked
as yet the strengthening of wisdom and understanding —"
and here Cicero stopped, lingered in mid-flight, in order to

send a long, long meaning look down upon the upturned blinking face of Oppianicus the Younger — "she seduced with those arts by which a man of his age can be snared." Oh silence, freighted silence! Cluentius turned his head slowly toward his stepbrother's seat; could see nothing at first, past many intervening heads. Then he saw the poor young head on the thin neck bend forward, face hidden again in the burying hands.

"Her daughter . . . monstrous sight of her mother as her husband's mistress . . . desired that no one else should know of her trouble . . . losing her youth . . . clasped in the arms of my client, her most devoted brother . . . lust over modesty, madness over sense . . . man is bound to endure a parent's offense in resignation and in silence, yes, but only where silence and endurance are possible —

"She comes! She comes!" And so great was the spell that all necks twisted, all eyes turned, as if to see Sassia moving down the very aisles. ". . . Ah no, she is just on the road — but she has organized this prosecution, she has marshaled her evidence, she comes to take delight in the mourning worn by the defendant — she is here now in spirit, and soon to be in flesh."

Unbearable . . . Unbearable . . . Cluentius' mind twisted and turned though he remained stiff and still on his bench. As of old, he fled from the unbearable into the refuge of reflection, turning his mind from all perception of the present, seeking eccentric comfort in the exercise of abstract thought.

He sought mechanically in his memory's storehouse for some of the notions which his old tutor Apollodorus had placed there under the heading "Consolations in Time of Trouble." Beauty? The old Greek voice came back to him, murmuring famous lines. But those lyrics, dealing with the beauty of life and its charm — shepherdesses, cheese, flutes in the shadow of trees, or winecups in a boudoir of Alexandria — it all tasted thin and bland. The great beauties Apollodorus had had to show had no consoling power, for they were the somber and terrible things of immortal tragedy, fed by springs from the dark heart of awful life. The sore mind of Cluentius turned from them.

Love . . . Shutting out of his mind all intuition of its horrors and glories, he directed his thought toward the light love that should be one of the refinements of life. Both he and Asuvius had long ago resolved, without much talk, without need of reason-searching, that marriage and ordinary family life were not to be part of their carefully designed fates. Probing into this resolution would have involved painful discussion of Cluentius' own family life, of the disasters which had shorn Asuvius of all his close kinsmen. So they did not discuss, only resolved.

Other arrangements were possible and much practiced, according to the tastes, sensibilities, resources of individuals. Cluentius remembered now Asuvius' gift of three years ago, a Greek girl of remarkable beauty and gentleness, from the same town and school as Asuvius' own favorite. She was delicate and lovely; she sang, and played an odd little Asiatic stringed instrument; the curve of her cheek as she turned her head to sip at the edge of a cup was enough to melt the heart. Her dancing was flawless, her speech carefully schooled. In the household of an aging *hetaera* of Athens she had learned these matters and others.

Cluentius tried to cool his burning mind with the thought of her, her slender arms, her cool skillful hands. With a slight shock, he knew for the first time why his pleasure in her had not lasted and had never become really a part of his private life; she lived in Larinum still, a part of his garden and his dining room, and her sweet voice had decorated many silent evenings; but that was all.

For she was a practitioner and a slave. She existed for her master's requirements. She knew this and welcomed it. She thought herself lucky in such a master, for he was gentle and generous. That he was Cluentius she neither knew nor cared to know. She cared for what concerned her, and he was gentle and generous. The arts of love were for her like the arts of Philogenes the old gardener and Chrysippus the painter: techniques, which she had mastered because she had aptitude, appropriate disposition and equipment, taste. Cluentius suddenly smiled, almost mirthfully, as he imagined what her one disappointment in him must have been, among so many unexpected leniencies.

He had not proved really interested in nor delighted by the more ingenious amatory artifices she had been able to offer him. He had gently insisted on plainness and simplicity in these matters. He had not, he thought ruefully though with no thought of change, really provided for the proper exercise of her full technical accomplishment.

Inquiry: could beauty and love wear other faces, represent a joy and a compound of delights born of understanding and the free intelligence?

Far off, the voice of Cicero thundered and hissed, listing the crimes of Oppianicus. ". . . killed the poor woman forthwith . . . his own sons, those innocents . . . the grandmother of our accuser, that poor lad there, and how many of his aunts, uncles, cousins have disappeared through those dark jaws . . . the poor lady's will forged, yes, her physician bribed, her ruin encompassed . . . Publius Asuvius, another poor young man . . . sand pits outside the Esquiline Gate, and there foully murdered . . . O savage and dangerous brute, this 'innocent man'! What perils have been forgotten here, in these eight years, while we thought only of the corruption of courts and forgot the ruin of lives!

"His *mother*, his *mother*, my client's *mother*. She hated him, but still she was his mother. And her hatred, that unfeeling woman —"

Unfeeling! A grim smile curved the fine lips of Cluentius, and he saw the mobile, working face of the Praetor give off for a moment a little spark of shock, and knew that Cicero had seen the smile. How many things she was, but how unjust that charge "unfeeling"! And as if he had never stopped thinking of the intelligences of love, Cluentius articulated in his mind the knowledge that his mother's hatred of him was deep and true as the best of loves, for it was based on an accurate and just understanding of his nature, based on intelligence, on the truth of two natures, his and hers. Son, enemy, victim, bah! She hated him because he was Cluentius, and she knew what and who he was.

That will of his to keep aloof and yet conserve the power to take action into his hands at final moments . . . that maintenance of reserve, that refusal to abandon judgment, that stone-founded unbreachable fortress of his mind and heart . . . she had turned from him when he was twelve because she could see the man he was becoming. She was waiting then, unknowingly, for the love of all her life; she might have thought, hoped . . . but then she saw what he was. And when her love came at last, the great machines of her destiny were visible to her seeing eyes, and she knew that in her son's nature lay the seeds of her loved husband's destruction.

A dark terrible thrill shook the lean body of Cluentius. The heat forgotten, he was cold. But the strange joy of knowledge and of final understanding lightened his mind, and he knew, as if he had been born for nothing but to know this, that there could exist in the world a love which was the other side of his mother's hatred: founded, like that, upon accurate and just understanding, upon the truth of two natures.

Through the recital of old wrongdoing, heard in detail now for the first time, Asuvia had sat firmly upright beside her uncle, her hand resting lightly on his arm. She too felt chilled in the eye of the afternoon sun. She turned her

head just slightly, feeling her long hair in the disarray of
mourning stir on the back of her gown, as she sought with
all her lively mind to convey a thought to her uncle without speaking to him — this thought: "This is of old time,
and we no longer care. We are in mourning here for Cluentius' sake, for his alone." She kept her eye on the back and
head of Cluentius, two bench-rows ahead of them.

She waited for him to turn. She thought that he would
turn, to see, after the story of her father's death, himself acquitted in her eyes, freed completely of any old association
with griefs not of his making. He did not turn; he sat
straight, and absorbed, as if he too heard the whole story
for the first time. Then, minutes later, he did turn and
look at her, with a most strange expression on his face. She
did not stop to wonder about the expression. She sent him
her own great singing look, out of her eyes blue as no sky
or sea were ever blue. She meant it to say: Just, innocent,
guiltless, honorable, brave, just! Cluentius saw in it a seascape and skyscape of love's sanities.

XVIII

I N THE SMALL STREET outside the Forum there was
a prearranged parting, and Cluentius went to Cicero's
house as the Praetor's guest for dinner and the night. No
words were exchanged as they toiled up the hill, their
crowd still around them. But Cicero's hand rested firmly on
the arm of his client, and Cluentius rejoiced in the contact.

After bathing they met in the smallest of the dining
rooms. They were alone. In the muted, courteously remote
tones which he had used for all social converse since the
opening of the pleadings, Cicero greeted Cluentius and
motioned him to recline.

"The pleadings close tomorrow," he said soberly. "The
question-and-answer period after the major speeches will be
insignificant. Accius does not excel at this exercise; I do,
and he will shrewdly lessen my chances to shine. So much
the better, friend, for the job will be done. I wished you to
be with me through this last night," he said with his broad
charming smile, "not to talk, not to prepare, really, for all
that is behind us even though the outcome is not yet known.
I just want you with me, under my roof. Only one caution:
you must strengthen your nerves a little — not that you

need strengthening in any vital way, my Cluentius, dear fellow — for the presence of your mother in the court to-morrow. I say no more of this. My speech will be closed at noon. The final hour before that closing will incorporate the reading of certain evidence, which I plan to enclose within the body of the speech itself."

"Evidence, great Cicero?" murmured Cluentius, creasing his brow in his attempt to concentrate.

"The character evidence, the formal depositions of fellow citizens in good standing, attesting to their opinion of your honor and uprightness. You recall, I told you that the municipal senate of Larinum had passed a resolution which all members signed? That sort of thing.

"*Now*," he added, as the slaves entered with the first dishes, "we shall say nothing. Nothing at all, my friend and brother." His voice was sweet and deep. ". . . until such time as we shall have dined, and our wine be poured, and we be alone again, at which time you will tell me anything you like, if you like; and I will answer, or not, as it shall please us both."

The first course was simple even for Cicero's never-elaborate table: small portions of salted fish, pickles, eggs, one abundant salad; for drink, the ancient honey-brew called *mulsum.* Cicero ate but a morsel of each platter, drank but a swallow. The slaves moved round the side-tables, prepared and served the meat. They ate in silence. As these dishes were taken away, the Praetor rose slowly from his couch. Glancing neither at slave nor guest, his whole face set in the mold of traditional dignities, he took some little salt-bread cakes from the tray under the fine silver salt-vessel on the table, walked with measured step, prescribed in centuries past, over to the small shrine of the household gods at one end of the modest room. He set the cakes on the narrow altar, spoke clearly some old grave words in their archaic forms, and returned to the table to break the cakes, and share them with his guest. Cluentius made the responses in the ancient formula. He had never before seen Cicero perform this old-fashioned ritual, nor any other man perform it so seriously.

Still nothing was said. A little dessert of apples was brought and consumed. The slaves poured wine and left the vessel and cups; a small brilliant lamp was brought in, for the twilight had made the one small window dark.

Cluentius drank silently at first. Then, as if giving a voice to private thoughts, he began quietly to tell Cicero of Asuvia's report to him concerning Sassia's religious practices. Silent, the Praetor listened.

"Priestess of revenge," he murmured in a low musical voice, as Cluentius again fell silent. "Sacrifice, ritual, purification, and renewal. Hm. Well, friend, we also act our part. Tonight as I went through the old things over there — with the household gods, you know — I thought of no household gods. An old story! But I thought of many households, of the ways and hearts of our ancestors; men of old time, men of old Rome." The Praetor's voice was so full of emotion that Cluentius looked up, startled. "They are much in my mind and heart, during the conduct of this case," said Cicero. "I consecrate this night to them, this night with you beneath my roof, Aulus Cluentius.

"For I too have my odd notions," he continued, twirling the stem of his graceful winecup in his large hands, with a smile of secret excitement curving his mouth. "We too, in other times, we of the Law of Rome, were priests. I meant always to speak of this to you tonight, even if you had not told me these other things. Tomorrow you will hear me and see me bending all the powers developed in me by gods and my own efforts, to make that jury believe you did not bribe your other jury. Already they believe that Oppianicus tried to poison you. You will sit there on your bench, wondering if your gift will be given, justice, acquittal as an innocent man. It *will*. If you are acquitted at all, it will be on those grounds you chose and wanted. But you must think of the means, the instruments I use, as devices of my mystery, parts of an arcane rite, procedures and ministrations not to be questioned by the profane. You must see them with the eyes of faith, Cluentius." He leaned forward, and a great intensity flowed between them. "And see me, Cluentius, as the priest of justice."

Cluentius raised his head to look the Praetor full in the face. Cicero's heavy features looked heavier than he had ever seen them, in that lamplight, composed in that solemnity.

But the pattern shifted and broke up; the hushed moment passed. The small lines at the eye-corners deepened and wrinkled, the blue eyes lit and shone brilliantly. Cicero began to laugh.

"It will not, however, be necessary," he said, "for you to watch me dance. Be thankful to the gods, Cluentius, for small marks of their favor."

The next morning, all Cicero's side sat in their places by sunrise. Cicero, not yet on the platform, talked quickly with Asuvius, behind one of the tribunal-posts. Asuvius left the court without a word to anyone, taking three slaves with him, leaving Asuvia accompanied only by her maid and the chief officer of his business, a freedman of many years' experience, who had served the older Asuvius before him and sat now with the dignity of white hairs, full citizenship, and the name of his old master, beside the straight form of that master's granddaughter. Asuvia whispered to him, asking about her uncle. The old freedman shook his head at her, scowling like a great-uncle, and then smiled. He leaned toward her, past her maid, and whispered: "Something of great importance, something which you will soon see . . ."

But his words were interrupted by a sudden huge babble of excitement, followed by a heavy hush.

Sassia's party had crossed the Forum, and now in the red-gold light of the new sun approached the benches of the tribunal. Her stepson walked at her side. His wife, her daughter, rode behind in a litter. Sassia walked erect as always, with her lithe swinging stride. Asuvia, watching her at first through Cluentius' eyes, suddenly saw her through her own, and shuddered with fear. Should she have to meet that wild gaze, stare at close quarters into that cold impassioned face? The maid Laetilla shrank murmuring against her side; she herself stood firm, resisting an impulse to clutch at the arm of old Lucius Asuvius, to run crazily toward Cluentius, to shriek for her uncle and old Axia. Perspiration stood on her young forehead, and she turned pale. But she stood firm, and told Laetilla, "Quiet! She has to pass on the other side! Quiet! She won't even see us, over here!"

Cluentius noted soberly, as if observing some procession of interesting foreigners, that Sassia wore the striped green-white-gold mantle, famous in Larinum before her husband's death. There was no article of Roman dress in all her costume. Her eyes glittered jewel-like, hawk-like, serpent-like in the full sunlight as she raised her head high to look at the tribunal. She seemed to see nothing and nobody but the ranged figures on the platform. Her eyes did not move when she moved forward, but remained fixed at last on the querulous face of the judge, the old face of Voconius Naso, who sat gaping in his carved chair, looking like a man who prefers not to believe his eyes.

The few women in the crowd on the benches began to speak in low hissing tones: Serpent! Serpent! Cruelest, vilest, beast, she-wolf, most infamous! And a low angry mutter went up from the crowd. The dark faces of Sassia's priests looked a bit gray; their eyes rolled, they moved closer together. Auria got out of her litter and moved along behind her mother, with the face of a sleepwalker.

On the platform of the tribunal Cicero came down to the edge, and struck the attitude of a pleader who has already begun his speech. The business of herald and judge, setting the formal terms of the day's proceedings, passed unnoticed; the words Cicero had spoken yesterday lived again in the troubled air, called into all remembering ears by the terrible, outraged look on his grave face.

Still, within an hour the whole crowd on the benches and the whole crowd of jurors on the platform were alike rocking and roaring with laughter. Cicero was telling the story of the trials of Oppianicus' agents eight years before; the verdicts given by the jury in these trials, he said, verdicts given without the slightest doubt or hesitation, had really committed those same jurors to a verdict of "guilty" on the case of Oppianicus. Cicero described the final proceedings in the trial held just before that of Oppianicus, when the poor harassed pleader for the defense kept saying in lofty tones, "Look back! Look back, upon the early years of these my clients!" — and then looking back, himself, saw the benches empty, for the clients themselves had stolen away from the trial in despair and in acknowledgment of the inevitable outcome. Cicero here let out a long bleat, and mimicked the backward glance, the astonishment and discomfiture of the agents' attorney. Even old Voconius smiled broadly in unaffected enjoyment.

Within two minutes Cicero was imitating the corrupt juror Staienus, agent of the bribery at Oppianicus' trial, and further laughter ran over the court. Then all laughter ceased as he leaned from the edge of the platform to pound home this section of his argument:

"*So,* who bribed? My client or Oppianicus? In that case

when Oppianicus alone was in danger, Oppianicus alone facing the verdict made inevitable by those former verdicts, Oppianicus alone had reason to fear; then Oppianicus alone, gentlemen, had reason to bribe! And we know why and how and whom he bribed! And we know that Staienus kept the money, and therefore the corrupt jurors, enraged, voted against Oppianicus! And we know that the good men on the jury, some of them at least, the fanatically good ones like my friend Claudius Niger here, knowing of bribery, knowing nothing of Staienus' theft, and hearing the corrupt jurors vote *against* Oppianicus, naturally concluded that these evil ones had been bribed to vote against him by my client! Their mistake was excusable, in that heated, stormy time; but that another Roman court, in these different, better times, should *repeat* this mistake — ah, no, gentlemen! Gentlemen, no!"

Cluentius listened grimly, as he had listened grimly the day before to the noble voice revealing the vile plot of Oppianicus against his upright stepson's life. He expelled emotion from his face, and kept his eyes empty of all feeling, mere instruments of physical perception, as he watched the Praetor come and go, gesturing, admonishing, dramatizing, performing. Lost in his mind's wanderings, he yet heard a voice from inside his heart, asking, asking, beseeching even, that he might still hear some sound of truth.

The Praetor began to speak, with great seriousness, of the trials following the condemnation of Oppianicus, in which the judge had been impeached and the court declared corrupt, Cluentius censured along with judge and jury. Deftly, precisely, Cicero recalled the political climate and the issues which had been involved; reminded that no subsequent tribunal nor censor had ever suggested for a moment that Oppianicus was innocent, though half Rome had since been led to believe that this was so; discredited the moving forces behind the accusations, explained away the action of the censors, all with a magnificent competence. Now Cluentius felt his heavy heart lift and lighten, his mind rejoice, at the splendid deployment of skills and powers.

Then his own name rang in his ears:

"You say, they censured Cluentius himself! Yes, but for nothing disgraceful, for no act in the course of his life was ever regrettable. None can be freer of blame than my client, more honorable, more careful in the observance of every duty — and, gentlemen, the censors themselves did not deny this! They state in their proclamation, which I shall read to you now, that they hold no opinion other than the general opinion concerning the honor, blamelessness, high character of my client. . . . They do but conform to a formality, which demands that if the jurors be censured, the accuser must share in the censure. . . ."

Cluentius had never seen the document nor heard its exact terms. Cicero read in the voice of a great actor reading a great poem. Surely now, now, the ring of truth would come . . . but the Praetor finished, and then began to speak of law, and the statutes applying to the case, and the prosecution's speech concerning Roman law and Roman justice. His voice was low and slow-moving, but an intensity so powerful radiated from his speaking figure that his hearers could sense immediately in his words the ring of major feeling:

"For law is the bond. Within the law are reposed the mind and heart, the judgment and the conviction. . . . The state without law would be the human body without mind, unable to make use of the parts which are like sinews, blood, and limbs. Magistrates, jurors, all of us, all, all, obey the law to the end that we may be free."

Cluentius, looking hard at the Praetor with all his attention, saw the heavy features again full of solemn passion. Tears, yes, tears in the blue eyes, and a note in the deep voice that rang so truly and so clearly that Cluentius felt in himself a deep stir of answering emotion.

Cicero had laughed at himself, after his words last night about the priesthood of justice. But he was serious. He had dismissed some solemn court proceedings as travesties on the law, he had called into question the good will and good faith of many Roman magistrates, he had mocked at verdicts, overthrown rulings, and thrown dust in the eyes of jurors; but in the last depths of his deep heart his love of the law of Rome lay hard and perfect, never to be altered or transformed. "Law is the bond of all the dignities which we in this state are privileged to enjoy." The Praetor of the City spoke with the ring of truth, believing what he said.

And after a brief skirmish with the nature of the statute — "You must admit, Titus Accius, that you were greatly mistaken in supposing that I should base my defense of my client's case not upon its merits but upon the legal aspect —" Cicero began to deal with the charges against his client's character. First, the charge that Cluentius had taken, in a group of slaves purchased from a confiscated estate, a free woman whom her husband had sued to recover.

"Actually, when Cluentius heard that this servant whom he had never even seen was a free woman, although purchased by him in good faith from a reputable broker, he immediately returned her to her husband, without any intervention of any court being necessary in any way. . . ."

Small charges of legacy-stealing, assault, etc.:

"How essentially trivial these charges, how substantially false, how easily refutable!"

And then, the poisoning charge.

"First, the prosecution asserts that my client instigated an attempt to poison young Oppianicus here, at a dinner which the boy gave to a large number of people on the, uh, *happy* occasion of his marriage. The poison was being offered to him in honey-brew when a certain young Balbutius playfully intercepted it, drank it, and instantly expired.

"Oh, friends, friends, gentlemen, what shameless lies are here! I call now some testimony. Who is to testify? The same man who testifies to his own grief, the father, the *father*, I say, of the young man in question; he who would have been ready, if a shadow of suspicion had crossed his anguished mind, to give evidence against Cluentius, now offers that evidence in his behalf, and comes in person to stand behind it. Read it!"

The clerk of the court stood up, held his tablets out in front of him, and cleared his throat. Cicero cut in:

"And you, sir, if I'm not asking too much, stand up for a few moments and nerve yourself for this painful but indispensable recital."

Cluentius twisted on his bench in astonishment, to look behind him. He saw, slowly rising above the sea of heads and shoulders, the aged form of the Senator Balbutius, a worthy of Larinum, one of the old friends of Cluentius' own father. Of his presence in Rome Cluentius had known nothing. As the clerk read, the old man kept his eyes fixed on Cluentius; even in his twisted, uncomfortable pose, the younger man did not think of abandoning this long, communicating gaze. The clerk read:

"I, Octavius Balbutius of Larinum, assert that my son on the day of his unhappy misfortune went to the dinner already suffering from indigestion, a chronic ailment with him; that he there ate heavily of a rich seafood stew, overindulging his appetite, as young men will do; was very ill when he came home, and died a natural if untimely death, attended by me, his mother, and our household physician, after an illness lasting several days. I do most firmly and believingly declare that Aulus Cluentius Habitus of

Larinum, my friend and the son of my old friend, had no share in this sad event. I do most firmly and believingly declare that Aulus Cluentius Habitus has never had nor ever in my opinion been capable of having any share in any criminal act, for he is a man free from blame, a just and upright man and the pride of our township."

The clerk's dry unfeeling voice read out these feeling words. The old man sat down and Cluentius turned round. The Praetor was watching him calmly. No actor's expression transformed the lawyer's face now; he looked simple and open, he looked like a man who feels that he need no longer lay any directing hand upon events, for they can now proceed on their right course without him. He spoke quietly and factually of the actual circumstances of Oppianicus' death. Cluentius listened half-dreamily, half-aware of some stir and disturbance in the rear of the court enclosure, but unwilling to look round. Cicero brought out the name of Sassia. He spoke of her first attempts to bring charges against Cluentius. He spoke of the marriage of young Oppianicus, of the slaves and the depositions — "forged this record of the inquiry . . . why no reputable witness? Why, why no complete record, kept for the jurors?" Dreading what must soon come, but unwilling to let his eyes stray for a moment from Cicero's face, Cluentius waited for the change from calm recital to fearful eloquence.

"Great heavens! So inhuman an abomination! No evil which from the first she has not plotted against her son! The whole elaborate charge is hers. Frenzy! Madness! Her son's accuser, thus fortified, she sent on to Rome. . . . On the news that my client's trial was at hand, she came flying hither with all speed.

"WHAT MANNER OF JOURNEY! How the citizens of the wayside towns flocked together in horror and disgust! They all felt this, that every place she passed needed some

ceremony of purification; not one but felt that the earth itself was suffering pollution from the feet of that accursed
mother!"

Splendor of loathing, dark flood of laden words . . .

". . . We have heard about her midnight sacrifices which
she thought secret, her infamous prayers and her unholy
vows . . . not knowing what we know, that the great and
true gods have spurned from their temples and their altars
forever this black frenzy of cruel hate." The voice was the
voice of the priest again: an invocation and a prayer.

Long silence from the Praetor, while the crowd on the
benches below raged, craned, muttered. Then the great
voice again, sober and consecrated:

"Gentlemen of the jury, chance has made you as gods, to
sway for all time the destiny of my client. Do not, I here
implore you, sacrifice to his mother's cruelty my client's
honorable past.

"For, jurors, you shall see now an unbelievable thing:
see it, I say, not hear of it only!

"Jurors! This is the time for the formal testimonials as to
my client's character. Jurors! Know now what you will find
hard to believe, in these weary and distrustful times. *All the
men of Larinum*, every citizen of able body and standing
proper to bear witness in a court of Roman law, all, *all* have
come the long journey in haste and peril, in their own
persons, to Rome, to bring my client in his danger all the
assistance in their power, by their strength of feeling and
their strength of numbers."

It was hard to believe. But it was true. As all the platform
and all the court enclosure and all the rings and crowds beyond gasped and shuffled, the spaces in the center of the
court were cleared, and the men of Larinum and its neighborhood began to enter. Asuvius guided them; he had
grouped them for some time now at the rear. His stewards
ushered and heralded. Long rows of benches were cleared.

"I myself call this roll," said Cicero in a voice of joy and pride. "No clerk shall do it. I know the names, I, a man of Arpinum, a man of townships, as well as a man of Rome." He took scrolls from the clerk and read name after name; the men of Larinum stood as he called them, and their neighbors, row upon row, erect and sober, each bearing all his marks of substance and distinction. "Plaetorius, Flaminius Elder and Younger, of the Magii alone twenty men, sixteen municipal senators. Lucius Papius and Gnaeus Papius Laena of Larinum, Roman businessmen and in their town senators, and ten kinsmen of high rank; Naevius; Octavius Baebius, known as well in Rome as in Larinum, all his famous clan; of the Aurii, thirty senior members of the family, from Teanum and other Apulian towns as well as Larinum; yes, gentlemen, families of Ferentum are here, from the Marrucini, from Luceria and all Apulia, Falernum, ten of the great family Numerius from Bovianum, every town in Samnium here represented!" Names, ranks, rolled from his mouth like prayers to old deities of Rome.

"Rise up, Aulus Cluentius, turn, face your friends, the men who have come to Rome for you, interrupting all business of their own in this most crowded time of year; businessmen, counselors, yes, Roman patricians also take their stand with these voyagers — you there, Helvidius, Volusenus, senators not of Larinum but of Rome, who have known my client and done business with him. Volumnius, Creticus, oh Quintus Claudius Marullus of Rome, friend of Cluentius not through any connection of family, but from services between you, from old knowledge of Cluentius' firm character and high courage!

"Know, men of Rome who stand here in our court, know, citizens, gentlemen of the jury, that these men have come when there was no necessity. We all know that a signed deposition is all that is needed, that it is what the law requires and finds sufficient. The Municipal Senate of Larinum, every

member of which is enrolled also in the order of businessmen of Rome, has passed the resolution in favor of Cluentius, but it has found suitable in this case to *send* no testimo-
nial, but to bring it. They wept when they passed it, the
grave councilors of Larinum, I know — they weep now!"

Cluentius in his ragged gown, his hands hanging at his
sides, stood facing the great standing group. On many old
faces, on some young ones, on these known to him for
many years and on some with which he had but slight acquaintance — on many and many, the great unabashed tears
of Italy flowed unchecked. Cicero was dry-eyed, but his
voice shook and his face worked. At Cluentius' knee, the
Greek slave wrote and wrote on his tablets, scribbling, wiping tears as he wrote.

"Love, gentlemen, trust and faith. Few have been so
beloved and honored by anyone of all his close connection,
by his own dearest kin, as this man, my Cluentius, is loved
and honored by a whole community."

And he began to read the testimony.

"Clean, upright, just . . . Gaius Babirius of Luceria de-
poses. . . . Marcus Papius of Larinum, that he would put
his life in this man's hands, and that his sister's son once did
so, and was saved. . . . Lucius Volumnius the Samnite, that
this man above all others has spoken words of truth and
performed acts of charity and generosity, all his life long.
. . ." Cicero's voice stuck; he passed the records to the
clerk, and the dry voice went on with the great cleansing
tide of words. Cluentius bowed his head and raised his hands
to cover his face. Asuvius and Asuvia moved over to him;
his friend's hand was on his shoulder, the shoulder of Asuvia
trembled against his upper arm as she stood at his side.

"Sit down. Sit down. Sit down. All but Cluentius, sit
down.

"And now, men of Rome, judges here, know that the

pains of all these people, and my own too, I add with pride, since I have as in ancient practice wanted to conduct this case singlehanded — our pains and your own spirit of justice and mercy, gentlemen, are assailed by one person alone. This *mother!* You see her, come at last to such a pass that she has lost all semblance to humanity save only her outward form." Here, as before, the whole weight of the court's impassioned attention bent upon one section of the enclosure, where she sat, head high, eyes cold and clear, the beautiful suave line of jaw and throat still visible in her stern profile, her mouth red with her own veins' red, as of old time and long memory. Cluentius, still standing, stared and stared. She looked like an artifact, an object made by hands and some bold designing brain. Her eyes were set in her white face like stones. Cluentius saw her for the last time, he knew; yet it was for the first. Her power was gone, all secret life had left her. When she should move, as she soon must, to leave this court, she would move like some elaborate fantastic engine, and would pass forever from his view.

"You, who grant aid to those most cruelly assailed," said Cicero in his priest's voice, "deliver Aulus Cluentius and restore him still a citizen to his town; give him back to his friends, neighbors, associates, whose love you have been privileged to see. Yours, judges, is this duty; rightly do we require you to set free at last from these disasters a good and innocent man, beloved and cherished by so many. Thereby may all men know that whatever meetings may be the place for prejudice, our courts of law are places for truth."

XIX

ATTICUS! Arrived, come at last!" They embraced, in the front court of Cicero's house.

"I have been here longer than you think," said Atticus with his cool smile. "Do you imagine that I could fail to arrive for your peroration, even at the cost of some haste in travel, which you know I abominate?"

Cicero began to laugh and tease. Atticus had not attended the final day of the hearing —

"After that speech, my roaring friend, what could possibly follow? I have heard that Accius all but resigned the *altercatio*, feeling no impulse to provoke you in any lively question-and-answer session."

"Between *his* deputation from Larinum, poor fellow, and *my* deputation from Larinum, frankly, the case was fought and won."

"What, modesty? Fortunately the best of my Greek doctors is with me on this journey — one could almost say I foresaw this illness of yours, my poor friend —" and they began to stroll about, gossiping of the statues Atticus had brought north to Rome, fixing their engagements for the next days.

"No, seriously, I must congratulate you," said Atticus. "More seriously than I am accustomed to do, since you know how I deplore your absorption in all this business at the expense of your studies — even when, as in our affair of the consuls, I break my own rules to take part. But I have to say it: you were right about this case. Feeling is so high now, the old facts of eight years ago so clearly re-established as favorable facts, rescued from the obscurities of political memory, that no one of our enemies will dare use your intervention as an arm against us in the big bribery matter. You've pulled it off, Marcus; I've nothing to say."

After a moment's silence Cicero spoke quietly.

"I did a good job, and I know it, as you know I know it. But I can't say I quite foresaw . . . It's been an odd case. I didn't know how deep, how strong in Larinum, was this feeling about Cluentius. I never thought to see the day when an army of municipal businessmen would leave their countinghouses like that, expose themselves like that, stand up in the Forum and weep like that. I looked at them and at Cluentius so hard that I failed to notice your presence, my Atticus; most unusual. Well, put it this way: I won't dis-guise from you my appreciation of my own powers. But one time, of all the times, the material was, was . . ."

"*Up* to those powers, Marcus? *Appropriate* to those powers?"

"Yes. Demanding; and rewarding — both in proportion."

"Cluentius has spoken to you since the trial? I suppose he can hardly have had the time — you were out so late last night, as I know too well."

"Business of *ours*, my Atticus. No, Cluentius comes this morning. After the crowd, I told him. So perhaps at any moment."

"You know how well informed I make myself, on all mat-ters of possible concern to you. I've already heard of an arrangement of considerable interest, made only last night, and at a late hour."

"You and your services! Well, *what?* Oh, stop that eternal grinning, man, *what* —"

"Cluentius' betrothal to the young Asuvia, the niece, you know."

"I know, yes, I know! Well, you please me, Atticus, though I can't say you surprise me. Very suitable; charming; yes, delightful."

"Well, Marcus, out with it! Why are you so halfhearted? You wrote of your admiration for the girl; all Rome knows your feeling for Cluentius. Oh! I see. You regret that you have already made those Piso arrangements for your own Tullia, you find yourself wistful, wishful —"

"Wistful! Wishful!" shouted the Praetor, nettled. "Don't be an idiot. You know how I worked on that thing with old Piso Frugi. But that's *just* it. The girl — I have nothing to say, for she could not, as a woman, be in any way improved. But what *is* marriage, my Atticus, an idyl, an eclogue, some eternal symposium, the mating of twin souls? Bah, and you know it; bah! A man must *think*.

"Atticus, the truth is that I want to approach Cluentius on an important matter. That quaestorship of the last elections, you know, that's fallen vacant because of the young Sempronius' death —"

"*That* quaestorship! But surely, for a man with absolutely no political background or connection —"

"The quaestorship, Atticus, is a *beginning* office, an *introductory* office, no matter what and where the particular quaestorship. No one could be more a new man than Cluentius, I agree. And yet, you know, the temperature of the air is such right now that if certain words were to be spoken in certain ears . . . and think, a man of our order, with a name like that, 'Cluentius,' a name which has come to mean 'decent, upright' as no other name has ever meant those things, such a man in a position of financial responsibility, there where some good can be done — Oh, I don't speak only of my consulship!"

"Marcus, I know."

"*But* — a marriage with a great political family. One of those young Sempronii — remember, the man has one of those lean fine faces that women . . . or the cousin of our old Metellus, *my* Metullus, not of the Metelli of Oppianicus . . . well, Asuvius is a substantial man, but no money really. All lost when his parents were ruined under Sulla. He has made his own fortune. I know, as you cannot, my own Atticus — it is not enough. Money *or* birth — only, why not both? The girl has neither. Oh, I know —"

Atticus said nothing, but looked sadly at his friend.

"Cicero," he said at last. "Look. Listen a minute. I confess to you, knowing you were engaged last night, I went to Asuvius' house to pay a call of congratulation on Aulus Cluentius. Your fault! The last hour of your speech, well, I wished to go. I heard of the betrothal then. But I heard also things which enable me to tell you that Cluentius will never launch himself on any career of Roman public office."

"You! You filled him full of your damned Epicurus! You preached retirement and the love of peace!"

"It is not my habit," said Atticus dryly, "to foist upon my unfortunate acquaintances my own views and urge them to do as I do. No, Cicero. He spoke to *me*. He is full of some plan for Larinum. He thinks of his father's old, poetic notions. He thinks of a new current of business between Larinum and the City, new tides of interest flowing both ways, many new associations. He will be here often, but his dreams of action now are centered round Larinum, his base of operations will be there. Not hard to understand, this feeling for the place, for *local* enterprise and dedication, when you think of what you made happen, at the end of the trial."

"Larinum! that backwater. I talked of Arpinum, but it was just breath. Rome —"

"I know where your heart is, and all your mind, Marcus. You know where are my heart and mind. Be sensible, feel a little, think a little! Let Aulus Cluentius think and feel as he wishes. He has deserved this."

The Praetor scowled and smiled.

"What a disease, this being always *right*. What a malady. No wonder that doctor goes everywhere with you."

Cluentius walked up the long hill to the Praetor's house unattended, as he had first come. A new and beautiful statue stood just inside the gate; beautiful, the cool ripple of Cicero's fountain, the fine delicate old face of the slave who led the guest in; and most beautiful, the figure of Cicero standing beside his friend, his face alight with intelligence, mirth, the gift of welcome. He held out both hands. As Cluentius came up to him, and the three clasped and murmured and greeted, so great a happiness seized the heart of the Praetor's client that he could say nothing for a moment, only smile and smile.

"I brought you —" he began at last.

Cicero turned aside and began to gesticulate — "*No*, my dear fellow, really —" but Atticus took his arm, shook him a little, and shut him up.

"This manuscript," said Cluentius, who had spent the morning acting on some advice he had asked of Atticus the night before.

"I swore by all the gods I'd take nothing from you, Aulus Cluentius," grumbled Cicero, "but Atticus thinks me ungracious; Atticus thinks me imperceptive. Atticus thinks — but I see what it is!" He all but grabbed it from Cluentius' hand. "Oh, rare! Oh, beautiful! Oh, *how* did you get that miserly, long-clawed old Caninus to part with it? Oh, Cluentius, how you can move the hearts of men, the stoniest!" And his eyes all ablaze with pleasure, the Praetor set skillfully about prolonging a most happy moment.

"Atticus," said Cicero in his voice of cheerful grumpiness, "I shall know every time I see that man, greet him, talk with him, watch him walk away from me, that the winning of this case, for which the whole Forum will be praising me for the next ten days and the rhetoric teachers maybe for the next hundred years, was in reality nothing at all, child's play, a game. Oh yes, I was rather neat about the jury-bribing and the prejudice. But so simple! The man is good, the man is just. Virtue shrieks out of every fold in his gown, every line in his face. Perhaps none could have done better than I, perhaps, well, *perhaps* none even so well.

"But Atticus, a new exercise occurs to me. Now that I have done this, and our affair of the elections, with so much weight on our side, is so sure in its outcome, when everything is over and the new year begins, and I am no longer Praetor, and can enter any case I choose, can be free to concentrate on the practice of the law and on the preparation of my election, what if I should try the impossible, the *real* impossible?"

"And if this difficult case was so easy, what then could be impossible, mighty friend?" said Atticus, grinning.

"To defend a man," said Cicero slowly, "against whom all Roman prejudice is ranged, as in this case. To defend a man, Atticus, who has no character at all that can be of any use to me as his attorney; whose character itself is the base of the prejudice, who is vile as his enemies say, a wolf among wolves."

"Do you think," asked Atticus sharply, "like Sassia, of resurrecting the late Statius Albius Oppianicus the Elder and arranging a case where you can appear in his defense?"

"No — let the earth rest on that restless man — or rather,

the obsidian lid of his sarcophagus in the chapel at Larinum. We don't need him. We have someone. Lucius Sergius Catilina, back from Africa to make trouble for us; back from Africa with his hoodlums, scum of the Popular party, so very useful perhaps to our coalition in the elections; back from Africa with all those extortion charges to face," said the Praetor slowly, his eyes glinting as he bit into a tart little apple, staring at his friend.

"You joke," said Atticus in a low voice.

"I joke," said Cicero soberly. There was a little silence.

"Oh, Marcus, Marcus," cried Atticus mournfully, "how long will it be? How long, before you make an end in itself out of the exercise of your great capacities? Before you lose yourself in the love of How, and forget the What —" and he was silent.

"Avoid pain, Epicurean," said Cicero, gently but unsmilingly.

"It pains me to hear you speak in this way of Catilina."

"You forget the Law. It is the Law; each man must have his advocate, no matter what his case."

"It pains me," repeated Atticus, "to hear you speak in this way of Catilina, and of your election too. Who are you? Not my Cicero — forgive me, my attachment to my friend —"

"Oh, Atticus!" said Cicero in the voice which could melt any chill, "look at me! Look, have an apple — *excellent*, dear fellow, real taste. There are many Ciceros," he went on, "and I'll go this far with you: yours is the best.

"Now put all the others from your mind. The case of Aulus Cluentius is closed, and he will leave for Larinum in the morning. We will be at our first meeting by dawn of that morning, and a day of scurry ahead of us. Such things, so alien to you, you must prepare for by long rest, and the pleasant converse of friends, and wholesome entertainment. I've a surprise for you: Torquatus dines with us tonight, we shall talk nothing but schoolboy philosophy, and old times; and I've got hold of this new Greek actor — they say his gestures are a new form of art, the wordless poem . . ." and the Praetor began to promise and console.

XX

UT CLUENTIUS did not leave in the morning, for at dawn a messenger came to him at the house of Asuvius, summoning him to Ostia at the water's edge, and a little sunken cellar in an odd old building.

"The Temple of Isis and Osiris," said the steward Hirtius. "Mostly sailors come here . . . none knew her to be here. She talked of taking ship for Alexandria, but I did not believe she would sail, for she gave no orders. I, I was not of the chosen ones, Lord, Cluentius, you know what I mean . . . I never could . . . so I knew less of her business in this last year than I did before. I was never allowed to come into these places. But she used me still for all arrangements on journeys. And she gave no orders here in Ostia. I became alarmed, I could not find them; at last I had to send in — I sent in her maid Rhodope, initiate, who knew —"

"She is down there?" asked Cluentius.

"Rhodope — no, you mean the Lady. Yes. And our young master Oppianicus."

"*Both* — but take me in."

"I dare not go in."

"Fool!" said Cluentius, and strode inside. He half expected to find the dark men he had seen in the Forum, and through Asuvia's descriptions, huddled in some corner with their rattles; but there was no one, and the smell of incense was old and faint. He went through a little curtained door, and down a second dank staircase.

The altars of the little sanctuary were lit with clumsy torches, set there beside the burnt-out lamps after the intruders had come in upon the scene. At the foot of the black altar of the middle wall lay the long prone body of Sassia, one arm flung over her dark head. Gold glittered in the flickering light, threads of the striped mantle which enshrouded her. Her face was half-hidden, but one cold smooth unmarred cheek shone dully white. Her mouth, thank the gods, was closed, no gaping or grimacing. The green hilt of a short Syrian sword seemed to fix her garment to her body, like a great grotesque jewel.

Slowly Cluentius raised his head to look for the body of young Oppianicus. There was a little stir behind him. He whirled, and saw the youth in a corner, not dead, not even wounded; sitting on a stool. He called him by name, but he did not answer. His pale face glimmered like Sassia's, his eyes were empty, and he kept the silence of one who has spoken his last word. With pity and gentleness, Cluentius raised him up, led him like a cripple, faltering, from the place.

"What . . . what happened there?" asked Hirtius.

"Who can know. Where are the priests?"

"Gone, sailed on the first evening we were here. It was then I thought that she did not mean to sail."

"Did they — were they down there with her?"

"Master, I do not know. I was at the inn. She told me nothing. Was it he — did they — was it she . . ."

"Who can know? Silence, Hirtius."

But Hirtius broke silence long enough to tell him that one of the great traveling carriages she had brought from

Larinum, one drawn by four white mules, carried the black sarcophagus from the chapel of her estate.

Cluentius stayed in Ostia for a day and a night, to arrange, among a colony of foreigners who knew nothing of his story or hers, for a double entombment. The wayside structure was ordered, and Hirtius commissioned to oversee the work. At its end, he was to receive his freedom and a sum of money left in trust with one of Cluentius' agents in Ostia.

"The anonymity of a harbor town," said Cluentius to Asuvia. "A tide of foreign faces, like the wash of the sea. In her last years she hated all things Roman. The manner of her death, who can know? We shall not concern ourselves with establishing any facts, here."

"We know what we need to know," said Asuvia in the light, astringent voice, all intelligence and mind, which she used to comfort Cluentius when matters of painful emotion were in question. "This was not her real death. Her life was over."

"We know what we need to know," repeated Cluentius slowly, smiling his slowly accustomed smile of delight in her.

"She was strange," said Asuvia, also slowly, and watching him with care. "Strange and beautiful. This death is strange, but has its beauty too. It is good, and right, that you have settled the burial in this way. I shall not forget her speeches to me in Larinum. We must forget much, but not her magnificence. She took and gave, both with magnificence." She spoke softly, still in that light dry voice, an old Greek formula: "May the earth be light."

But she thought in her private mind: I am a liar! for I know I can never forgive, and will never forget, that what she gave magnificently to Oppianicus was what she meanly took from you, Cluentius.

And still . . . and still . . . her mind raced in the silence. I shall soften after all, she thought, for the mind must see clearly through the heart's hatred. What she took from you, she gave not only to Oppianicus but to me. If she had been otherwise, and done otherwise, you would be different, and I do not want you different. If she had been otherwise, you would not have come to me, you would long since have belonged to others; most unfortunate, since it so happens that only I can know and love you as is necessary and suitable, not only you, but all your work and all your ways. So, after all, and on second thought . . . farewell, and may the earth be light.

"The house is to be torn down, the whole estate turned into a farm," he continued quietly. "The income, of course, from the property will be Auria's. She will stay indefinitely in the South now; if she comes to Larinum, she will naturally stay with us. We, you and I, will manage the farm for her. As her brother . . . that child, she kept saying 'as my brother' . . ."

"Of course," said Asuvia lightly, "you must remember, as her brother, it won't be forever. Auria in a little while will be pretty again. The divorce will leave her free to be what she always was when I saw her; how she laughed, how blue-eyed she was, Cluentius, you can't think. He was never real to her, that poor boy. She'll know, knowing you, that she needn't worry about his care, or anything like that. So, before very long, there'll be a wedding, then children, lots of agents and contracts, all that sort of thing —"

"All that sort of thing," said Cluentius, smiling again. "Tedious."

"Very tedious," agreed Asuvia, smiling back, and they began to talk of the arrangements for the delayed departure.

In the sunlight of the next morning the party left for Larinum. The case was closed.